THE BURNING BRIDGE

THE RANGER'S APPRENTICE SERIES

www.rangersapprentice.com.au

Book One: The Ruins of Gorlan
Children's Book Council of Australia Notable Book 2005
Finalist for the 2004 Aurealis Award — Children's Novel

Book Two: The Burning Bridge
Children's Book Council of Australia Notable Book 2006

Book Three: The Icebound Land
Highly commended in the 2005 Aurealis Awards for
Children's Novel

Book Four: Oakleaf Bearers
Finalist for the 2006 Aurealis Award — Children's Novel

Book Five: The Sorcerer in the North
Children's Book Council of Australia Notable Book 2007

Book Six: The Siege of Macindaw
Children's Book Council of Australia Notable Book 2008

Book Seven: Erak's Ransom
Children's Book Council of Australia Notable Book 2008
Winner of the Australian Book Industry Award —
Book of the Year for Older Children 2008

Book Eight: The Kings of Clonmel
Children's Book Council of Australia Notable Book 2009
Shortlisted for the 2008 Young Australians
Best Book Award — Older Readers

Book Nine: Halt's Peril
Shortlisted for the Australian Book Industry Award —
Book of the Year for Older Children 2010

THE BURNING
BRIDGE

JOHN FLANAGAN

RANDOM HOUSE AUSTRALIA

A Random House book
Published by Random House Australia Pty Ltd
Level 3, 100 Pacific Highway, North Sydney NSW 2060
www.randomhouse.com.au

First published by Random House Australia in 2005
This edition first published in 2009

Addresses for companies within the Random House Group can be found at
www.randomhouse.com.au/offices.

National Library of Australia
Cataloguing-in-Publication Entry

Author: Flanagan, John, 1944–
Title: The burning bridge / John Flanagan
Edition: 2nd ed.
ISBN: 978 1 86471 905 5 (pbk.)
Series: Flanagan, John, 1944– Ranger's apprentice bk. 2
Target audience: For primary school age
Dewey number: A823.4

Cover illustration by Jeremy Reston
Cover design by www.blacksheep-uk.com
Internal design by Mathematics
Typeset in 12/15 pt Caslon Classico by Midland Typesetters, Australia
Printed and bound by Griffin Press, South Australia

This one is for Katy.

Araluen, Picta and Celtica

Year 643 Common Era

Prologue

alt and Will had been trailing the Wargals for three days. The four heavy-bodied, brutish creatures, foot soldiers of the rebel warlord Morgarath, had been sighted passing through Redmont Fief, heading north. Once word reached the Ranger, he had set out to intercept them, accompanied by his young apprentice.

'Where could they have come from, Halt?' Will asked during one of their short rest stops. 'Surely we've got Three Step Pass well and truly bottled up by now?'

Three Step Pass provided the only real access between the Kingdom of Araluen and the Mountains of Rain and Night, where Morgarath had his headquarters. Now that the Kingdom was preparing for the coming war with Morgarath, a company of infantry and archers had been sent to reinforce the small permanent garrison at the narrow pass until the main army could assemble.

'That's the only place where they can come in sizeable

numbers,' Halt agreed. 'But a small party like this could slip into the Kingdom by way of the barrier cliffs.'

Morgarath's domain was an inhospitable mountain plateau that towered high above the southern reaches of the Kingdom. From Three Step Pass in the east, a line of sheer, precipitous cliffs ran roughly due west, forming the border between the plateau and Araluen. As the cliffs swung south-west, they plunged into another obstacle called the Fissure — a huge split in the earth that ran out to the sea, and separated Morgarath's lands from the kingdom of the Celts.

It was these natural fortifications that had kept Araluen, and neighbouring Celtica, safe from Morgarath's armies for the past sixteen years. Conversely, they also provided the rebel warlord with protection from Araluen's forces.

'I thought those cliffs were impassable?' Will said.

Halt allowed himself a grim smile. 'Nowhere is ever really impassable. Particularly if you have no respect for how many lives you lose trying to prove the fact. My guess is that they used ropes and grapnels and waited for a moonless night and bad weather. That way, they could slip past the border patrols.'

He stood, signifying that their rest stop was at an end. Will rose with him and they moved towards their horses. Halt gave a small grunt as he swung into the saddle. The wound he had suffered in the battle with the two Kalkara still troubled him a little.

'My main concern isn't where they came from,' he continued. 'It's where they're heading, and what they have in mind.'

The words were barely spoken when they heard a shout from somewhere ahead of them, followed by a commotion of grunting and, finally, the clash of weapons.

'And we may be about to find out!' Halt finished.

He urged Abelard into a gallop, controlling the horse with his knees as his hands effortlessly selected an arrow and nocked it to the string of his massive longbow. Will scrambled into Tug's saddle and galloped after him. He couldn't match Halt's hands-free riding skill. He needed his right hand for the reins as he held his own bow ready in his left hand.

They were riding through sparse woodland, leaving it to the sure-footed Ranger horses to pick the best route. Suddenly, they burst clear of the trees into a wide meadow. Abelard, under his rider's urging, slid to a stop, Tug following suit beside him. Dropping the reins to Tug's neck, Will's right hand instinctively reached for an arrow from his quiver and nocked it ready.

A large fig tree grew in the middle of the cleared ground. At the base of it there was a small camp. A wisp of smoke still curled from the fireplace and a pack and blanket roll lay beside it. The four Wargals they had been tracking surrounded a single man, who had his back to the tree. For the moment his long sword held them at bay, but the Wargals were making small feinting movements towards him, trying to find an advantage. They were armed with short swords and axes and one carried a heavy iron spear.

Will drew in a sharp breath at the sight of the creatures. After following their trail for so long, it was a shock to come upon them so suddenly in plain sight. Bear-like in build, they had long muzzles and massive, yellow canine fangs, exposed now as they snarled at their prey. They were covered in shaggy fur and wore black leather armour. The man was dressed similarly and his voice cracked in fear as he repelled their tentative attacks.

'Stand back! I'm on a mission for Lord Morgarath. Stand back, I order you! I order you in Lord Morgarath's name!'

Halt nudged Abelard around, allowing him room to draw the arrow he had ready on the string.

'Drop your weapons! All of you!' he shouted. Five pairs of eyes swung towards him as the four Wargals and their prey turned in surprise. The Wargal with the spear recovered first. Realising that the swordsman was distracted, he darted forward and ran the spear into his body. A second later, Halt's arrow buried itself in the Wargal's heart and he fell dead beside his stricken prey. As the swordsman sank to his knees, the other Wargals charged at the two Rangers.

Shambling and bear-like as they might be, they covered ground with incredible speed.

Halt's second shot dropped the left-hand Wargal. Will fired at the one on the right and realised instantly that he had misjudged the brute's speed. The arrow hissed through the space where the Wargal had been a second before. His hand flew to his quiver for another arrow and he heard a hoarse grunt of pain as Halt's third shot buried itself in the chest of the middle creature. Then Will loosed his second arrow at the surviving Wargal, now terrifyingly close.

Panicked by those savage eyes and yellow fangs, he snatched as he released and knew that his arrow would fly wide and the Wargal was almost upon him.

As the Wargal snarled in triumph, Tug came to his

master's aid. The little horse reared and lashed out with his front hooves at the horrific creature in front of him. Unexpectedly, he also danced forward a few steps, towards the threat, rather than retreating. Will, caught by surprise, clung to the pommel of the saddle.

The Wargal was equally surprised. Like all its kind, it had a deep-seated instinctive fear of horses — a fear born at the Battle of Hackham Heath sixteen years ago, where Morgarath's first Wargal army had been decimated by Araluan cavalry. It hesitated now for a fatal second, stepping back before those flashing hooves.

Halt's fourth arrow took it in the throat. At such short range, the arrow tore clean through. With a final grunting shriek, the Wargal fell dead on the grass.

White-faced, Will slid to the ground, his knees nearly giving way beneath him. He clung to Tug's side to stay upright. Halt swung down quickly and moved to the boy's side. His arm went round him.

'It's all right, Will.' His deep voice cut through the fear that filled Will's mind. 'It's over now.'

But Will shook his head, horrified by the rapid train of events.

'Halt, I missed . . . twice! I panicked and I missed!' He felt a deep sense of shame that he had let his teacher down so badly. Halt's arm tightened around him and he looked up at the bearded face and the dark, deep-set eyes.

'There's a big difference between shooting at a target and shooting at a charging Wargal. A target isn't usually trying to kill you.' Halt added the last few words in a more gentle tone. He could see that Will was in shock. And no wonder, he thought grimly.

'But . . . I missed . . .'

'And you've learned from it. Next time you won't miss. Now you know it's better to fire one good shot than two hurried ones,' Halt said firmly. Then he took Will's arm and turned him towards the camp site under the fig tree. 'Let's see what we have here,' he said, putting an end to the subject.

The black-clad man and the Wargal lay dead beside each other. Halt knelt beside the man and turned him over, whistling softly in surprise.

'It's Dirk Reacher,' he said, half to himself. 'He's the last person I would have expected to see here.'

'You know him?' Will asked. His insatiable curiosity was already helping him to put the horror of the previous few minutes to one side, as Halt had known it would.

'I chased him out of the Kingdom five or six years ago,' the Ranger told him. 'He was a coward and a murderer. He deserted from the army and found a place with Morgarath.' He paused. 'Morgarath seems to specialise in recruiting people like him. But what was he doing here . . .?'

'He said he was on a mission for Morgarath,' Will suggested but Halt shook his head.

'Unlikely. The Wargals were chasing him and only Morgarath could have ordered them to do that, which he'd hardly do if Reacher really was working for him. My guess is that he was deserting again. He'd run out on Morgarath and the Wargals were sent after him.'

'Why?' Will asked. 'Why desert?'

Halt shrugged. 'There's a war coming. People like Dirk try to avoid that sort of unpleasantness.'

He reached for the pack that lay by the camp fire and began to rummage through it.

'Are you looking for anything in particular?' Will asked. Halt frowned as he grew tired of looking through the pack and dumped its contents onto the ground instead.

'Well, it strikes me that if he were deserting Morgarath and coming back to Araluen, he'd have to bring something to bargain for his freedom. So . . .' His voice died away as he reached for a carefully folded parchment among the spare clothes and eating utensils. He scanned it quickly. One eyebrow rose slightly. After almost a year with the grizzled Ranger, Will knew that was the equivalent of a shout of astonishment. He also knew that if he interrupted Halt before he had finished reading, his mentor would simply ignore him. He waited until Halt folded the parchment, stood slowly and looked at his apprentice, seeing the question in the boy's eyes.

'Is it important?' Will asked.

'Oh, you could say so,' Halt told him. 'We appear to have stumbled on Morgarath's battle plans for the coming war. I think we'd better get them back to Redmont.'

He whistled softly and Abelard and Tug trotted to where their masters waited.

From the trees several hundred metres away, carefully downwind so that the Ranger horses would catch no scent of an intruder, unfriendly eyes were upon them. Their owner watched as the two Rangers rode away from the scene of the small battle. Then he turned south, towards the cliffs.

It was time to report to Morgarath that his plan had been successful.

One

It was close to midnight when the single rider reined in his horse outside the small cottage set in the trees below Castle Redmont. The laden pack pony trailing behind the saddle horse ambled to a halt as well. The rider, a tall man who moved with the easy grace of youth, swung down from the saddle and stepped up onto the narrow verandah, stooping to avoid the low-lying eaves. From the lean-to stable at the side of the house came the sound of a gentle nickering and his own horse's head rose as he answered the greeting.

The rider had raised his fist to knock at the door when he saw a light come on behind the curtained windows. He hesitated. The light moved across the room and, a second or so later, the door opened before him.

'Gilan,' Halt said, without any note of surprise in his voice. 'What are you doing here?'

The young Ranger laughed incredulously as he faced his former teacher.

'How do you do it, Halt?' he asked. 'How could you possibly know it was me arriving in the middle of the night, before you'd even opened the door?'

Halt shrugged, gesturing for Gilan to enter the house. He closed the door behind him and moved to the neat little kitchen, opening the damping vent on the stove and sending new life flaring into the wood coals inside. He tossed a handful of kindling into the stove and set a copper kettle on the hot plate over the fire chamber, shaking it first to make sure there was plenty of water in it.

'I heard your horse some minutes ago,' he said. 'Then, when I heard Abelard call a greeting, I knew it had to be a Ranger horse.' He shrugged again. Simple when you explained it, the gesture said. Gilan laughed again in reply.

'Well, that narrowed it down to fifty people, didn't it?' he said. Halt cocked his head to one side with a pitying look.

'Gilan, I must have heard you stumbling up that front step a thousand times when you were studying with me,' he said. 'Give me credit for recognising that sound once more.'

The younger Ranger spread his hands in a gesture of defeat. He unclasped his cloak and hung it over the back of a chair, moving a little closer to the stove. It was a chilly night and he watched Halt measuring coffee into a pot with some anticipation. The door to the rear room of the house opened and Will entered the small living room, his clothes pulled on hastily over his nightshirt, his hair still tousled from sleep.

'Evening, Gilan,' he said casually. 'What brings you here?'

Gilan looked from one to the other in something like despair. 'Isn't anybody surprised when I turn up in the middle of the night?' he asked, of no one in particular. Halt, busy by the stove, turned away to hide a grin. A few minutes earlier, he'd heard Will moving hurriedly to the window as the horse drew closer to the cottage. Obviously, his apprentice had overheard Halt's exchange with Gilan and was doing his best to emulate his own casual approach to the unexpected arrival. However, knowing Will as he did, Halt was sure that the boy was burning with curiosity over the reason for Gilan's sudden appearance. He decided he'd call his bluff.

'It's late, Will,' he said. 'You may as well go back to bed. We have a busy day tomorrow.'

Instantly, Will's nonchalant expression was replaced by a stricken look. The suggestion from his master was tantamount to an order. All thought of appearing casual departed instantly.

'Oh, please, Halt!' the boy exclaimed. 'I want to know what's going on!'

Halt and Gilan exchanged a quick grin. Will was actually hopping from one foot to another as he waited for Halt to rescind the suggestion that he should go to bed. The grizzled Ranger kept a straight face as he set three steaming mugs of coffee on the kitchen table.

'Just as well I made three cups then, isn't it?' he said and Will realised that he'd been having his leg pulled. He shrugged, grinning, and sat down with his two seniors.

'Very well, Gilan, before my apprentice explodes with curiosity, what is the reason for this unexpected visit?'

'Well, it has to do with those battle plans you discovered

last week. Now we know what Morgarath has in mind, the King wants the army ready on the Plains of Uthal before the dark of the next moon. That's when Morgarath plans to break out through Three Step Pass.'

The captured document had told them a great deal. Morgarath's plan called for five hundred Skandian mercenaries to make their way through the swamps of the fenlands and attack the Araluan garrison at Three Step Pass. With the Pass undefended, Morgarath's main army of Wargals would be able to break out and deploy into battle order on the Plains.

'So Duncan plans to beat him to the punch,' Halt said, nodding slowly. 'Good thinking. That way we control the battlefield.'

Will nodded in his turn and said in an equally grave voice, 'And we'll keep Morgarath's army bottled up in the Pass.'

Gilan turned slightly to hide a grin. He wondered if he had tried to copy Halt's mannerisms when he was an apprentice, and decided that he probably had.

'On the contrary,' he said, 'once the army's in place, Duncan plans to withdraw, then fall back to prepared positions and let Morgarath out onto the Plains.'

'Let him out?' Will's voice went up in pitch with surprise. 'Is the King crazy? Why would . . .'

He realised that both Rangers were looking at him, Halt with one eyebrow raised and Gilan with a quizzical smile playing at the corners of his mouth.

'I mean . . .' He hesitated, not sure if questioning the King's sanity might constitute treason. 'No offence or anything like that. It's just —'

'Oh, I'm sure the King wouldn't be offended to hear that a lowly apprentice Ranger thought he was crazy,' said Halt. 'Kings usually love to hear that sort of thing.'

'But Halt . . . to let him out, after all these years? It seems . . .' He was about to say 'crazy' again but thought better of it. He thought suddenly of his recent encounter with the Wargals. The idea of thousands of those vile beasts streaming unopposed out of the Pass made his blood run cold.

It was Halt who answered first. 'That's just the point, Will — *after all these years*. We've spent sixteen years looking over our shoulders at Morgarath, wondering what he's up to. In that time, we've had our forces tied up patrolling the base of the cliffs and keeping watch over Three Step. And he's been free to strike at us any time he likes. The Kalkara were the latest example, as you know only too well.'

Gilan glanced admiringly at his former teacher. Halt had instantly seen the reasoning behind the King's plan. Not for the first time, he understood why Halt was one of the King's most respected advisers.

'Halt's right, Will,' he said. 'And there's another reason. After sixteen years of relative peace, people are growing complacent. Not the Rangers, of course, but the village people who provide men at arms for our army, and even some of the barons and battlemasters in remote fiefs to the north.'

'You've seen for yourself how reluctant some people are to leave their farms and go to war,' Halt put in. Will nodded. He and Halt had spent the past week travelling to outlying villages in Redmont Fief to raise the levies of men who would make up the bulk of the army. On more than one occasion, they had been met with outright hostility — hostility that melted away as Halt exerted the full force of his personality and reputation.

'As far as King Duncan is concerned, now is the time to settle this,' Gilan continued. 'We're as strong as we'll ever be and any delay will only weaken us. This is the best opportunity we'll have to get rid of Morgarath once and for all.'

'All of which still begs my original question,' Halt said. 'What brings you here in the middle of the night?'

'Orders from Crowley,' Gilan said crisply. He placed a written despatch on the table and Halt, after an enquiring look at Gilan, unrolled it and read it. Crowley was the Commandant of the Rangers, Will knew, the most senior of all the fifty Rangers in the Corps. Halt read, then rolled the orders closed again.

'So you're taking despatches to King Swyddned of the Celts,' he said. 'I assume you're invoking the mutual defence treaty that Duncan signed with him some years ago?'

Gilan nodded, sipping appreciatively at the fragrant coffee. 'The King feels we're going to need all the troops we can muster.'

Halt nodded thoughtfully. 'I can't fault his thinking there,' he said softly. 'But . . .?' He spread his hands in a questioning gesture. If Gilan were taking despatches to Celtica, the sooner he got on with it the better, the gesture seemed to say.

'Well,' said Gilan, 'it's an official embassy to *Celtica*.' He laid a little stress on the last word and suddenly Halt nodded his understanding.

'Of course,' he said. 'The old Celtic tradition.'

'Superstition, more like it,' Gilan answered, shaking his head. 'It's a ridiculous waste of time as far as I'm concerned.'

'Of course it is,' Halt replied. 'But the Celts insist on it so what can you do?'

Will looked from Halt to Gilan and back again. The two Rangers seemed to understand what they were talking about. To Will, they might as well have been speaking Espanard.

'It's all very well in normal times,' Gilan said. 'But with all these preparations for war, we're stretched thin in every area. We simply don't have the people to spare. So Crowley thought . . .'

'I think I'm ahead of you,' said Halt and, finally, Will could bear it no longer.

'Well, I'm way behind you!' he burst out. 'What on earth are you two talking about? You are speaking Araluan, aren't you, and not some strange foreign tongue that just sounds like it, but makes no sense at all?'

Two

Halt turned slowly to face his impulsive young apprentice, and raised his eyebrows at the outburst. Will, subsiding, muttered, 'Sorry, Halt,' and the older Ranger nodded.

'I should think so. It's more than obvious that Gilan is asking if I'll release you to accompany him to Celtica.'

Gilan nodded confirmation of the fact and Will frowned, puzzled by the sudden turn of events. 'Me?' he said incredulously. 'Why me? What can I do in Celtica?'

The moment the words had left his mouth, he regretted them. He should have learnt by now never to give Halt that sort of opening. Halt pursed his lips as he considered the question.

'Not much, probably. The real question is, can you be spared from duty here? And the answer to that is "definitely".'

'Then why...' Will gave up. They would either explain or they wouldn't. And no amount of asking would make Halt deliver that explanation a second sooner than he chose to. In fact, he was beginning to think that the more questions he asked, the more Halt actually enjoyed keeping him dangling. It was Gilan who took pity on him, perhaps remembering how close-mouthed Halt could be when he chose.

'I need you to make up the numbers, Will,' he said. 'Traditionally, the Celts insist that an official embassy be made up of three people. And to be honest, Halt's right. You're one who can be spared from the main effort here in Araluen.' He grinned a little ruefully. 'If it makes you feel any better, I've been given the mission because I'm the most junior Ranger in the Corps.'

'But why three people?' Will asked, seeing that Gilan at least seemed disposed to answer questions. 'Can't one deliver the message?'

Gilan sighed. 'As we were saying, it's a superstition among the Celts. It goes back to the old days of the Celtic Council, when the Celts, the Scotti and the Hibernians were one alliance. They were ruled then by a triumvirate.'

'The point is,' Halt interrupted, 'of course Gilan can take the message to them. But if he's a sole messenger, they'll keep him waiting and fob him off for days, or even weeks, while they dither over form and protocol. And we don't have that sort of time to waste. There's an old Celtic saying that covers it: *One man may be deceit. Two can be conspiracy. Three is the number I trust.*'

'So you're sending me because you can do without me?' Will said, somewhat insulted by the thought. Halt decided that it was time to massage his young ego a little — but only a little.

'Well, we can, as a matter of fact. But you can't send just anyone on these embassies. The three members have to have some sort of official status or position in the world. They can't be simple men at arms, for example.'

'And you, Will,' Gilan added, 'are a member of the Ranger Corps. That will carry a certain amount of weight with the Celts.'

'I'm only an apprentice,' Will said, and was surprised when both men shook their heads in disagreement.

'You wear the Oakleaf,' Halt told him firmly. 'Bronze or silver, it doesn't matter. You're one of us.'

Will brightened visibly at his teacher's statement. 'Well,' he said, 'when you put it like that, I'd be delighted to join you, Gilan.'

Halt regarded him dryly. It was obviously time for the ego-stroking to end, he thought. Deliberately, he turned to Gilan.

'So,' he said, 'can you think of anyone else who's totally unnecessary to be the third member?'

Gilan shrugged, smiling as he saw Will subside. 'That's the other reason Crowley sent me here,' he said. 'Since Redmont is one of the larger fiefs, he thought you might be able to spare someone else from here. Any suggestions?'

Halt rubbed his chin thoughtfully, an idea forming. 'I think we might have just the person you need,' he said. He turned to Will. 'Perhaps you'd better get some sleep. I'll give Gilan a hand with the horses and then we'll go up to the castle.'

Will nodded. Now that Halt mentioned sleep, he felt an irresistible urge to yawn. He rose and headed for his small room.

'See you in the morning, Gilan.'

'Bright and early,' Gilan smiled and Will rolled his eyes in mock horror.

'I knew you'd say that,' he replied.

Halt and Gilan strolled through the fields towards Castle Redmont in companionable silence. Gilan, attuned to his old teacher's ways, sensed that Halt had something he wanted to discuss, and before too long, the older Ranger broke the silence.

'This embassy to Celtica could be just what Will needs,' he said. 'I'm a little worried about him.'

Gilan frowned. He liked the irrepressible young apprentice. 'What's the problem?' he asked.

'He had a bad time of it when we ran into those Wargals last week,' Halt said. 'He thinks he's lost his nerve.'

'And has he?'

Halt shook his head decisively. 'Of course not. He's got more courage than most grown men. But when the Wargals charged us, he rushed his shot and missed.'

Gilan shrugged. 'No shame in that, is there? After all, he's not yet sixteen. He didn't run, I take it?'

'No. Not at all. He stood his ground. Even got another shot away. Then Tug backed the Wargal off so I could finish it. He's a good horse, that one.'

'He has a good master,' Gilan said and Halt nodded.

'That's true. Still, I think a few weeks away from all of these war preparations will be good for the boy. It might get his mind off his troubles if he spends some time with you and Horace.'

'Horace?' Gilan asked.

'He's the third member I'm suggesting. One of the Battleschool apprentices and a friend of Will's.' Halt thought for a few moments then nodded to himself. 'Yes. A few weeks with people closer to his own age will do him good. After all, folk do say I can be a little grim from time to time.'

'You, Halt? Grim? Who could say such a thing?' Gilan said. Halt glanced at him suspiciously. Gilan was, all too obviously, just managing to keep a straight face.

'You know, Gilan,' he said, 'sarcasm isn't the lowest form of wit. It's not even wit at all.'

Even though it was after midnight, the lights were still burning in Baron Arald's office when Halt and Gilan reached the castle. The Baron and Sir Rodney, Redmont's Battlemaster, had a lot of planning to do, preparing for the march to the Plains of Uthal, where they would join the rest of the Kingdom's army. When Halt explained Gilan's need, Sir Rodney was quick to see where the Ranger's thinking was headed.

'Horace?' he said to Halt. The small, bearded Ranger nodded almost imperceptibly.

'Yes, it's not a bad idea at all,' the Battlemaster continued, pacing the room as he thought it over. 'He has the sort of status you need for the task — he's a Battleschool member, even if he is only a trainee. We can spare him from the force leaving here at the end of the week and . . .' At this he paused and looked meaningfully at Gilan. 'You might even find he's a useful person to have along.'

The younger Ranger looked at him curiously and Sir Rodney elaborated: 'He's one of my best trainees — a real natural with a sword. He's already better than most members of the Battleschool. But he does tend to be a bit formal and inflexible in his approach to life. Perhaps an assignment with two undisciplined Rangers might teach him to loosen up a little.'

He smiled briefly to show that he meant no offence by the joke, then glanced at the sword Gilan wore at his hip. It was an unusual weapon for a Ranger. 'You're the one who studied with MacNeil, is that right?'

Gilan nodded. 'The Swordmaster. Yes, that was me.'

'Hmmm,' muttered Sir Rodney, regarding the tall young Ranger with new interest. 'Well, you might see your way clear to giving Horace a few pointers while you're on the road. I'd take it as a favour and you'll find he's a quick learner.'

'I'd be glad to,' Gilan replied. He thought that he'd like to see this apprentice warrior. He knew from his time as Halt's apprentice that Sir Rodney wasn't given to overstating praise for any of the students in the Battleschool.

'Well, that's settled then,' Baron Arald said, anxious to get back to planning the thousand and one details of the march to Uthal. 'What time will you be leaving, Gilan?'

'As soon after sun-up as I can, sir,' Gilan replied.

'I'll have Horace report to you before first light,' Rodney told him. Gilan nodded, sensing that the meeting was over. The Baron's next words confirmed it.

'Now if you two will excuse us, we'll get back to the relatively simple business of planning a war,' he said.

Three

The sky was heavy with sullen rain clouds. Somewhere the sun may have been rising, but here there was no sign of it, just a dull, grey light that filtered through the overcast and gradually, reluctantly, filled the sky.

As the little party crested the last ridge, leaving the massive shape of Castle Redmont behind them, the new day finally gave in to the clouds and it began to rain — a cold spring rain. It was light and misting, but persistent. At first, it ran off the riders' treated woollen cloaks. But, eventually, it began to soak into the fibres. After twenty minutes or so, all three were hunched in their saddles, trying to retain as much body warmth as they could.

Gilan turned to his two companions as they plodded along, eyes down, hunched over their horses' necks. He smiled to himself, then addressed Horace, who was keeping a position slightly to the rear, alongside the pack pony Gilan was leading.

'Well then, Horace,' he said, 'are we giving you enough adventure for the moment?'

Horace wiped the misting rain from his face, and grimaced ruefully.

'Less than I'd expected, sir,' he replied. 'But it's still better than close order drill.'

Gilan nodded and grinned at him.

'I imagine it is at that,' he said. Then he added kindly: 'There's no need to ride back there, you know. We Rangers don't stand on ceremony too much. Come and join us.'

He nudged Blaze with his knee and the bay horse stepped out to open a gap. Horace eagerly urged his horse forward, to ride level with the two Rangers.

'Thank you, sir,' he said gratefully. Gilan cocked an eyebrow at Will.

'Polite, isn't he?' he mused. 'Obviously manners are well taught in the Battleschool these days. Nice to be called "sir" all the time.'

Will grinned at the kindly meant jibe. Then the smile faded from his face as Gilan continued thoughtfully.

'Not a bad idea to have a bit of respect shown. Perhaps you could call me sir as well,' he said, turning his face away to study the treeline to one side, so that Will couldn't see the faint trace of a grin that insisted on breaking through.

Aghast, Will choked over his answer. He couldn't believe his ears.

'Sir?' he said finally. 'You really want me to call you sir, Gilan?' Then, as Gilan frowned slightly at him, he amended hurriedly and in great confusion: 'I mean, sir! You want me to call you sir . . . sir?'

Gilan shook his head. 'No. I don't think "sir-sir" is suitable. Nor "Sir Gilan". I think just the one sir would do nicely, don't you?'

Will couldn't think of a polite way of phrasing what was in his mind, and gestured helplessly with his hands. Gilan continued.

'After all, it'll do nicely to keep us all remembering who's in charge of this party, won't it?'

Finally, Will found his voice. 'Well, I suppose it will, Gil . . . I mean, sir.' He shook his head, surprised at this sudden demand for formality from his friend. He rode in silence for a few minutes, then heard an explosive sneezing sound from beside him as Horace tried, unsuccessfully, to smother his giggling. Will glared at him, then turned suspiciously to Gilan.

The young Ranger was grinning all over his face as he eyed the apprentice. He shook his head in mock sorrow.

'Joking, Will. Joking.'

Will realised his leg was being pulled again, and this time with Horace's full knowledge.

'I kne-ew,' he replied huffily, dragging the word out into two syllables to show his disdain. Horace laughed out loud. This time, Gilan joined in.

They travelled south all day, finally making camp in the first line of foothills on the road to Celtica. Around midafternoon, the rain had slowly begun to peter out, but the ground around them was still sodden.

They searched under the thickest-foliaged trees for dry, dead wood, and gradually collected enough for a small camp fire. Gilan joined in with the two apprentices, sharing the work among the three of them, and they ate their meal in an atmosphere of friendship and shared experience.

Horace, however, was still a little in awe of the tall young Ranger. Will eventually realised that, by teasing him, Gilan was doing his best to set Horace at ease, making sure that he didn't feel left out. Will found himself warming to Halt's former apprentice even more than before. He reflected thoughtfully that he still had a lot to learn about managing people.

He knew that he faced at least another four years' training before he finished his apprenticeship. Then, he supposed, he'd be expected to carry out clandestine missions, gather intelligence about the Kingdom's enemies and perhaps lead elements of the army, just as Halt did. The thought that one day he would have to depend on his own wits and skill was a daunting one. Will felt secure in the company of experienced Rangers like Halt or Gilan. Their knowledge and ability invested them with a reassuring aura of invincibility and he wondered if he would ever be able to take his place alongside them. Right now, he told himself glumly, he doubted it.

He sighed. Sometimes, it seemed that life was determined to be confusing. Less than a year ago, he had been a nameless, unknown orphan in Castle Redmont's Ward. Since then he had begun to learn the skills of a Ranger, and basked in the admiration and praise of everyone at Redmont Fief when he had helped the Baron, Sir Rodney and Halt defeat the terrifying beasts known as the Kalkara.

He glanced across at Horace, the childhood enemy who had become his friend, and wondered if he felt the same bewildering conflict of emotions. The memory of their days in the Ward together reminded him of his other friends — George, Jenny and Alyss, now apprenticed to their own Craftmasters. He wished he'd had time to say goodbye to them before leaving for Celtica. Particularly Alyss. He shifted uncomfortably as he thought of her. Alyss had kissed him after that night at the inn and he still remembered the soft touch of her lips.

Yes, he thought, particularly Alyss.

Across the camp fire, Gilan observed Will through half-closed eyes. It wasn't easy being Halt's apprentice, he knew. Halt was a near-legendary figure and that laid a heavy burden on anyone apprenticed to him. There was a lot to live up to. He decided that Will needed a little distraction.

'Right!' he said, springing lithely to his feet. 'Lessons!'

Will and Horace looked at each other.

'Lessons?' said Will, in a pleading tone of voice. After a day in the saddle, he was hoping more for his bedroll.

'That's right,' Gilan said cheerfully. 'Even though we're on a mission, it's up to me to keep up the instruction for you two.'

Now it was Horace's turn to be puzzled. 'For me?' he asked. 'Why should I be taught any Ranger skills?'

Gilan picked up his sword and scabbard from where they lay beside his saddle. He withdrew the slender, shining blade from its plain leather receptacle. There was a faint hiss as it came free and the blade seemed to dance in the shifting firelight.

'Not Ranger skills, my boy. Combat skills. Heaven knows, we'll need them as sharp as possible before too long. There's a war coming, you know.' He regarded the heavy-set boy before him with a critical eye. 'Now, let's see what you know about that toothpick you're wearing.'

'Oh, right!' said Horace, sounding a little more pleased about this turn of events. He never minded a little sword practice and he knew it wasn't a Ranger skill. He drew his own sword confidently and stood before Gilan, point politely lowered to the ground. Gilan stuck his own sword point-first into the soft earth, and held out his hand for Horace's.

'May I see that, please?' he asked. Horace nodded and handed it to Gilan hilt-first.

Gilan hefted it, tossed it lightly, then swung it experimentally a few times.

'See this, Will? This is what you look for in a sword.'

Will looked at the sword, unimpressed. It looked plain to him. The blade was simple and straight. The hilt was leather wrapped around the steel tang and the crosspiece was a chunky piece of brass. He shrugged.

'It doesn't look special,' he said apologetically, not wanting to hurt Horace's feelings.

'It's not how they look that counts,' said Gilan. 'It's how they feel. This one, for example. It's well balanced so you can swing it all day without getting overtired, and the blade is light but strong. I've seen blades twice this thick snapped in half by a good blow from a cudgel. Fancy ones, too,' he added, with a smile, 'with engravings and inlays and jewels.'

'Sir Rodney says jewels in the hilt are just unnecessary weight,' said Horace. Gilan nodded agreement.

'What's more, they tend to encourage people to attack you and rob you,' he said. Then, all business again, he returned Horace's sword and took up his own.

'Very well, Horace, we've seen that the sword is good quality. Let's see about its owner.'

Horace hesitated, not sure what Gilan intended.

'Sir?' he said awkwardly. Gilan gestured to himself with his left hand.

'Attack me,' he said cheerfully. 'Have a swing. Take a whack. Lop my head off.'

Still Horace stood uncertainly. Gilan's sword wasn't in the guard position. He held it negligently in his right hand, the point downwards. Horace made a helpless gesture.

'Come on, Horace,' Gilan said. 'Let's not wait all night. Let's see what you can do.'

Horace put his own sword point-first into the earth.

'But you see, sir, I'm a trained warrior,' he said. Gilan thought about this and nodded.

'True,' he said. 'But you've been training for less than a year. I shouldn't think you'll chop too much off me.'

Horace looked to Will for support. Will could only shrug. He assumed that Gilan knew what he was doing. But he hadn't known him long, and, he'd never seen him so much as draw his sword, let alone practise with it. Gilan shook his head in mock despair.

'Come on, Horace,' he said. 'I do have a vague idea what this is all about.'

Reluctantly, Horace swung a half-hearted blow at Gilan. Obviously, he was worried that, if he should penetrate the Ranger's guard, he was not sufficiently experienced to pull the blow and avoid injuring him. Gilan didn't even raise his sword to protect himself. Instead, he swayed easily to one side and Horace's blade passed harmlessly clear of him.

'Come on!' he said. 'Do it as if you mean it!'

Horace took a deep breath and swung a full-blooded roundhouse stroke at Gilan.

It was like poetry, Will thought. Like dancing. Like the movement of running water over smooth rocks. Gilan's sword, seemingly propelled only by his fingers and wrist, swung in a flashing arc to intercept Horace's blow. There was a ring of steel and Horace stopped, surprised. The parry had jarred his hand through to the elbow. Gilan raised his eyebrows at him.

'That's better,' he said. 'Try again.'

And Horace did. Backhands, overhead cuts, round arm swings.

Each time, Gilan's sword flicked into position to block the stroke with a resounding clash. As they continued, Horace swung harder and faster. Sweat broke out on his forehead and his shirt was soaked. Now he had no thought of trying not to hurt Gilan. He cut and slashed freely, trying to break through that impenetrable defence.

Finally, as Horace's breath was coming in ragged gasps, Gilan changed from the blocking movement that had been so effective against Horace's strongest blows. His sword clashed against Horace's, then whipped around in a small, circular motion so that his blade was on top. Then, with a slithering clash, he ran his blade down Horace's, forcing the apprentice's sword point down to the ground. As the point touched the damp earth, Gilan swiftly put one booted foot on it to hold it there.

'Right, that'll do,' he said calmly. Yet his eyes were riveted on Horace's, making sure the boy knew that the practice session was over. Sometimes, Gilan knew, in the heat of the moment, the losing swordsman could try for just one more cut — at a time when his opponent had assumed the fight was over.

And then, all too often, it was.

He saw now that Horace was aware. He stepped back lightly from him, moving quickly out of the reach of the sword.

'Not bad,' said Gilan approvingly. Horace, mortified, let his sword drop to the turf.

'Not bad?' he exclaimed. 'It was terrible! I never once looked like . . .' He hesitated. Somehow, it didn't seem polite to admit that for the last three or four minutes, he'd been trying to hack Gilan's head from his shoulders. He finally managed to compromise by saying: 'I never once managed to break through your guard.'

'Well,' Gilan said modestly, 'I have done this sort of thing before, you know.'

'Yes,' panted Horace. 'But you're a Ranger. Everyone knows Rangers don't use swords.'

'Apparently, this one does,' said Will, grinning. Horace, to his credit, smiled wearily in return.

'You can say that again.' He turned respectfully to Gilan. 'May I ask where you learned your swordsmanship, sir? I've never seen anything like it.'

Gilan shook his head in mock reproof. 'There you go again with the "sir",' he said. Then, in answer: 'My

Swordmaster was an old man. A northerner named MacNeil.'

'MacNeil!' Horace whispered in awe. 'You don't mean *the* MacNeil? MacNeil of Bannock?'

Gilan nodded. 'He's the one,' he replied. 'You've heard of him then?'

Horace nodded reverently. 'Who hasn't heard of MacNeil?'

And at that stage, Will, tired of not knowing what was going on, decided to speak up.

'Well, I haven't, for one,' he said. 'But I'll make tea if anyone chooses to tell me about him.'

Four

'So tell me about this Neil person,' said Will, as the three of them settled comfortably by the fire, steaming mugs of herb tea warming their cupped hands.

'MacNeil,' Horace corrected him. 'He's a legend.'

'Oh, he's real enough,' said Gilan. 'I should know. I practised under him for five years. I started when I was eleven, then, at fourteen, I was apprenticed to Halt. But he always gave me leave of absence to continue my work with the Swordmaster.'

'But why did you continue to learn the sword after you started training as a Ranger?' Horace asked.

Gilan shrugged. 'Maybe people thought it was a shame to waste all that early training. I certainly wanted to continue, and my father is Sir David of Caraway Fief, so I suppose I was given some leeway in the matter.'

Horace sat up a little straighter at the mention of the name.

- 31 -

'Battlemaster David?' he said, obviously more than a little impressed. 'The new supreme commander?'

Gilan nodded, smiling at the boy's enthusiasm. 'The same,' he agreed. Then, seeing that Will was still in the dark, he explained further: 'My father has been appointed supreme commander of the King's armies, since Lord Northolt was murdered. He commanded the cavalry at the Battle of Hackham Heath.'

Will's eyes widened. 'When Morgarath was defeated and driven into the mountains?'

Both Horace and Gilan nodded. Horace continued the explanation enthusiastically.

'Sir Rodney says his co-ordination of the cavalry with flanking archers in the final stage of the battle is a classic of its kind. He still teaches it as an example of perfect tactics. No wonder your father was chosen to replace Lord Northolt.'

Will realised that the conversation had moved away from its original gambit.

'So what did your father have to do with this MacNeil character?' he asked, returning to the subject.

'Well,' said Gilan, 'my father was a former pupil as well. It was only natural that MacNeil should gravitate to his Battleschool, wasn't it?'

'I suppose so,' Will agreed.

'And it was only natural that I should come under his tutelage as soon as I could swing a sword. After all, I was the Battlemaster's son.'

'So how was it that you became a Ranger?' Horace asked. 'Weren't you accepted as a knight?'

Both Rangers looked at him quizzically, somewhat

amused by his assumption that a person only became a Ranger after failing to become a knight or a warrior. In truth, it was only a short time since Will had felt the same way, but now he conveniently overlooked the fact. Horace became aware of the extended lull in the conversation, then of the looks they were giving him. All of a sudden, he realised his gaffe, and tried to recover.

'I mean . . . you know. Well, most of us want to be knights, don't we?'

Will and Gilan exchanged glances. Gilan raised an eyebrow. Horace blundered on.

'I mean . . . no offence or anything . . . but everyone I know wants to be a warrior.' His embarrassment lessened as he pointed a forefinger at Will. 'You did yourself, Will! I remember when we were kids, you used to always say you were going to Battleschool and you'd be a famous knight!'

Now it was Will's turn to feel uncomfortable. 'And you always sneered at me, didn't you, and said I'd be too small?' he said.

'Well, you were!' said Horace, with some heat.

'Is that right?' Will replied, angrily. 'Well, does it occur to you that maybe Halt had already spoken to Sir Rodney and said he wanted me as an apprentice? And that's the reason why I wasn't selected for Battleschool? Has that ever occurred to you?'

Gilan interrupted at this point, gently stopping the argument before it got any further out of hand.

'I think that's enough of childhood squabbles,' he said firmly. Both boys, each ready with another verbal barb, subsided a little awkwardly.

'Oh . . . yes. Right,' mumbled Will. 'Sorry.'

Horace nodded several times, embarrassed at the petty scene that had just occurred. 'Me too,' he said. Then, curiosity piqued, he added: 'Is that how it happened, Will? Did Halt tell Sir Rodney not to pick you because he wanted you for a Ranger?'

Will dropped his gaze and picked at a loose thread on his shirt.

'Well . . . not exactly,' he said, then admitted, 'And you're right. I always did want to be a knight when I was a kid.' Then, turning quickly to Gilan, he added, 'But I wouldn't change now, not for anything!'

Gilan smiled at the two of them. 'I was the opposite,' he said. 'Remember, I grew up in the Battleschool. I may have started my training with MacNeil when I was eleven, but I began my basic training at around nine.'

'That must have been wonderful,' Horace said with a sigh. Surprisingly, Gilan shook his head.

'Not to me. You know what they say about distant pastures always looking greener?'

Both boys looked puzzled by this.

'It means you always want what you haven't got,' he said, and they both nodded their understanding. 'Well, that's the way I was. By the time I was twelve, I was sick to death of the discipline and drills and parades.' He glanced sidelong at Horace. 'There's a bit of that goes on in Battleschool, you know.'

The heavy-set boy sighed. 'You're telling me,' he agreed. 'Still, the horsemanship and practice combats are fun.'

'Maybe,' said Gilan. 'But I was more interested in the life the Rangers led. After Hackham Heath, my father and Halt had become good friends and Halt used to come visiting. I'd see him come and go. So mysterious. So adventurous. I started to think what it might be like to come and go as you please. To live in the forests. People know so little about Rangers, it seemed like the most exciting thing in the world to me.'

Horace looked doubtful. 'I've always been a little scared of Halt,' he said. 'I used to think he was some kind of sorcerer.'

Will snorted in disbelief. 'Halt? A sorcerer?' he said. 'He's nothing of the kind!'

Horace looked at him, pained once again. 'But you used to think the same thing!' he said.

'Well . . . I suppose so. But I was only a kid then.'

'So was I!' replied Horace, with devastating logic.

Gilan grinned at the two of them. They were both still boys. Halt had been right, he thought. It was good for Will to be spending some time in company with someone his own age.

Will turned to the older Ranger. 'So did you ask Halt to take you as an apprentice?' he asked, then, before receiving any answer, continued, 'What did he say to that?'

Gilan shook his head. 'I didn't ask him anything. I followed him one day when he left our castle and headed into the forest.'

'You followed him? A Ranger? You followed a Ranger into the forest?' said Horace. He didn't know whether to be impressed by Gilan's courage or appalled at his fool-hardiness. Will sprang to Gilan's defence.

'Gil's one of the best unseen movers in the Ranger Corps,' he said quickly. 'The best, probably.'

'I wasn't then,' said Gilan ruefully. 'Mind you, I

thought I knew a bit about moving without being seen. I found out how little I actually did know when I tried to sneak up on Halt as he stopped for a noon meal. First thing I knew was his hand grabbed me by the scruff of the neck and threw me in a stream.'

He smiled at the memory of it.

'I suppose he sent you home in disgrace then?' asked Horace, but Gilan shook his head again, a distant smile still on his face as he remembered that day.

'On the contrary, he kept me with him for a week. Said I wasn't too bad at sneaking around the forest and I might have some talent as an unseen mover. He started to teach me about being a Ranger — and by the end of the week, I was his apprentice.'

'How did your father take it when you told him?' Will asked. 'Surely he wanted you to be a knight like him? I guess he was disappointed.'

'Not at all,' said Gilan. 'The strange thing was, Halt had told him that I'd probably be following him into the forest. My father had already agreed that I could serve as Halt's apprentice, before I even knew I wanted to.'

Horace frowned. 'How could Halt have known that?'

Gilan shrugged and looked at Will meaningfully.

'Halt has a way of knowing things, doesn't he, Will?' he asked, grinning. Will remembered that dark night in the Baron's office, and the hand that had shot out of the darkness to seize his wrist. Halt had been waiting for him that night. Just as he'd obviously waited for Gilan to follow him.

He looked deep into the low embers of the fire before he answered.

'Maybe, in his own way, he is a kind of a sorcerer,' he said.

The three companions sat in comfortable silence for a few minutes, thinking about what had been discussed. Then Gilan stretched and yawned.

'Well, I'm for sleep,' he said. 'We're on a war footing these days so we'll set watches. Will, you're first, then Horace, then me. 'Night, you two.'

And so saying, he rolled himself into his grey-green cloak and was soon breathing deeply and evenly.

Five

They were on the road again before the sun was barely clear of the horizon. The clouds had cleared now, blown away by a fresh southerly wind, and the air was crisp and cold as their trail started to wind higher into the rocky foothills leading to the border with Celtica.

The trees grew more stunted and gnarled. The grass was coarse and the thick forest was replaced by short, windblown scrub.

This was a part of the land where the winds blew constantly, and the land itself reflected its constant scouring action. The few houses they saw in the distance were huddled into the side of hills, built of stone walls and rough thatch roofs. It was a cold, hard part of the Kingdom and, as Gilan told them, it would become harder as they entered Celtica itself.

That evening, as they relaxed around the camp fire, Gilan continued with Horace's instruction in swordsmanship.

'Timing is the essence of the whole thing,' he said to the sweating apprentice. 'See how you're parrying with your arm locked and rigid?'

Horace looked at his right arm. Sure enough, it was locked, stiff as a board. He looked pained.

'But I have to be ready to stop your stroke,' he explained.

Gilan nodded patiently, then demonstrated with his own sword. 'Look . . . see how I'm doing it? As your stroke is coming, my hand and arm are relaxed. Then, just before your sword reaches the spot where I want to stop it, I make a small counterswing, see?'

He did so, using his hand and wrist to swing the blade of his sword in a small arc. 'My grip tightens at the last moment, and the greater part of the energy of your swing is absorbed by the movement of my own blade.'

Horace nodded doubtfully. It seemed so easy for Gilan.

'But . . . what if I mistime it?'

Gilan smiled widely. 'Well, in that case, I'll probably just lop your head off your shoulders.' He paused. Horace obviously wasn't too pleased with that answer. 'The idea is *not* to mistime it,' Gilan added gently.

'But . . .' the boy began.

'And the way to develop your timing is?' Gilan interrupted. Horace nodded wearily.

'I know. I know. Practice.'

Gilan beamed at him again. 'That's right. So, ready? One and two and three and four, that's better, and three and four . . . No! No! Just a small movement of the wrist . . . and one and two . . .'

The ring of their blades echoed through the camp site.

Will watched with some interest, heightened by the fact that he wasn't the one who was working up a sweat.

After a few days of this, Gilan noticed that Will seemed a little too relaxed. He was sitting running a stone down the edge of his sword after a practice session with Horace when he glanced quizzically at the apprentice Ranger.

'Has Halt shown you the double knife sword defence yet?' he asked suddenly. Will looked up in surprise.

'The double knife . . . what?' he asked uncertainly. Gilan sighed deeply.

'Sword defence. Damn! I should have realised that there'd be more for me to do. Serves me right for taking two apprentices along with me.' He stood up with an exaggerated sigh, and motioned for Will to follow him. Puzzled, the boy did.

Gilan led the way to the clear ground where he and Horace had been practising their swordsmanship. Horace was still there, making shadow lunges and cuts at an imaginary foe as he counted time to himself under his breath. Sweat ran freely down his face and his shirt was dark with it.

'Right, Horace,' called Gilan. 'Take a break for a few minutes.'

Gratefully, Horace complied. He lowered the sword, and sank onto the trunk of a fallen tree.

'I think I'm getting the feel of it,' he said. Gilan nodded approvingly.

'Good for you. Another three or four years and you might just have it mastered.' He spoke cheerfully, but Horace's face dropped as the prospect of long years of weary practice stretched out in front of him.

'Look on the bright side, Horace,' Gilan said. 'By that time, there'd be less than a handful of swordsmen in the Kingdom who could best you in a duel.'

Horace's face brightened somewhat, then sagged again as Gilan added: 'The only trick is, knowing who those handful are. Be most uncomfortable if you accidentally challenged one of them and then found out, wouldn't it?'

He didn't wait for an answer, but turned to the smaller boy.

'Now, Will,' he said. 'Let's see those knives of yours.'

'Both of them?' Will hesitated and Gilan rolled his eyes to heaven. The expression was remarkably like the one that Halt used when Will asked one question too many.

'Sorry,' Will mumbled, unsheathing his two knives and holding them out to Gilan. The older Ranger didn't take them. He quickly inspected their edges and checked to see that the fine layer of rust proofing oil was on them. He nodded, satisfied, when he saw everything was as it should be.

'Right,' he said. 'Saxe knife goes in your right hand, because that's the one you use to block a sword cut . . .'

Will frowned. 'Why would I need to block a sword cut?'

Gilan leaned forward and rapped him none too gently on the top of his head with his knuckles.

'Well, perhaps to stop it splitting your skull might be a good reason,' he suggested.

'But Halt says Rangers don't fight at close quarters,' Will protested. Gilan nodded agreement.

'It's certainly not our role. But, if the occasion arises when we have to, it's a good idea to know how to go about it.'

As they'd been talking, Horace had risen from his spot on the log and moved closer to watch them. He interrupted, a trifle scornfully.

'You don't think a little knife like that is going to stop a proper sword, do you?' he asked. Gilan raised one eyebrow at him.

'Take a closer look at that "little knife" before you sound so certain,' he invited. Horace held out his hand for the knife. Will quickly reversed it and placed its hilt into Horace's hand.

Will had to agree with Horace. The saxe knife was a large knife. Almost a short sword, in fact. But compared to a real sword, like Horace's or Gilan's, it seemed woefully inadequate.

Horace swung the knife experimentally, testing its balance.

'It's heavy,' he said finally.

'And hard. Very, very hard,' Gilan told him. 'Ranger knives are made by craftsmen who've perfected the art of hardening steel to an amazing degree. You'd blunt your sword edge against that, and barely leave a nick on it.'

Horace pursed his lips. 'Even so, you've been teaching me the idea of movement and leverage all week. There's a lot less leverage in a short blade like this.'

'That's true,' Gilan agreed. 'So we have to find another source of leverage, don't we? And that's the shorter knife. The throwing knife.'

'I don't get it,' said Horace, the frown deepening between his eyebrows. Will didn't either, but he was glad the other boy had admitted his ignorance first. He adopted a knowing look as he waited for Gilan to explain. He should have known better. The Ranger's sharp eyes missed very little.

'Well, perhaps Will could explain it for you?' Gilan said pleasantly.

He cocked his head at Will expectantly. Will hesitated.

'Well . . . it's the . . . ah . . . um . . . the two knife defence,' he stammered. There was a long pause as Gilan said nothing, so Will added, just a little doubtfully: 'Isn't it?'

'Of course it is!' Gilan replied. 'Now would you care to demonstrate?' He didn't even wait for Will's reply, but went on with barely a pause: 'I thought not. So, please, allow me.'

He took Will's saxe knife and withdrew his own throwing knife from its sheath. Then he gestured to Horace's sword with the smaller knife.

'Right then,' he said, all business. 'Pick up your sticker.'

Horace did so, doubtfully. Gilan gestured him out to the centre of the practice area, then took a ready stance. Horace did the same, sword point up.

'Now,' said Gilan, 'try an overhand cut at me.'

'But . . .' Horace gestured unhappily to the two smaller weapons in Gilan's grasp. Gilan rolled his eyes in exasperation.

'When will you two learn?' he asked. 'I do know what I'm doing. Now get on with it!'

He actually shouted the last words at Horace. The big apprentice, galvanised into action, and conditioned to instant obedience to shouted commands by his months spent on the drill field, swung his sword in a murderous overhand cut at Gilan's head.

There was a ringing clash of steel and the blade stopped dead in the air. Gilan had crossed the two Ranger knives in front of it, the throwing knife supporting the saxe knife blade, and blocked the cut easily. Horace stepped back, a little surprised.

'See?' said Gilan. 'The smaller knife provides the support, or the extra leverage, for the bigger weapon.' He addressed these remarks mainly to Will, who looked on with great interest. Then he spoke to Horace again. 'Right. Underhand cut please.'

Horace swung underhand. Again, Gilan locked the two blades and blocked the stroke. He glanced at Will, who nodded his understanding.

'Now, side cut,' Gilan ordered. Again, Horace swung. Again, the sword was stopped cold.

'Getting the idea?' Gilan asked Will.

'Yes. What about a straight thrust?' he asked. Gilan nodded approvingly.

'Good question. That's a little different.' He turned back to Horace. 'Incidentally, if you're ever facing a man using two knives, thrusting is your safest and most effective form of attack. Now, thrust please.'

Horace lunged with the point of his sword, his right foot leading the way in a high-stepping stamp to deliver extra momentum to the stroke. This time, Gilan used only the saxe knife to deflect the blade, sending it gliding past his body with a slither of steel.

'We can't stop this one,' he instructed Will. 'So we simply deflect it. On the positive side, there's less force behind a thrust, so we can use just the saxe knife.'

Horace, meeting no real resistance to the thrust, had

stumbled forward as the blade was deflected. Instantly, Gilan's left hand was gripping a handful of his shirt and had pulled him closer, until their shoulders were almost touching. It happened so quickly and casually that Horace's eyes widened in surprise.

'And this is where a short blade comes in very handy indeed,' Gilan pointed out. He mimed an underarm thrust with the saxe knife into Horace's exposed side. The boy's eyes widened even further as he realised the full implications of what he had just been shown. His discomfort increased as Gilan continued his demonstration.

'And of course, if you don't want to kill him, or if he's wearing a mail shirt, you can always use the saxe blade to cripple him.'

He mimed a short swing to the back of Horace's knee, bringing the heavy, razor-sharp blade to a halt a few centimetres from his leg.

Horace gulped. But the lesson still wasn't over.

'Or remember,' Gilan added cheerfully, 'this left hand, holding his collar, also has a rather nasty, rather sharp stabbing blade attached to it.' He waggled the short, broad-bladed throwing knife to bring their attention to it.

'A quick thrust up under the jaw and it's goodnight swordsman, isn't it?'

Will shook his head in admiration.

'That's amazing, Gilan!' he breathed. 'I've never seen anything like it.'

Gilan released his grip on Horace's shirt and the boy stepped back quickly, before any more demonstrations of his vulnerability might be made.

'We don't make a lot of noise about it,' the Ranger admitted. 'It's preferable to run into a swordsman who doesn't know the dangers involved in the double knife defence.' He glanced apologetically at Horace. 'Naturally, it's taught in the Kingdom's Battleschools,' he added. 'But it's a second year subject. Sir Rodney would have shown you next year.'

Will stepped forward into the practice ground. 'Can I try it?' he asked eagerly, unsheathing his throwing knife.

'Of course,' said Gilan. 'You two may as well practise together in the evenings from now on. But not with real weapons. Cut some practice sticks to use.'

Horace nodded at the wisdom of this. 'That's right, Will,' he said. 'After all, you're just starting to learn this and I wouldn't want to hurt you.' He thought about it, then added with a grin, 'Well, not too badly, anyway.'

The grin faded as Gilan corrected him. 'That's one reason, of course,' said the Ranger. 'But we also don't have the time for you to be re-sharpening your sword every night.'

He glanced meaningfully down at Horace's blade. The apprentice followed his gaze and let out a low moan. There were two deep nicks in the edge of his blade, obviously from the overhand and underhand cuts that Gilan had blocked. One glance told Horace that he'd spend at least an hour honing and sharpening to get rid of them. He looked questioningly at the saxe knife, hoping to see the same result there. Gilan shook his head cheerfully and brought the heavy blade up for inspection.

'Not a mark,' he said, grinning. 'Remember, I told you that Ranger knives are specially made.'

Ruefully, Horace rummaged in his pack for his sharpening steel and, sitting down on the hard-packed sand, began to draw it along the edge of his sword.

'Gilan,' Will said. 'I've been thinking . . .'

Gilan raised his eyebrows to heaven in mock despair. Again, the expression reminded Will forcefully of Halt. 'Always a problem,' said the Ranger. 'And what did you think?'

'Well,' began Will slowly, 'this double knife business is all well and good. But wouldn't it be better just to shoot the swordsman before he got to close quarters?'

'Yes, Will. It certainly would,' Gilan agreed patiently. 'But what if you were about to do that and your bowstring broke?'

'I could run and hide,' he suggested, but Gilan pressed him.

'What if there were nowhere to run? You're trapped against a sheer cliff. Nowhere to go. Your bowstring just broke and an angry swordsman is coming at you. What then?'

Will shook his head. 'I suppose then I'd have to fight,' he admitted reluctantly.

'Exactly,' Gilan agreed. 'We avoid close combat wherever possible. But if the time comes when there's no other choice, it's a good idea to be prepared, isn't it?'

'I guess,' Will said. Then Horace chimed in with a question.

'What about an axeman?' he said. Gilan looked at him, nonplussed for a moment.

'An axeman?' he asked.

'Yes,' said Horace, warming to his theme. 'What about

if you're facing an enemy with a battleaxe? Do your knives work then?'

Gilan hesitated. 'I wouldn't advise anyone to face a battleaxe with just two knives,' he said carefully.

'So what should I do?' Will joined in. Gilan glared from one boy to the other. He had the feeling he was being set up.

'Shoot him,' he said shortly. Will shook his head, grinning.

'Can't,' he said. 'My bowstring's broken.'

'Then run and hide,' said Gilan, between gritted teeth.

'But there's a cliff,' Horace pointed out. 'A sheer drop behind him and an angry axeman coming at him.'

'What do I do?' prompted Will.

Gilan took a deep breath and looked them both in the eye, one after the other.

'Jump off the cliff. It'll be less messy that way.'

Six

Baron Arald shoved the heavy parchment scroll to one side and looked up at Lady Pauline in exasperation.

'Pauline, do you understand what this idiot is getting at?' he asked. The head of Castle Redmont's Diplomatic Service nodded.

'In principle, I do, my lord,' she said. Arald made a frustrated gesture.

'Then in principle, please explain it to me,' he said, adding in an undertone, 'as if I don't have enough on my plate planning for war without this sort of nonsense.'

Lady Pauline suppressed a smile. Arald had a well-known dislike of legal documents with their whereifs, wheretofores and notwithstandings.

'Sir Montague of Cobram Keep is obliged to supply a draft of four knights and thirty men at arms when called upon,' she began.

'And I take it he is refusing to do so?' said the Baron wearily.

'Not exactly, sir,' she replied. 'He is willing to supply the men. He is unwilling to place them, or himself, under your command.'

Arald frowned. 'But he *is* under my command,' he said. 'Cobram Keep is within the boundaries of Redmont Fief and I am his lord. And commander.'

Pauline nodded agreement. 'Correct, my lord. But he does have a case. A very tenuous one, I must say, but a case nonetheless.'

Arald's face, already flushed with annoyance, became a little redder. 'How can he have a case?' he demanded. 'His castle is within my boundaries. I am the lord of Redmont Fief. He is my tenant. I am his commander. End of story. Ipso facto. Case-o closed-o.'

'As he sees it, my lord, the whole thing hinges on a treaty signed by his great-great-granduncle and the present king's great-great-grandfather, when Cobram Keep became part of the Kingdom of Araluen — and the Fief of Redmont. At that time, Cobram Keep was allowed to retain a certain level of independence.'

'That's ridiculous! You can't run a kingdom like that! What was Duncan's great-great-whatever-he-was thinking?'

'It was a gesture only, my lord. The said independence would apply only to certain matters of civil administration — the right to perform and register marriages, for example — not military matters.'

'Well then!' Arald exclaimed, throwing his arms wide. 'If that's the case, where is the problem?'

'The intent is obvious, my lord, in context. But this treaty was drawn up by lawyers, so there is a certain ambiguity in the wording.'

'Ambiguity is always certain when lawyers are involved,' Arald said. His face brightened. He rather liked that piece of wordplay. It struck him as quite droll. He looked hopefully for a smile from Lady Pauline, but in vain. Deciding she must have missed it, he began again.

'You see, you said "a certain ambiguity" and I said, "Ambiguity is always certain when" —'

'Yes, yes, my lord. Quite so,' Pauline said, cutting him off. Arald looked disappointed. She continued: 'Nigel and I have gone through the treaty, and the letter, and Nigel has drafted a reply. He has found seventeen points of law where Montague has grossly misrepresented the intent of the treaty. In short, he has destroyed Montague's case most comprehensively.'

'He's good at that,' Arald said, smiling once again. This time, Pauline smiled with him.

'None better, my lord,' she said.

'So what's our next move?' the Baron asked. Pauline proffered the letter she had mentioned, but he waved it away. If Nigel and Pauline were happy with it, he knew it would be watertight. Pauline nodded. She appreciated the trust he placed in her.

'Very well, my lord. We'll do a final draft and I thought I might have one of my students deliver it.'

She replaced the draft letter in a thin leather folder and withdrew another document, laying it on the table in front of her and smoothing it out so that it lay flat.

'Now, my lord, there is another matter we must discuss . . .'

She saw the pained expression on the Baron's face. She knew he didn't want to discuss it.

'You're talking about this brouhaha with Halt, I suppose? I really don't have the time,' he said, making dismissive gestures at her.

'Nonetheless, my lord, it is a brouhaha that we must make time for.' She tapped the document with one forefinger. 'This is a summary of the brouhaha in question, my lord.'

Arald glanced up at her. She seemed to be quite fond of that word, he thought. Or she was gently making fun of his choice of it in the first place. But Lady Pauline's face gave nothing away. She continued: 'If you care to look through it?'

He reached for it reluctantly. Pauline had known that he would try to avoid the subject. It was distasteful for all of them, but unfortunately, it had to be resolved. At that moment, there was a heavy-handed knock at the door to the Baron's office and, grateful for any interruption, he hastily called, 'Come in!'

Pauline frowned at the distraction. It was Sir Rodney, head of the Redmont Battleschool. He threw the door open and entered with a little more than his usual energy. He was talking before he had even crossed the threshold.

'My lord, you're simply going to have to do something about Halt!' he said. Then, noticing Lady Pauline, he made a small gesture of apology. 'Oh, sorry, Pauline, didn't see you there.'

Lady Pauline inclined her head in acknowledgment of the apology. The Craftmasters at Redmont were all good friends. There was no petty jealousy between them, none of the manoeuvring for influence and favour that plagued some fiefs.

The Baron sighed deeply. 'What has he done now?'

'Do I sense another brouhaha in the making?' Lady Pauline said innocently and he glanced suspiciously at her. She seemed not to notice.

'Well, one of my fourth-year apprentices was stupid enough to make a remark about Will and Horace being sent off on a soft assignment. Said that's all they were good for.'

'Oh, dear,' said Lady Pauline. 'I do hope he didn't make this remark in Halt's hearing?'

'Unfortunately, yes,' said Rodney. 'He's not a bad lad. All muscle and bone, mind you, and a good deal of that between his ears. But he was feeling his oats a little and told Halt to mind his own business.' He paused, then added, by way of explanation, 'Everyone's a little jumpy, what with all the preparations for war.'

'So how is the lad?' Arald asked.

Rodney shrugged. 'The infirmary says there's no lasting damage. He'll be back on duty in a few days' time. But the point is, I can't have Halt going around damaging my apprentices. I'm going to need them soon.'

Arald toyed with one of the quill pens on his desk. 'He's definitely been difficult these past few days,' he said. 'It's like having a bear with a sore head around the castle. In fact, I think I might prefer a bear with a sore head. It would be less disruptive.'

'We were about to discuss Halt's behaviour as you arrived, Rodney,' Lady Pauline said, taking the opportunity to return the conversation to the case in hand. 'There's been a complaint about him from Sir Digby of Barga.'

'Digby?' Rodney said, a frown touching his face. 'Didn't he try to shortchange us on his draft of men?'

'Exactly,' said the Baron. 'We're having a lot of that going on at the moment. So I sent Halt to straighten matters out. Thought it might be a good idea to give him something to keep him busy.'

'So what's Digby got to complain about?' Rodney asked. It was obvious from his tone that he felt no sympathy for the recalcitrant commander of Barga Hold.

The Baron gestured for Lady Pauline to explain.

'Apparently,' she said, 'Halt threw him into the moat.'

Seven

'**W**here the devil is everyone?'

Gilan brought Blaze to a halt and looked around the deserted border post. There was a small guardhouse by the side of the road, barely large enough to keep two or three men sheltered from the wind. Further back was a slightly larger garrison house. Normally, at a small, remote border post like this, there would be a garrison totalling half a dozen men, who would live in the garrison house and take shifts at the guardhouse by the road.

Like the majority of buildings in Celtica, both structures were built in the grey sintered stone of the region, flat river stones that had been split lengthwise, with roof tiles of the same material. Wood was scarce in Celtica. Even fires for heating used coal or peat wherever possible. Whatever timber was available was needed for shoring up the tunnels and galleries of Celtica's iron and coal mines.

Will looked around him uneasily, peering into the scrubby heather that covered the windswept hills as if expecting a sudden horde of Celts to rise up from it. There was something unnerving about the near silence of the spot — there was no sound but the quiet sighing of the wind through the hills and heather.

'Perhaps they're between shifts?' he suggested his voice seeming unnaturally loud.

Gilan shook his head. 'It's a border post. It should be garrisoned at all times.'

He swung down from the saddle, making a motion for Will and Horace to stay mounted. Tug, sensing Will's uneasiness, sidestepped nervously in the road. Will calmed him with a gentle pat on the neck. The little horse's ears went up at his master's touch and he shook his head, as if to deny that he was in any way edgy.

'Could they have been attacked and driven off?' Horace asked. His mindset always worked towards fighting, which Will supposed was only natural in a Battleschool apprentice.

Gilan shrugged as he pushed open the door of the guardhouse and peered inside.

'Maybe,' he said, looking round the interior. 'But there doesn't seem to be any sign of fighting.'

He leaned against the doorway, frowning. The guardhouse was a single-roomed building, with minimal furnishing of a few benches and a table. There was nothing here to give him any clue as to where the occupants had gone.

'It's only a minor post,' he said thoughtfully. 'Perhaps the Celts have simply stopped manning it. After all, there's been a truce between Araluen and Celtica for over thirty years now.' He pushed himself away from the doorway and jerked a thumb towards the garrison house.

'Maybe we'll find something down there,' he said.

The two boys dismounted. Horace tethered his horse and the pack pony to the counterweighted bar that could swing down to close the road. Will simply let Tug's reins fall to the ground. The Ranger horse was trained not to stray. He took his bow from the leather bow scabbard behind the saddle and slung it across his shoulders. Naturally, it was already strung. Rangers always travelled with their bows ready for use. Horace, noticing the gesture, loosened his sword slightly in its scabbard and they set off after Gilan for the garrison house.

The small stone building was neat, clean and deserted. But here at least there were signs that the occupants had left in a hurry. There were a few plates on a table, bearing the dried-out remains of food, and several closet doors hung open. Items of clothing were scattered on the floor in the dormitory, as if their owners had hurriedly crammed a few belongings into packs before leaving. Several of the bunks were missing blankets.

Gilan ran a forefinger along the edge of the dining room table, leaving a wavy line in the layer of dust that had gathered there. He inspected the tip of his finger and pursed his lips.

'They didn't leave recently,' he said.

Horace, who had been peering into the small supply room under the stairs, started at the sound of the Ranger's voice, bumping his head on the low door sill.

'How can you tell?' he asked, more to cover his own

embarrassment than out of real curiosity. Gilan swept an arm around the room.

'Celts are neat people. This dust must have settled since they left. At a guess, I'd say the place has been empty for at least a month.'

'Maybe it's like you said,' Will suggested, coming down the steps from the command room. 'Maybe they decided they didn't need to keep this post manned any more.'

Gilan nodded several times. But his expression showed he wasn't convinced.

'That wouldn't explain why they left in a hurry,' he said. He swept his arm around the room. 'Look at all of this — the food on the table, the open closets, the clothes scattered on the floor. When people close down a post like this, they clean up and take their belongings with them. Particularly Celts. As I said, they're very orderly.'

He led the way outside again and swept his gaze around the deserted landscape, as if hoping to find some clue to the puzzle there. But there was nothing visible except their own horses, idly cropping the short grass that grew by the guardhouse.

'The map shows the nearest village is Pordellath,' he said. 'It's a little out of our way but perhaps we can find out what's been going on here.'

Pordellath was only five kilometres away. Because of the steep nature of the land, the path wound and zigzagged up the hillsides. Consequently, they had almost reached the little village before it came in sight. It was late in the day and both Will and Horace were feeling the pangs of hunger. They hadn't stopped for their normal noon meal, initially because they'd been in a hurry to reach the border post, then because they had pressed on to Pordellath. There would be an inn in the village and both boys were thinking fondly of a hot meal and cool drinks. As a result of this preoccupation, they were surprised when Gilan reined in as the village came into sight around the shoulder of a hill, barely two hundred metres away.

'What the hell is going on here?' he asked. 'Look at that!'

Will and Horace looked. For the life of him, Will couldn't see what might be bothering the young Ranger.

'I don't see anything,' he admitted. Gilan turned to him.

'Exactly!' he agreed. 'Nothing! No smoke from the chimneys. No people in the streets. It looks as empty as the border post!'

He nudged Blaze with his knees and the bay horse broke into a canter on the stony road. Will followed, with Horace's horse a little slower to respond. Strung out in a line, they clattered into the village, finally drawing rein in the small market square.

There wasn't much to Pordellath. Just the short main street by which they'd entered, lined with houses and shops on either side, and widening into the small square at the end. It was dominated by the largest structure which was, in Celtic fashion, the Riadhah's dwelling. The Riadhah was the hereditary village head man — a combined clan chief, mayor and sheriff. His authority was absolute and he ruled unchallenged over the villagers.

When there were any villagers for him to rule. Today there was no Riadhah. There were no villagers. Only the faint, dying echoes of the horses' hooves on the cobbled surface of the square.

'Hello!' Gilan shouted, and his voice echoed down the narrow main street, bouncing off the stone buildings, then reaching out to the surrounding hills.

'Oh – oh – oh . . .' it went, gradually tailing away into silence. The horses shifted nervously again. Will was reluctant to seem to correct the Ranger, but he was uneasy at the way he was advertising their presence here.

'Maybe you shouldn't do that?' he suggested. Gilan glanced at him, a trace of his normal good humour returning as he sensed the reason for Will's discomfort.

'Why's that?' he asked.

'Well,' Will said, glancing nervously around the deserted market square, 'if somebody has taken away the people here, maybe we don't want them to know that we've arrived.'

Gilan shrugged. 'I think it's a little late for that,' he said. 'We came galloping in here like the King's cavalry, and we've been travelling the road completely in the open. If anybody was looking out for us, they would have already seen us.'

'I suppose so,' said Will doubtfully.

Horace, meanwhile, had edged his horse up close to one of the houses and was leaning down from the saddle to peer in under the low windows, trying to see inside. Gilan noticed the movement.

'Let's take a look around,' he said, and dismounted.

Horace wasn't terribly eager to follow his example.

'What if this is some kind of plague or something?' he said.

'A plague?' asked Gilan.

Horace swallowed nervously. 'Yes. I mean, I've heard of this sort of thing happening years and years ago; whole towns would be wiped out by a plague that would sweep in and just . . . sort of . . . kill people where they stood.' As he said it, he was edging his horse away from the building, and out to the centre of the square. Will inadvertently began to follow suit. The moment Horace had raised the idea, he'd had pictures of the three of them lying dead in the square, faces blackened, tongues protruding, eyes bulging from their final agonies.

'So this plague could just come out of thin air?' Gilan asked calmly. Horace nodded several times.

'Nobody really knows how they spread,' he said. 'I've heard that it's the night air that carries plague. Or the west wind, sometimes. But however it travels, it strikes so fast there's no escape. It simply kills you where you stand.'

'Every man, woman and child in its path?' Gilan prompted. Again, Horace's head nodded frantically.

'Everyone. Kills 'em stone dead!'

Will was beginning to feel a lumpy dryness in the back of his throat, even as the other two were speaking. He tried to swallow and his throat felt raspy. He had a moment of panic as he wondered if this wasn't the first sign of the onset of the plague. His breath was coming faster and he almost missed Gilan's next question.

'And then it just . . . dissolves the dead bodies away into thin air?' he asked mildly.

'That's right!' Horace began, then realised what the Ranger had said. He hesitated, looked around the deserted village and saw no signs of people struck dead where they stood. Will's throat, coincidentally, suddenly lost that lumpy, raspish feeling.

'Oh,' said Horace, as he realised the flaw in his theory. 'Well, maybe it's a new strain of plague. Maybe it does sort of dissolve the bodies.'

Gilan looked at him sceptically, his head to one side.

'Or maybe there were one or two people who were immune, and they buried all the bodies?' Horace suggested.

'And where are those people now?' Gilan asked. Horace shrugged.

'Maybe they were so sad that they couldn't bear to live here anymore,' he said, trying to keep the theory alive a little longer.

Gilan shook his head. 'Horace, whatever it was that drove the people away from here, it wasn't the plague.' He glanced at the rapidly darkening sky. 'It's getting late. We'll take a look around, then find a place to stay the night.'

'Here?' said Will, his voice cracking with nerves. 'In the village?'

Gilan nodded. 'Unless you want to camp out in the hills,' he suggested. 'There's precious little shelter and it usually rains at night in these parts. Personally, I'd rather spend the night under a roof — even a deserted one.'

'But . . .' Will began and then could find no rational way to continue.

'I'm sure your horse would rather spend the evening under cover than out in the rain too,' Gilan added gently, and that tipped the balance with Will. His basic instinct was to look after Tug, and it was hardly fair to condemn the pony to a wet, uncomfortable night in the hills just because his owner was afraid of a few empty houses. He nodded and swung down from the saddle.

Eight

'Into his own moat, you say?' said Sir Rodney. He paused to think about the fact. Lady Pauline noticed that he didn't seem overly shocked by Halt's action. If anything, there was a look of grim satisfaction on the Battlemaster's face.

The Baron frowned at Rodney's tacit approval. 'I know the man deserved it,' he said, 'but we can't have people going around throwing knights into the moat. It's not . . . diplomatic.'

Lady Pauline raised one elegant eyebrow. 'Indeed not, sir,' she said.

'And Halt has been altogether too high-handed about it all,' he continued. 'I'm going to have to speak to him about it. Most severely.'

'Someone certainly should,' Pauline agreed.

Rodney grunted a reluctant assent. 'He definitely needs taking in hand.'

'You wanted to see me, my lord?' said a familiar voice,

and they all turned guiltily toward the door, which Rodney had left open when he barged in.

Halt stood there, clad in his grey-and-green mottled cloak, his face half hidden in the shadows of the deep cowl. It was uncanny, the Baron thought, how the man could appear almost without a sound. Now Arald, like his two Craftmasters, was conscious that he had been caught talking about Halt behind his back. He flushed in embarrassment, while Sir Rodney cleared his throat noisily. Only Lady Pauline appeared unconcerned – and she had a lifetime of practice at appearing unconcerned.

'Aaahhhh . . . yes . . . Halt. Of course. Of course. Come in, won't you? Shut the door behind you, there's a good fellow.' As he said these last words, Baron Arald shot a baleful glance at Sir Rodney, who shrugged guiltily.

Halt nodded greetings to Lady Pauline and Sir Rodney, then moved to stand before the Baron's massive desk.

There was a long and increasingly awkward silence as the Ranger stood waiting. Arald cleared his throat several times, not sure where to begin. Inevitably, it was Lady Pauline who broke the impasse.

'I imagine you're wondering why the Baron asked to see you, Halt,' she said, relieving the tension in the room and forcing Halt to say something – anything – at the same time.

The Ranger, taciturn as ever, glanced at Pauline, then the Baron, and replied in as few words as possible. 'Yes, my lord.'

But it was a start and now Baron Arald had been given a chance to gather his thoughts and overcome his embarrassment. He brandished the letter in Halt's general direction.

'This . . .' He managed in time not to say 'brouhaha' again. The word was being grossly overused, he thought. 'This . . . business with Sir Digby, Halt. It's just no good. No good at all!'

'I agree, my lord,' Halt said, and the Baron sat back in his chair, a little surprised and quite a bit relieved.

'You do?' he said.

'Yes, my lord. The man is a nincompoop and a fool. Even worse, he took me for a fool as well. I suppose I can understand that he might want to keep some of his men for the planting season. But to try to hide them in the forest from a Ranger? Why, that was a downright insult. The man needed to be taught a lesson.'

'But was it your place to teach him, Halt?' the Baron asked. Now Halt raised one eyebrow in reply.

'I don't recall seeing anyone else prepared to do so, my lord.'

'Perhaps Halt acted in haste – in the heat of the moment?' Lady Pauline interjected, trying to give Halt a graceful way out of the situation.

But the Ranger simply looked at her, then back to the Baron, and said, 'No. It was pretty well thought through. And I didn't rush at all. I took my time.'

Lady Pauline shrugged. The Baron's expression showed his exasperation. He would be willing to give Halt some leeway in this matter if the Ranger would only allow it. But Halt was obviously determined to be pig-headed.

'Then there are no mitigating circumstances, Halt,' he said firmly. 'You have acted excessively. I have no choice but to reprimand you.'

Halt considered the matter before replying. 'An awkward situation, my lord, since I am not technically answerable to you. I answer to Ranger command and, ultimately, to the King.'

The Baron opened his mouth to answer, then closed it again. Halt was right. As the Ranger attached to Redmont Fief, he was required to co-operate with the Baron, but he was independent of the Baron's authority. That fact and Halt's intentionally unhelpful manner were beginning to get under the Baron's skin. Once again, it was Lady Pauline who suggested a compromise.

'Perhaps you could inform Halt, in an official manner, that you are displeased with his actions,' she said.

The Baron considered the suggestion. It had merit, he thought. But the wording could be a little stronger.

' "Displeased" is too mild a word, Pauline. I would rather use the word "vexed".'

'I would be most discomforted to know you were vexed, my lord,' Halt said, with just the slightest trace of mockery in his tone. The Baron turned a piercing glare on him. Don't take this too far, it warned him.

'Then we shall make it "*extremely* vexed", Lady Pauline,' he said meaningfully. 'I leave it to you to put it in the right form.' He looked from her to Halt. 'You will receive the official notification of my displeasure tomorrow, Halt.'

'I tremble in anticipation, my lord,' said Halt, and the Baron's eyebrows drew together angrily.

'I think that will be all, Halt,' he said, very obviously restraining his temper. Lady Pauline shook her head slightly at Halt's sardonic tone. He was walking a very fine line, she thought. The Ranger now bowed slightly to Baron Arald, turned and left, closing the door quietly behind him.

The Baron let his breath out in an angry sigh.

'The man is impossible!' he said. 'In all the time I've known him, I have never seen him like this. He's touchy, bad-tempered, sarcastic! What on earth is the matter with him?'

Sir Rodney shook his head. Like the Baron, he had known Halt for many years, and counted him as a friend.

'Something is obviously bothering him,' he said. 'But what?'

'Perhaps he's lonely,' Lady Pauline said thoughtfully, and both men looked at her in amazement.

'Lonely? Halt?' said Sir Rodney incredulously. 'Halt's never been lonely in his life! He lives alone. He likes it that way!'

'He did,' said Lady Pauline, 'but things have been different for the past year or so, haven't they?'

'You mean . . . Will?' the Baron asked.

'Think about it. Halt has only ever had two apprentices. There was Gilan, five or six years ago. And now Will. And he's a rather special young man.'

The Baron nodded, not sure she was right but willing to listen. 'He's that, all right.'

Lady Pauline was warming to her theme now. 'He's amusing and interesting and talkative and cheerful. I should imagine he's brightened Halt's life quite considerably.'

'Not only that,' Rodney put in, 'but he saved Halt's life as well.'

'Exactly,' said Lady Pauline. 'There's a very special

bond that's developed between those two. Halt has become as much a surrogate father as a mentor to Will. And now he's sent him away. I think he's missing him. He'd never admit it, but I think he's been enjoying having a young person around.'

She paused to see what the Baron thought. He was nodding agreement.

'You could be right, Lady Pauline,' he said. 'You could be right.' He considered the matter for some seconds, then said thoughtfully, 'You know, it might be a good idea if you were to have a talk with him.'

'I, my lord?' said Lady Pauline. 'Why would I have more influence over him than anyone else?'

'Well,' said the Baron, 'I just thought that since you and he were once . . .' Something in Lady Pauline's expression stopped him from going further. 'You know?' he finished weakly.

'I'm afraid I don't, my lord,' she said. 'What is it that I should know?'

'Well, it's just that people have always said . . . you know . . . that you and Halt were once . . .' He realised he was floundering and he stopped once more. Lady Pauline was smiling expectantly at him. But the smile didn't reach her eyes. They were like ice. The Baron looked around for help and noticed Sir Rodney. He appealed to him for confirmation.

'Rodney, you've heard what people say, haven't you?'

But the Battlemaster was an experienced campaigner and he knew when a tactical retreat was the wisest course.

'I'm afraid I have no idea what you're talking about, my lord,' he said. 'I never listen to idle gossip,' he added, a little smugly. Arald shot him a baleful look. Just you wait, it said. Rodney saw it, read the message there and shrugged. He'd take the Baron's anger over Lady Pauline's any day of the week.

'A wise policy, Sir Rodney,' Lady Pauline told him. Then, turning back to the Baron, she continued, 'But perhaps I do have a suggestion that might ease the problem with Halt.'

The Baron seized the lifeline eagerly. 'That's splendid, my lady! Splendid! And in point of fact, that's all I meant when I said that you might talk to him. After all, you are a very wise woman. Very wise.'

Lady Pauline hid a smile with some difficulty. For a moment, she played with the idea of teasing him further — pretending to equate wisdom with advancing years. But she felt he had suffered enough.

'You're too kind, my lord. Altogether too kind.'

The Baron breathed a sigh of relief that the conversation had veered away from dangerous ground. He had handled it very adroitly, he thought. Women were always susceptible to flattery, after all.

'So what is this excellent idea of yours?' he said, piling it on a little more. Lady Pauline hesitated just long enough to let him know she could see right through him, then continued.

'Well, sir, since Halt is missing his apprentice, I thought we might look at replacing young Will for a week or two.'

'Replace him?' Arald said, puzzled. 'We can hardly give Halt a new apprentice for two weeks, my lady.'

'No, my lord,' she agreed. 'But I thought I might lend him one of mine.'

It was Rodney who was first to see where she was heading.

'Young Alyss,' he said, 'the tall blonde one?'

Lady Pauline inclined her head in his direction and smiled. Sir Rodney found himself wondering about the rumoured relationship between Pauline and Halt. She was tall, elegant and graceful. And even now that her blonde hair was streaked with grey, she was still an exceptional beauty.

'Exactly,' she said. 'I mentioned I'm planning to send Alyss on her first independent mission. I thought we might ask Halt to escort her. I'm sure his presence would be good for her confidence.'

Baron Arald was tugging thoughtfully at his short beard.

'She's a rather solemn lass, isn't she?' he asked, but Lady Pauline shook her head.

'On the contrary, my lord, she has a delightfully dry sense of wit. And a beautiful smile. We've been encouraging her to make greater use of it.'

'And you think a week or so in her company might snap Halt out of this black mood he's in?'

'Well, if he's looking after her, it'll take his mind off his own troubles,' Lady Pauline replied. 'In addition, Alyss is young and free-spirited — and quite beautiful. I think her company might be enough to cheer up any man. Even grim old Halt,' she added, smiling.

The Baron smiled too. 'She sounds just like her teacher.'

And this time, it was no idle flattery.

Nine

There were no answers to be found in Pordellath. The three companions went through the village and found the same signs of sudden departure that they had seen at the border post. There was evidence of some hasty packing, but in the majority of houses, most of the occupants' possessions were still in place. Everything spoke of a population that had departed in a hurry, taking what they could carry on their backs and little more. Tools, utensils, clothes, furniture and other personal goods had been left behind. But they could find no clue as to where the people of Pordellath had gone. Or why they had departed.

As it began to grow dark, Gilan finally called an end to their search. They returned to the Riadhah's house, where they unsaddled the horses and rubbed them down in the shelter of the small porch at the front of the building.

They spent an uneasy night in the house. At least, Will did and he assumed Horace was as uncomfortable as he was. Gilan, for his part, seemed relatively unperturbed, rolling himself into his cloak and falling instantly asleep when Will relieved him after the first watch. But Gilan's manner was more subdued than normal and Will guessed that the Ranger was more concerned by this baffling turn of events than he was letting on.

As he stood his watch, Will was amazed at how much noise a house could make. Doors creaked, floors groaned, the ceiling seemed to sigh with every breath of wind outside. And the village itself seemed full of loose items that would bang and clatter as well, bringing Will to a nervous, wide-eyed attention as he sat by the unglazed window in the front room of the house, the wooden shutters hooked back to keep them secure.

The moon seemed keen to join in on the subterfuge as well, soaring high above the village and casting deep pools of shadow between the houses of the village. Shadows that seemed to move slightly when you caught sight of them out of the corner of your eye, then stopped as soon as you stared directly at them.

More movement came as clouds flew across the face of the moon, alternately causing the main square to be illuminated, then plunged into sudden darkness.

Just after midnight, as Gilan had predicted, a steady rain set in and the other noises were joined by the gurgle of running water and the plash-plash-plash of drops falling off eaves and into puddles below.

Will woke Horace to take over the watch at around two in the morning. He piled up a stack of cushions and bed-covers on the floor of the main room, wrapped his cloak around him and lay down.

Then he lay awake for another hour and a half, listening to the creaks, the groans, the gurgles and the splashes, wondering whether Horace had dropped off to sleep and whether, even now, some unseen horror was creeping up on the house, bloodthirsty and unstoppable.

He was still worrying about it when he finally fell asleep.

They were on the road early the following morning. The rain had stopped just before dawn and Gilan was keen to press on to Gwyntaleth, the first large town on their route, and find some answers to the puzzles that they had found so far in Celtica. They had a quick, cold breakfast, washed down with icy water from the village well, then saddled up and rode out.

They wound down the stony path from the village, taking their time on the uneven surface. But when they hit the main road once more, they urged their horses into a canter. They held the canter for twenty minutes, then rested the horses by riding at a walk for the next twenty. They maintained that alternating, steady pattern through the morning.

They ate a quick meal in the middle of the day, then rode on. This was the principal mining area of Celtica and they passed at least a dozen coal or iron mines: large black holes cut into the sides of hills and mountains, surrounded by timber shoring and stone buildings. Nowhere, however, did they see any sign of life. It was as if the inhabitants of Celtica had simply vanished from the face of the earth.

'They may have deserted their border post, and even their villages,' Gilan muttered once, almost to himself. 'But I've never yet met a Celt who would desert a mine while there was an ounce of metal still to be torn from it.'

Eventually, in midafternoon, they came over a crest and there, in a valley dropping away from them, were the neat rows of stone roofs that formed Gwyntaleth township. A small spire in the centre of the town marked a temple — the Celts had their own unique religion, which had to do with the gods of fire and iron. A larger tower formed the main defensive position for the town.

They were too far away to make out whether there might be any movement of people in the streets. But, as before, there was no sign of smoke from the chimneys and, even more significantly, according to Gilan, no noise.

'Noise?' Horace asked. 'What kind of noise?'

'Banging, hammering, clanking,' Gilan answered him briefly. 'Remember, the Celts don't just mine iron ore. They work the iron as well. With the breeze blowing from the south-west as it is, we should be able to hear the forges at work, even from this distance.'

'Well, let's go see then,' Will said, and began to urge Tug forward. Gilan, however, put up a hand to restrain him.

'I think perhaps I might go on ahead alone,' he said slowly, his eyes never leaving the town in the valley below them. Will looked at him, puzzled.

'Alone?' he asked and Gilan nodded.

'You noted yesterday that we were making ourselves pretty obvious when we rode into Pordellath. Perhaps it's time we became a little more circumspect. Something is going on and I'd like to know what it is.'

Will had to agree that it made good sense for Gilan to go on alone. After all, he was possibly the best unseen mover in the Ranger Corps, and Rangers were the best unseen movers in the Kingdom.

Gilan motioned for them to fall back from the crest they were standing on, and down the other side to a spot where a small gully formed a sheltered camp site, out of the wind.

'Set up a camp here,' he told them. 'No fires. We'll have to stay with cold rations until we know what's going on. I should be back some time after dark.'

And with that, he wheeled Blaze and trotted him back over the crest and down the road towards Gwyntaleth.

Will and Horace took half an hour or so to set up the camp site. There was little to do. They attached their tarpaulin to some scrubby bushes growing out of the stone wall of the gully, weighing down the other end with rocks. At least there were plenty of them. This gave them a triangular shelter in case the rain set in again. Then they prepared a fireplace in front of the shelter. Gilan had said no fires, but if he arrived back in the middle of the night and changed those orders, they might as well be ready.

It took a considerably longer time to stack a supply of firewood. The only real source was the scrubby heather that covered the hillsides. The roots and branches of the bush were tough but highly flammable. The two boys hacked out a reasonable supply, Horace using the small hatchet he carried in his pack and Will his saxe knife. Eventually, with all their housekeeping taken care of, they sat on either side of the empty fireplace, their backs leaning against rocks. Will spent a few minutes running his sharpening stone over the saxe knife, restoring its razor-sharp edge.

'I really prefer camping in forest areas,' Horace said, shifting his back for the tenth time against the unyielding rock behind him.

Will grunted in reply. But Horace was bored and kept on talking, more for the sake of having something to do than because he really wanted to.

'After all, in a forest, you have lots of firewood, ready to hand. It just falls out of the trees for you.'

'Not while you wait,' Will disagreed. He, too, was talking more for the sake of it than anything else.

'No. Not while you wait. Usually it's already happened before you arrive,' Horace said. 'Plus in a forest, you've usually got pine needles or leaves on the ground. And that makes for a softer sleeping place. And there are logs and trees to sit on and lean against. And they have a lot fewer sharp edges than rock.'

Again, he wriggled his back to a temporarily more comfortable spot. He glanced up at Will, rather hoping that the apprentice Ranger might disagree with him. Then they could argue to pass the time. Will however, merely grunted again. He inspected the edge of his saxe knife, slid the knife back into its scabbard and lay back. Uncomfortable, he sat up again, undid the knife belt and draped it over his pack, along with his bow and quiver. Then he lay back, his head on a flat piece of stone. He closed his eyes. The sleepless night he had spent had left him drained and flat.

Horace sighed to himself, then took out his sword and began honing its edge — quite unnecessarily, as it was already razor-sharp. But it was something to do. He rasped away, glancing occasionally at Will to see if his friend was asleep. For a moment, he thought he was, but then the smaller boy suddenly squirmed around, sat up and reached for his cloak. Bundling it up, he put it on the flat stone he was using as a head rest, then lay back again.

'You're right about forests,' he said crankily. 'Much more comfortable places to camp.'

Horace said nothing. He decided his sword was sharp enough and slid it back into its oiled leather scabbard, leaning the sheathed weapon against the rock face beside him.

He watched Will again, as he tried to find a comfortable spot. No matter how he twisted and squirmed, there was always a pebble or a piece of rock poking into his back or side. Five or ten minutes passed, then Horace finally said:

'Want to practise? It'll pass the time.'

Will opened his eyes and considered the idea. Reluctantly, he admitted to himself that he was never going to get to sleep on this hard, stony ground.

'Why not?' He rummaged in his pack for his practice weapons, then joined Horace on the far side of the tent, where he was scraping a practice circle in the sandy gully floor. The two boys took up their positions, then, at a nod from Horace, they began.

Will was improving but Horace was definitely the master at this exercise. Will couldn't help admiring the speed and balance he showed as he wielded the wooden sword in a dazzling series of backhands, forehands, side cuts and overheads. Furthermore, when he knew he had beaten Will's defensive posture, he would, at the last moment, hold back from whacking him. Instead, he would lightly touch the spot where his blow would have fallen, to demonstrate the point.

He didn't do it with any sense of superiority, either. Weapons practice, even with wooden weapons, was a serious part of Horace's life nowadays. It wasn't something to crow about when you were better than your opponent. Horace had learned only too well in dozens of practice bouts at the Battleschool that it never paid to underestimate an opponent.

Instead, he used his superior ability to help Will, showing him how to anticipate strokes, teaching him the basic combinations that all swordsmen used and the best way to defeat them.

As Will ruefully acknowledged, knowing how to do it was one thing. Actually doing it was an entirely different matter. He realised how much his former enemy had matured and wondered if the same changes were evident in himself. He didn't think so. He didn't feel any different. And whenever he saw himself in a mirror he didn't seem to look any different either.

'Your left hand is dropping too far,' Horace pointed out as they paused between bouts.

'I know,' Will said. 'I'm expecting a side cut and I want to be ready for it.'

Horace shook his head. 'That's all very well, but if you drop it too far, it's easy for me to feint a side cut then swing up into an overhand. See?'

He showed Will the action he was describing, beginning the sword in a wide sideways sweep then, with a powerful wrist movement, taking it up into a high swinging downward stroke. He stopped the wooden blade a few centimetres from Will's head and the Ranger apprentice saw that his counterstroke would have been far too late.

'Sometimes I think I'll never learn these things,' he said.

Horace patted him encouragingly on the shoulder. 'Are you kidding?' he asked. 'You're improving every day. And besides, I could never shoot or use those throwing knives the way you do.'

Even while they had been on the road, Gilan had insisted that Will practise his Ranger skills as often as was practical. Horace had been impressed, to say the least, when he had seen how adept the smaller boy had become. Several times, he had shuddered when he thought what might happen if he had to face an archer such as Will. His accuracy with the bow was uncanny, as far as Horace was concerned. He knew that Will could place arrows into every gap in his armour if he chose. Even into the narrow vizor slit of a full-face jousting helmet.

What he didn't appreciate was that Will's accuracy was nothing more than average as far as Ranger standards were concerned.

'Let's try it again,' Will suggested wearily. But another voice interrupted them.

'Let's not, little boys. Let's put down our nasty sharp sticks and stand very still, shall us?'

The two apprentices whirled around at the words. There, at the mouth of the small U-shaped gully where they had built their camp, stood two ragged-looking figures. Both were heavily bearded and unkempt and both were dressed in a strange mixture of clothing — some of it tattered and threadbare, while some items were new and obviously very costly. The taller of the two wore a richly brocaded satin vest, but it was thick with dirt. The other sported a scarlet hat with a bedraggled feather in it. He also carried an iron-spiked wooden club, holding it in a hand that was swathed in a dirty bandage. His companion had a long sword, jagged and nicked along the edges. He flourished it now at the two boys.

'Come on now, you boys. Sharp sticks're danger-orius for the likes of you,' he said, and let go a hoarse, guttural laugh.

Will's hand dropped automatically to reach for the saxe knife, encountering nothing. With a sinking feeling, he realised that his knife belt, bow and quiver were all neatly piled on the far side of the fireplace, where he had been sitting. The two intruders would stop him before he could reach them. He cursed himself for his carelessness. Halt would be furious, he thought. Then, looking at the sword and club, he realised that Halt's annoyance might be the least of his worries.

Ten

The girl was smiling at him again. Halt sensed it. It was as if he could actually *feel* the smile radiating at him. He knew if he were to glance sideways at her, where she was riding just a few paces away from him, he would see it once more.

But he couldn't help himself. He looked and there it was. Wide, friendly and infectious. In spite of himself, it made him want to smile back in return and that would never do. Halt hadn't spent years cultivating a grim, unapproachable manner just to have it dispelled by this girl and her smile.

He glared at her instead. Alyss's smile widened.

'Why, Halt,' she said cheerfully, 'what a grim face that is to ride alongside.'

They had left Castle Redmont the previous day for the short ride to Cobram Keep. Halt had agreed readily when Lady Pauline had asked him to escort Alyss on her first assignment – in point of fact, he would have agreed to most things suggested by the head of Redmont's Diplomatic Service. Of course, as a Courier, Alyss rated an official guard of two mounted men at arms, and they rode a few metres to the rear. But Pauline had suggested that Alyss might need advice or counsel in dealing with Sir Montague. Halt had agreed to provide it if necessary.

What Lady Pauline hadn't mentioned was Alyss's innate friendliness and the fact that she was so eminently *likeable*. And cheerful, he thought, and that reminded him of someone else. He had been missing Will's lively presence over the past week or so, he admitted. After years of living by himself, attending to the secret and sometimes frightening business of the Kingdom, he had enjoyed the light and laughter that Will brought to his life. Now Will was far away, on his way to the Celtic court, and Halt himself had sent him there. He realised that the boy's absence left a void in his life. Reluctantly, he told himself that he must be growing old — and sentimental.

Now here was this girl, barely sixteen but already poised and sure of herself, chiding him gently for his black mood and grim countenance and fixing him with that damned smile.

'And such a silent face as well,' she mused to herself. He realised that he had been ill-mannered and she didn't deserve that.

'My apologies, Lady Alyss,' he said curtly. Travelling on official business, Alyss was entitled to be addressed as 'Lady Alyss'. She frowned at his formality.

'Oh, come now, Halt. Is that any way for friends to speak to each other?'

He glanced at her now. The smile was still lurking there

at the corners of her mouth. The frown was an artifice. She was gently teasing him, he realised, and he determined that he would not give her the satisfaction of rising to her bait.

'Are we friends, Lady Alyss?' he said, and she inclined her head thoughtfully. The action reminded him of Lady Pauline and he realised how much this girl was like her mentor. He remembered Pauline when she was much younger. It could have been her riding beside him, he thought.

'I would hope so, Halt. After all, I am a friend of Will's and I'm apprenticed to one of *your* oldest friends, I believe. Doesn't this give us some kind of . . . special relationship?'

'I am your escort, Lady,' he replied and his tone left no doubt that the conversation should end there.

With most people, that would have been the result. Halt could be quite a forbidding figure when he chose. And many people clung to the belief that Rangers dabbled in black magic, and so were people who should not be annoyed. Obviously, however, this girl wasn't one of those people.

'As you say, you're my escort. And I'm very grateful that you are. But that's not to say that we can't be friends as well. After all, it's quite daunting to be on my first assignment.' She paused, and then said quietly, 'I'm not altogether sure that I'm up to it, as a matter of fact.'

'Of course you are!' Halt said immediately. 'Pauline knows her business. If you weren't "up to it", as you put it, she would never have entrusted the mission to you. She thinks very highly of you, you know,' he added.

'She's an amazing woman,' Alyss said, and the

admiration in her voice was obvious. 'I've looked up to her for years. She's succeeded so well in what is generally regarded as a man's world.'

Halt nodded agreement. 'Amazing is a good word for her. She's courageous, honest and enormously intelligent. Smarter than most men too. Baron Arald saw those qualities in her years ago. She was the one who convinced him that women are more suited to the diplomatic role than men.'

'I've heard people say that. Why does he think that way?'

Halt shrugged. 'He feels women are more inclined to talk things through, whereas men tend to resort to physical methods more quickly.'

'So, for example, Lady Pauline would never resort to throwing someone into a moat if they were being objectionable?' she said, and Halt glanced up at her sharply. Her face was totally deadpan. Pauline had trained her well, he thought.

'No,' he agreed. 'But I didn't say that she's always right. Some people deserve to be thrown into moats.'

He realised now that he had been chattering on with her for some minutes, in spite of his determination to maintain his usual grim, tight-lipped manner. She had drawn him out like an angler luring a fish to the hook, and he wasn't sure how she had done it. And now she was smiling at him again. He harrumphed noisily and turned away to scan the woods on either side.

This far to the west, there was little danger to be expected. And his horse Abelard would alert him if there were any enemies or wild beasts lurking in the bushes nearby. But scanning the terrain gave him an opportunity to break off the conversation.

Alyss watched him curiously. She had seen him around Redmont for years, of course. But when Lady Pauline had introduced them the day before, she had been surprised to realise that he was at least a head shorter than she was. A lot of men were, though. She was an exceptionally tall girl and she carried herself erect. But Halt had an amazing reputation — a seven-foot-tall reputation, she mused. He was famous throughout the Kingdom and one tended to think of him as a larger-than-life character. Seen close-up, he was surprisingly small in stature. Like Will, she thought, and that set her to wondering.

'What qualities does a Ranger need, Halt?' she asked.

He glanced back at her. Once bitten, twice shy, he thought. She wasn't going to draw him out into an extended conversation again.

'A propensity for silence is a good one,' he said, and she smiled, genuinely amused at something.

'Somehow I can't see Will managing that,' she said. She and Will had grown up together as orphans in the Castle Ward. He was probably her oldest friend.

In spite of himself, Halt's lips twitched in what was almost a smile.

'No. He does tend to chatter, doesn't he?' he agreed. Then, realising that she might think he was criticising the boy, he continued quickly, 'But that's part of being a Ranger as well. He's always asking questions. He's always curious, always ready to learn more. A good Ranger needs that. Eventually, he'll learn to curb his tongue a little.'

'Not entirely, I hope,' said Alyss. 'I can't imagine Will

becoming grim and forbidding and taciturn, like' — she hesitated and amended what she was about to say — 'some people.'

Halt raised one eyebrow at her. 'Some people?' he repeated, and she shrugged.

'Nobody particular in mind.' Then, changing tack, she said, 'He's very brave, isn't he? I mean, you must be proud of what he's done.'

Halt nodded. 'He has true courage,' he said. 'He can feel fear, he can be afraid. But it doesn't stop him from doing what he has to. Mindless courage isn't any sort of real courage at all.'

'You've trained him well,' Alyss said, but Halt shook his head.

'The training is important. But the qualities have to be there from the beginning. You can't teach courage and honesty. There's a basic openness and lack of malice in Will.'

'You know,' she said confidentially 'when I was a child, I always said I was going to marry him.'

Inwardly, he smiled at her words. *When I was a child.* She was barely more than a child now, he thought. Then he changed his mind. She was a Courier. An apprentice to the Diplomatic Service. She wore the bronze laurel branch and that meant she was very much more than a child.

'You could do a lot worse,' he said finally, and she glanced across at him.

'Really?' she said. 'Do you think diplomats and Rangers make a good match, Halt?' Her tone was just too innocent, too casual. He knew exactly what she was getting at and this time he wasn't going to be drawn. He was not going to discuss any relationship that might or might not have existed between himself and the beautiful Lady Pauline.

He met her gaze very evenly for some moments, then said, 'I think we might stop here for lunch. This is as good a place as any.'

Alyss's mouth twitched with a smile again. But this time it was a slightly rueful one.

'You can't blame a girl for trying,' she said.

Eleven

Will felt Horace's hand on his shoulder as the bigger boy began to pull him back from the two bandits.

'Back away, Will,' Horace said quietly.

The man with the club laughed. 'Yes, Will, you back away. You stay away from that nasty little bow I see over there. We don't hold no truck with bows, do us, Carney?'

Carney grinned at his companion. 'That we don't, Bart, that we don't.' He looked back at the two boys and frowned angrily. 'Didn't we tell you to drop those sticks?' he demanded, his voice rising in pitch and very, very ugly in tone. Together, the two men began to advance across the clearing.

Horace's grip now tightened and he jerked Will to one side, sending him sprawling. As he fell, he saw Horace turn to the rocks behind him and grab up his sword. He flicked it once and the scabbard sailed clear of the blade. That easy action alone should have warned Bart and Carney that they were facing someone who knew more than a little about handling weapons. But neither of them was overly bright. They simply saw a boy of about sixteen. A big boy, perhaps, but still a boy. A child, really, with a grown-up weapon in his hand.

'Oh dear,' said Carney. 'Have we got our daddy's sword with us?'

Horace eyed him, suddenly very calm. 'I'll give you one chance,' he said, 'to turn around and leave now.'

Bart and Carney exchanged mock terrified looks.

'Oh dear, Bart,' said Carney. 'It's our one chance. What'll us do?'

'Oh dear,' said Bart. 'Let's run away.'

They began to advance on Horace and he watched them coming. He had the practice stick in his left hand now and the sword in his right. He tensed, balanced on the balls of his feet as they advanced on him, Carney with the rusty, ragged-edged sword snaking in front of him and Bart with the spiked cudgel laid back on his shoulder, ready for use.

Will scrambled to his feet and began to move towards his weapons. Seeing the action, Carney, moved to cut him off. He hadn't gone a pace when Horace attacked.

He darted forward and his sword flashed in an overhead cut at Carney. Startled by the sheer speed of the apprentice warrior's move, Carney barely had time to bring his own blade up in a clumsy parry. Thrown off balance and totally unprepared for the surprising force and authority behind the stroke, he stumbled backwards and sprawled in the dust.

In the same instant, Bart, seeing his companion in trouble, stepped forward and swung the heavy club in a vicious arc at Horace's unprotected left side. His expectation was for Horace to try to leap back to avoid the blow. Instead, the apprentice warrior stepped forward. The practice stick in his left hand flicked up and outwards, catching the heavy cudgel in its downward arc and deflecting it away from its intended line. The club's spiked head thudded dully into the stony ground and Bart let go a deep 'whoof' of surprise, the impact jarring his arm from shoulder to wrist.

But Horace wasn't finished yet. He continued the forward lunge, and now he and Bart stood shoulder to shoulder. It was too close for Horace to use the blade of his sword. Instead, he swung his right fist, hammering the heavy brass pommel of his sword hilt into the side of Bart's head.

The bandit's eyes glazed and he collapsed to his knees, semi-conscious, head swaying slowly from side to side.

Carney, back-pedalling furiously through the sand, had regained his feet. Now he stood watching Horace, puzzled and angry. Unable to grasp the fact that he and his companion had been bested by a mere boy. Luck, he thought. Sheer, dumb luck!

His lips formed into a snarl and he gripped the sword tightly, advancing once more on the boy, mouthing threats and curses as he went. Horace stood his ground, waiting. Something in the boy's calm gaze made Carney hesitate. He should have gone with his first instincts and given the fight away then and there. But anger overcame him and he started forward again.

By now, he was paying no attention to Will. The Ranger's apprentice darted around the camp site, grabbing his bow and quiver and hastily stepping his right foot through the recurve to brace the bow against his left while he slid the string up into its notch.

Quickly, he selected an arrow and nocked it to the string. He was about to draw back when a calm voice behind him said:

'Don't shoot him. I'd rather like to see this.'

Startled, he turned to find Gilan behind him, almost invisible in the folds of his Ranger cloak, leaning non-chalantly on his longbow.

'Gilan!' he began, but the Ranger made a sound for silence.

'Just let him go,' he said softly. 'He'll be fine as long as we don't distract him.'

'But . . .' Will began desperately, looking to where his friend was facing a full-grown, very angry man. Sensing his concern, Gilan hurried to reassure him.

'Horace will handle him,' he said. 'He really is very good, you know. A natural, if ever I saw one. That bit with the practice stick and the hilt strike was sheer poetry. Lovely improvisation!'

Shaking his head in wonder, Will turned back to the fight. Now Carney attacked, hacking and lunging and cutting with a blind fury and terrifying power. Horace gradually gave way before him, his own sword moving in small, semi-circular actions that blocked every cut and hack and thrust and jarred Carney's wrist and elbow with the strength and impenetrability of his defence. All the while, Gilan was whispering an approving commentary beside Will.

'Good boy!' he said. 'See how he's letting the other

fellow start proceedings? Gives him an idea of how skilful he might be. Or otherwise. My God, he's got the timing of that defensive swing just about perfect! Look at that! And that! Terrific!'

Now Horace had apparently decided not to back away any further. Continuing to parry Carney's every stroke with obvious ease, he stood his ground, letting the bandit expend his strength like the sea breaking on a rock. And as he stood, Carney's strokes became slower and more ragged. His arm was beginning to ache with the effort of wielding the long, heavy sword. He was really more accustomed to using a knife to the back of most of his opponents and he hadn't looked for this engagement to go past one or two crushing, hacking strokes to break down the boy's guard before killing him. But his most devastating blows had been flicked aside with apparent contempt.

He swung again, losing his balance in the follow-through. Horace's blade caught his, spun it in a circle, holding it with his own, then let it rasp down its length until their crosspieces locked.

They stood there, eye to eye, Carney's chest heaving, Horace absolutely calm and totally in control. The first worm of fear appeared in Carney's stomach as he realised that, boy or not, he was hopelessly outmatched in this contest.

And at that point, Horace went on the attack.

He drove his shoulder into Carney's chest, unlocking their blades and sending the bandit staggering back. Then, calmly, Horace advanced, swinging his sword in confusing, terrifying combinations. Side, overhead, thrust. Side, side, backhand, overhead. Thrust. Thrust. Thrust. Forehand.

Backhand. One combination flowed smoothly into the next and Carney scrambled desperately, trying to bring his own blade between himself and the implacable sword that seemed to have a life and an inexhaustible energy all its own. He felt his wrist and arm tiring, while Horace's strokes grew stronger and firmer until finally, with a dull and final CLANG, Horace simply beat the sword from his numbed grasp.

Carney sank to his knees, sweat pouring off him and running into his eyes, chest heaving with exertion, waiting for the final stroke that would end it all.

'Don't kill him, Horace!' called Gilan. 'I'd like to ask him some questions.'

Horace looked up, surprised to see the tall Ranger standing there. He shrugged. He wasn't really the type to kill an opponent in cold blood anyway. He flicked Carney's sword to one side, way out of reach. Then, setting one boot against the defeated bandit's shoulder, he shoved him over in the dust on his side.

Carney lay there, sobbing, unable to move. Terrified. Worn out. Physically and mentally defeated.

'Where did you come from?' Horace asked Gilan indignantly. 'And why didn't you give me a hand?'

Gilan grinned at him. 'You didn't seem to need one, from what I could see,' he replied. Then he gestured behind Horace to where Bart was slowly rising from his kneeling position, shaking his head as the effect of the hilt strike began to wear off.

'I think your other friend needs a little attention,' he suggested. Horace turned and casually raised his sword, swinging it to clang, flat-bladed, against Bart's skull.

Another small moan and Bart went face down in the sand.

'I really think you might have said something,' he said.

'I would have if you were in trouble,' Gilan said. Then he moved across the clearing to stand over Carney. He seized the bandit by the arm and dragged him upright, frogmarching him across the clearing to throw him, none too gently, against the rock face at the far side. As Carney began to sag forward, there was a hiss of steel on leather and Gilan's saxe knife appeared at his throat, keeping him upright.

'It seems these two caught you napping?' Gilan asked Will. The boy nodded, shamefaced. Then, as the full import of the comment sank in, he asked:

'Just how long have you been here?'

'Since they arrived,' Gilan said. 'I hadn't gone far when I saw them skulking through the rocks. So I left Blaze and doubled back here, trailing them. Obviously they were up to no good.'

'Why didn't you say something then?' Will asked incredulously.

For a moment, Gilan's eyes hardened. 'Because you two needed a lesson. You're in dangerous territory, the population seems to have mysteriously disappeared and you stand around practising sword craft for all the world to see and hear.'

'But,' Will stammered, 'I thought we were supposed to practise?'

'Not when there's no one else to keep an eye on things,' Gilan pointed out reasonably. 'Once you start practising like that, your attention is completely distracted. These two made enough noise to alert a deaf old granny. Tug even gave you a warning call twice and you missed it.'

Will was totally crestfallen. 'I did?' he said and Gilan nodded. For a moment, his gaze held Will's, until he was sure the lesson had been driven home and the point taken. Then he nodded slightly, signifying that the matter was closed. Will nodded in return. It wouldn't happen again.

'Now,' said Gilan, 'let's find out what these two beauties know about the price of coal.'

He turned back to Carney, who was now going quite cross-eyed as he tried to watch the gleaming saxe knife pressed against his throat.

'How long have you been in Celtica?' Gilan asked him. Carney looked up at him, then back to the heavy knife.

'Tuh-tuh-tuh-ten or eleven days, my lord,' he stammered eventually.

Gilan made a pained face. 'Don't call me "my lord",' he said, adding as an aside to the two boys, 'These people always try to flatter you when they realise they're in trouble. Now . . .' He returned his gaze to Carney. 'What brought you here?'

Carney hesitated, his eyes sliding away from Gilan's direct gaze so that the Ranger knew he was going to lie even before the bandit spoke.

'Just . . . wanted to see the sights, my . . . sir,' he amended, remembering at the last moment Gilan's instruction not to call him 'my lord'. Gilan sighed and shook his head with exasperation.

'Look, I'd just as soon lop your head off here and now. I really doubt that you have anything useful to tell me.

But I'll give you one last chance. Now let's have THE TRUTH!'

He shouted the last two words angrily, his face suddenly only a few centimetres away from Carney's. The sudden transition from the languid, joking manner he had been using came as a shock to the bandit. Just for a few seconds, Gilan let his good-natured shield slip and Carney saw through to the white hot anger that was just below the surface. In that instant, he was afraid. Like most people, he was nervous of Rangers. Rangers were not people to make angry. And this one seemed to be very, very angry.

'We heard there were good pickings down here!' he answered immediately.

'Good pickings?' Gilan asked and Carney nodded dutifully, the flood gates of conversation now well and truly open.

'All the towns and cities deserted, like. Nobody there to guard them, and all their valuables left lying around for us'n to take as we chose. We didn't harm nobody though,' he concluded, a little defensively.

'Oh no. You didn't harm them. You just crept in while they were gone and stole everything of value that they owned,' Gilan told him. 'I should think they'd be almost grateful for your contribution!'

'It was Bart's idea, not mine,' Carney tried and Gilan shook his head sadly.

'Gilan?' Will said tentatively, and the Ranger turned to look at him. 'How would they have heard that the towns were deserted? We didn't hear a thing.'

'Thieves' grapevine,' Gilan told the two boys. 'It's like the way vultures gather whenever an animal is in trouble.

The intelligence network between thieves and robbers and brigands is incredibly fast. Once a place is in trouble, word spreads like wildfire and they come down on it in their scores. I should imagine there are plenty more of them through these hills.'

He turned back to Carney as he said it, prodding the saxe knife a little deeper into the flesh of his neck, just holding it back so that it didn't draw blood.

'Aren't there?' he asked. Carney went to nod, realised what might happen if his neck moved, gulped instead and whispered:

'Yes, sir.'

'And I should imagine you've got a cave somewhere, or a deserted mine tunnel, where you've stowed the loot you've stolen so far?'

He eased the pressure on the knife and this time Carney was able to manage a nod. His fingers fluttered towards the belt pouch that he wore at his waist, then stopped as he realised what he was doing. But Gilan had caught the gesture. With his free hand, he ripped open the pouch and fumbled inside it, finally withdrawing a grubby sheet of paper, folded in quarters. He passed it to Will.

'Take a look,' he said briefly and Will unfolded the paper, revealing a clumsily drawn map with reference points, directions and distances all indicated.

'They've buried their loot, by the look of this,' he said and Gilan nodded, smiling thinly.

'Good. Then without their map, they won't be able to find it again,' he said, and Carney's eyes shot wide open in protest.

'But that's ours . . .' he began, stopping as he saw the dangerous glint in Gilan's eyes.

'It was stolen,' the Ranger said, in a very low voice. 'You crept in like jackals and stole it from people who are obviously in deep trouble. It's not yours. It's theirs. Or their family's, if they're still alive.'

'They're still alive,' said a new voice from behind them. 'They've run from Morgarath — those he hasn't already captured.'

Twelve

Sir Montague kept Alyss waiting for over an hour before deigning to receive her.

Halt and Alyss waited in the anteroom to Montague's office. Halt stood to one side, leaning impassively on his longbow. Montague was an oaf, he thought. As a Courier on official business Alyss should have been greeted without delay. Obviously aware of her youth, the Master of Cobram Keep was attempting to assert his own importance by treating her as an everyday messenger.

He watched the girl approvingly as she sat, straight-backed, in one of the hard chairs in the anteroom. She appeared calm and unflustered in spite of the insult she was being offered. She had changed from her riding clothes when they were a few kilometres from the castle and she was now dressed in the simple but elegant white gown of a Courier. The bronze laurel branch pin, the symbol of her authority, fastened a short blue cape at her right shoulder.

For his part, Halt had left his distinctive mottled

Ranger's cloak folded on the pommel of Abelard's saddle. His longbow and quiver, however, he retained. He never went anywhere without them.

Alyss glanced up at him and he nodded, almost imperceptibly, to her. *Don't let him make you angry.* She returned the nod, acknowledging the message. Her hands, which were clenched into fists on her knees, slowly relaxed as she took several deep breaths.

This girl is very good, Halt thought.

Montague's secretary had obviously been well briefed by his master. After peremptorily waving Alyss to a chair and leaving Halt to stand, he had busied himself with paperwork and resolutely ignored them — rising several times to take items in to the inner office. Finally, at the sound of a small bell tinkling from beyond the door, he looked up and gestured toward the office.

'You can go in now,' he said disinterestedly. Alyss frowned slightly. Protocol dictated that a Courier should be properly announced, but the man obviously had no intention of doing so. She rose gracefully and moved toward the door, Halt following. That got the secretary's attention.

'You can wait here, forester,' he said rudely. Without the cloak, there was little to distinguish Halt from a yeoman. He was dressed in simple brown leggings, soft leather boots and a green surcoat. The double knife scabbard had apparently escaped the secretary's notice. Or perhaps he didn't realise its significance.

'He's with me,' Alyss said. The unmistakable tone of authority in her voice stopped the man cold. He hesitated, then rose from behind the desk and moved toward Halt.

'Very well. But you'd better leave that bow with me,' he said, without quite the certainty that he had displayed earlier. He held out his hand for the bow, then met Halt's eyes. He saw something very dangerous there and he actually flinched.

'All right, all right. Keep it if you must,' he muttered. He backed away, more than a little flustered, retreating behind the secure bulk of his desk. Halt opened the door for Alyss, then followed her as she entered the office.

Montague of Cobram was seated at a large oaken table that served as a desk. He was studying a letter and didn't look up from it as Alyss approached. Halt was willing to bet that the letter was about something totally unimportant. The man was playing silly mind games, he thought.

But Alyss was up to the challenge. She stepped forward and produced a heavy scroll from her sleeve, slapping it briskly down on the table before Montague. He started in surprise, looking up. Halt hid a smile.

'Alyss Mainwaring, Sir Montague, Courier from Castle Redmont. My credentials.'

Montague wasn't just an oaf, Halt thought. He was a fop as well. His satin doublet was formed in alternating quarters of scarlet and gold. His reddish-blond hair was left in overlong curls, framing a somewhat chubby face with slightly bulging blue eyes and a petulant mouth. He was of average height, but of somewhat more than average weight. He would be passably handsome, Halt supposed, if he could shed some weight, but the man obviously liked to indulge himself. Montague recovered now from his momentary surprise and leaned back in his chair, adopting a languid, slightly disapproving tone.

'Good heavens, girl, you can't come in here throwing your credentials on the desk like that! Don't they teach good manners at Castle Redmont these days?'

He looked distastefully at the scroll and shoved it to one side.

'They teach protocol, Sir Montague,' Alyss replied, very evenly. 'And it requires that you examine and acknowledge my credentials before we proceed.'

'Yes, yes, yes,' Montague said, waving a dismissive hand at the scroll. 'Take it as read. Take it as read. Now, girl, what brings you here?'

Halt interjected quietly, 'The correct form of address, Sir Montague, is "Lady Alyss".'

Montague looked at Halt in genuine surprise, as if he considered him some lower form of life who lacked the ability of speech.

'Is that so, forester?' he said. 'And what might your name be?'

Alyss went to speak, but a warning glance from Halt stopped her. He replied, still in the same quiet tone, 'Some people call me Arratay, Sir Montague. It's Gallican,' he added mildly.

Montague raised his eyebrows in mock surprise. 'Gallican, you say? How exotic! Well, Master *Arratay*, perhaps you could leave the talking to me and young Alyss here, would that suit you?'

Halt shrugged and Montague took the movement for assent.

'Wonderful.' Then, dismissing Halt, he turned his attention back to Alyss. 'So, sweetheart, what do you have for me? A letter, perhaps? Some self-important note from Fat Baron Arald, I'll be bound?'

There were two small spots of colour in Alyss's cheeks, the only outward sign of the anger that was building up inside her at the man's offhanded manner. She produced Nigel's heavy linen envelope from the satchel she wore at her side and offered it across the desk.

'I have an official legal position, prepared under Baron Arald's seal. He requests that you study it.'

Montague made no move to take the letter.

'Set it down. I'll look at it when I have time.'

'The Baron requests that you look at it now, sir. And give me your answer.'

Montague rolled his eyes to heaven and took the envelope. 'Oh, very well, if it will make you happy.' He sliced the envelope and took out the sheet of parchment inside it, skimming through it, muttering to himself, 'Yes . . . yes . . . seen it . . . heard it before . . . nonsense . . . rubbish . . . nonsense.'

He set the page down and pushed it away from him, shaking his head wearily.

'When will you people learn? You can send me all the letters you like. The fact remains, Cobram is an independent hold, owing no allegiance to Redmont Fief. The treaty makes that very clear.'

'I'm instructed to draw your attention to Items Three and Five in the letter, sir. And paragraph nine as well. They make it quite clear that the wording of the treaty is faulty and your claim to independence is totally spurious,' Alyss replied.

And now, for the first time, Montague shed the air of world-weariness that he'd assumed. He stood angrily.

'Spurious!' he shouted. 'Spurious? Who the devil are you, a little girl in a grown-up's dress, to come in here insulting me and saying my claim is spurious? How dare you!'

Alyss stood her ground, unmoved by his sudden anger.

'I repeat, sir, you are requested to read those items,' she said quietly. Instead, Montague threw the letter down on the desk between them.

'And I refuse!' he shouted. Then his eyes narrowed. 'I know who's behind this. I see the hand of that sour-faced shrew Lady Pauline here!'

Now Alyss's own anger flared. 'You will speak respectfully of Lady Pauline, sir!' she warned him. But Montague was too angry to stop.

'I'll speak of her, all right! I'll tell you this. She's a woman meddling in a man's world, where she has no place. She should have found a husband years ago and raised a brood of squalling babies. Surely there's a deaf and half-blind man somewhere who would have taken her.'

'Sir!' said Alyss, her own voice rising. 'You are going too far!'

'Is that right, sweetheart?' Montague replied sarcastically. 'Well, let me give you some advice. Get away from that shrill, pinch-faced witch while you still have time. Find a husband and learn to cook. That's all women are good for, girl. Cooking and raising the babies!'

Halt stepped forward before Alyss could reply. 'The correct form of address,' he repeated quietly, 'is not "girl" or "sweetheart". It is "Lady Alyss". You will show respect for the laurel branch that this Courier wears. And you will show respect for Lady Pauline as well.'

For a moment, Montague was too startled to reply. First a girl, now a common forester had told him how to behave!

'Oh, is that so?' he raged. 'I'll show you respect!' He picked up the letter and tore it in half. Then he did the same to the scroll bearing Alyss's credentials. 'There's my respect! Now get out!'

Very carefully, Halt set his longbow to one side, leaning it against a chair. Alyss raised a warning hand.

'Halt, don't get into trouble on my behalf,' she said. But Halt looked at her and shook his head.

'Lady Alyss, this . . . fop . . . has insulted you, your Baron, your mentor and the Diplomatic Service as a whole. He has shown absolute disregard for the laurel branch you wear. And by destroying your credentials, he has committed a crime that warrants a jail term.'

Alyss considered his words for a second or two. Then she nodded. Montague had been more than rude to her. His behaviour was totally beyond acceptance.

'You're right,' she said. 'Carry on.'

But Montague had heard nothing after the word 'Halt'. The entire Kingdom knew the legendary Ranger's reputation and the Master of Cobram Keep paled now and stepped back as the grim-faced figure came toward him.

'But you said . . . you said your name was . . .' He struggled to remember it. Halt smiled at him. It was the smile of a wolf.

'Arratay? Yes, well, more correctly, *Arretez*. It's Gallican for "Halt". My pronunciation has never been good.'

His hand shot forward and locked in the scarlet-and-gold collar of the other man's doublet. The satin tore momentarily, then Halt gained a firmer grip and dragged the struggling knight across the table toward him.

Montague was taller and heavier than Halt. But Halt's hands, arms, shoulders and back were conditioned by years of drawing the massive longbow, with its pull weight of sixty kilograms. The thousands of arrows he had shot, over and over again, had turned his muscles into steel cord. Montague was dragged off his feet and hoisted across his own desk.

'The question is,' said Halt, glancing at Alyss, 'what should we do with him?' She hesitated, then that wonderful smile spread over her face.

'I wonder,' she said, 'does this castle have a moat?'

A group of servants were busy emptying the privy buckets into the moat when they were startled by a sudden drawn-out cry. They looked up in time to see a scarlet-and-gold-clad figure sail out of a first-storey window, turn over once and then land with an enormous splash in the dark, rancid waters. They shrugged and went back to work.

'I suppose I'll be in trouble again now,' Halt said as they were riding home. Alyss glanced at him. He didn't look very repentant.

'I doubt it,' she said. 'Once people hear my report, I should think they'll say Montague got off lightly. After all, phrases like "Fat Baron Arald" and "sour-faced shrew" won't exactly endear him to Baron Arald or Lady Pauline. And he did sign an acceptance of the letter in the end.

As the official Courier on this mission, I thank you for your service.'

Halt bowed slightly from the saddle. 'It's been a pleasure working with you,' he said, and they rode in companionable silence for a while.

'I suppose you'll be leaving with the army soon?' she said after a few minutes, and when Halt nodded, she continued: 'I'll miss you. How will I ever carry out diplomatic missions without someone to throw unpleasant nobles out the window?'

'I'll miss you too.' Halt smiled. And he realised that he meant it. He enjoyed being around young people – enjoyed their energy, their freshness, their idealism. 'You're a good influence on a jaded, old, bad-tempered Ranger.'

'You'll soon have Will back to keep you busy,' she said. 'You *really* miss him, don't you?'

The Ranger nodded. 'More than I realised.'

Alyss urged her horse close beside his and leaned over to kiss him on the cheek. 'That's for Will when you see him.'

A ghost of a smile touched Halt's face.

'You'll understand if I don't pass it on in person?' he said.

Alyss smiled and leaned over to kiss him again.

'And that's for you, you jaded, bad-tempered old Ranger.'

A little surprised by her own impulsiveness, she urged her horse ahead of him. Halt touched one hand to his cheek and looked after the slim blonde figure.

If I were twenty years younger, he began.

Then he sighed and had to be honest with himself. Make that thirty years, he thought.

Thirteen

If she hadn't spoken, they would have taken her for a boy. It was the soft voice that gave her away. She stood at the edge of the camp site, a slender figure with blonde hair cut short — to a boy's length — dressed in a ragged tunic, breeches and soft leather boots, bound up to the knee. A stained and torn sheepskin vest seemed to be her only protection against the cold mountain nights for she wore no cloak and carried no blankets. Just a small bandanna tied into a bundle which, presumably, contained all her belongings.

'Where the devil did you spring from?' Gilan asked, turning to face her. He sheathed his saxe knife as he did so and allowed Carney to fall gratefully to his knees, exhausted.

The girl, who Will could now see was around his own age and, underneath a liberal coating of dirt, remarkably pretty, gestured vaguely.

'Oh . . .' She paused uncertainly, trying to gather her

thoughts, and Will realised she was close to the point of exhaustion. 'I've been hiding out in the hills for several weeks now,' she said finally. Will had to admit she looked as if she had been.

'Do you have a name?' asked Gilan, not unkindly. He too could see the girl was worn out.

She hesitated. She appeared uncertain as to whether to give them her name or not.

'Evanlyn Wheeler, from Greenfield Fief,' she said. Greenfield was a small coastal fief in Araluen. 'We were here visiting friends . . .' She stopped and looked away from Gilan. She seemed to be thinking for a second, before she amended the statement. 'Rather, my mistress was visiting friends, when the Wargals attacked.'

'Wargals!' Will said, the word jerked from him, and she turned a level pair of brilliant green eyes upon him. As he looked into them, he realised she was more than pretty. Much, much more. She was beautiful. The strawberry blonde hair and green eyes were complimented by a small, straight nose and a full mouth that Will thought would look quite delightful if she were smiling. But right now, a smile was a long way from the girl's thoughts. She gave a sad little lift of her shoulders as she answered him.

'Where did you think all the people have gone?' she asked him. 'Wargals have been attacking towns and villages throughout this part of Celtica for weeks now. The Celts couldn't stand against them. They were driven out of their homes. Most of them escaped to the South-West Peninsula. But some were captured. I don't know what's happened to them.'

Gilan and the two boys exchanged looks. Deep down, they'd all been expecting to hear something of the kind. Now, it was out in the open.

'I thought I saw Morgarath's hand behind all this,' Gilan said softly and the girl nodded, tears forming in her eyes. One of them slid down her cheek, tracking its way through the grime there. She put a hand to her eyes, and her shoulders began to shake. Quickly, Gilan stepped forward and caught her just before she fell. He lowered her gently to the ground, leaning her against one of the rocks that the boys had positioned around the fireplace. His voice was gentle and compassionate now.

'It's all right,' he said to her. 'You're safe now. Just rest here and we'll get you something hot to eat and drink.' He glanced quickly at Horace. 'Get a fire going, please, Horace. Just a small one. We're fairly sheltered here and I think we can risk it. And Will,' he added, raising his voice so that it carried clearly, 'if that bandit makes another move to get away, would you mind shooting him through the leg?'

Carney, who had taken the opportunity created by Evanlyn's surprising appearance to begin crawling quietly away towards the surrounding rocks, now froze where he was. Gilan threw an angry glare at him, then revised his orders.

'On second thoughts, you do the fire, Will. Horace, tie those two up.'

The two boys moved quickly to the tasks he had set them. Satisfied that everything was in hand, Gilan now removed his own cloak and wrapped it around the girl. She had covered her face with both hands and her shoulders were still shaking, although she made no noise. He put his arms around her and murmured gently, reassuring her once more that she was safe.

Gradually, her silent, racking sobs diminished and her breathing became more regular. Will, engaged in heating a pot of water for a hot drink, looked at her in some surprise as he realised that she'd fallen asleep. Gilan motioned for silence and said quietly:

'She's obviously been under a great strain. It's best to let her sleep. You might prepare one of those excellent stews that Halt taught you to make. '

In his pack, Will carried a selection of dried ingredients that, when blended together in boiling water and simmered, resulted in delicious stews. They could be augmented by any fresh meat and vegetables that the travellers picked up along the way but, even without them, they made a far tastier meal than the cold rations the three had been eating that day.

He set a large bowl of water over the fire and soon had a delicious beef stew simmering and filling the cold evening air with its scent. At the same time, he produced their dwindling supply of coffee and set the enamel pot full of water in the hot embers to the side of the main fire. As the water bubbled and hissed to boiling point, he lifted the lid of the pot with a forked stick and tossed in a handful of grounds. Soon the aromatic scent of fresh coffee mingled with the stew and their mouths began to water. Around the same time, the savoury smells must have penetrated Evanlyn's consciousness. Her nose twitched delicately, then those startling green eyes flicked open. For a second or two, there was alarm in them as she tried to remember where she was. Then she caught sight of Gilan's reassuring face and she relaxed a little.

'Something smells awfully good,' she said and he grinned at her.

'Perhaps you could try a bowlful and then tell us what's been going on in these parts.' He made a sign to Will to fill an enamel bowl with the stew. It was Will's own bowl, as they didn't have any spare eating utensils. His stomach growled as he realised he'd have to wait until Evanlyn had finished before he could eat. Horace and Gilan, of course, simply helped themselves.

Evanlyn began wolfing down the savoury stew with an enthusiasm that showed she hadn't eaten in days. Gilan and Horace also set to quite happily. A whining voice came from the far rock wall, where Horace had tied the two bandits, sitting them back to back.

'Can we have something to eat, sir?' asked Carney. Gilan barely paused between mouthfuls and threw a disdainful glance at them.

'Of course not,' he said, and went back to enjoying his dinner.

Evanlyn seemed to realise that, aside from the bandits, only Will wasn't eating. She glanced down at the plate and spoon she was holding, looked at the identical implements being used by Gilan and Horace, and seemed to realise what had happened.

'Oh,' she said, looking apologetically at Will, 'would you like to . . .?' She offered the enamel plate to him. Will was tempted to share it with her, but realised that she must be nearly starving. In spite of her offer, he could see that she was hoping he'd refuse. He decided that there was a difference between being hungry, which he was, and starving, which she was, and shook his head, smiling at her.

'You go ahead,' he said. 'I'll eat when you've finished.'

He was a little disappointed when she didn't insist, but went back to wolfing down great spoonfuls of the stew, pausing occasionally for a deep draught of hot, freshly brewed coffee. As she ate, it seemed that a little colour returned to her cheeks. She cleaned the plate and looked wistfully at the stewpot still hanging over the fire. Will took the hint and ladled out another healthy dollop of stew and she set to once again, hardly pausing to breathe. This time, when the plate was empty, she smiled shyly and handed it back to him.

'Thanks,' she said simply and he ducked his head awkwardly.

'S'all right,' he mumbled, filling the plate again for himself. 'I suppose you were pretty hungry.'

'I was,' she agreed. 'I don't think I've eaten properly in a week.'

Gilan hitched himself into a more comfortable position by the small fire they kept burning. 'Why not?' he asked. 'I would have thought there was plenty of food left in the houses? You could have taken some of that?'

She shook her head, her eyes showing the fear that had gripped her for the previous few weeks. 'I didn't want to risk it,' she said. 'I didn't know if there'd be more of Morgarath's patrols around, so I didn't dare go into any of the towns. I found a few vegetables and the odd piece of cheese in some of the farmhouses, but precious little else.'

'I think it's time you told us what you know about events here,' Gilan told her and she nodded agreement.

'Not that I know too much. As I said, I was here with . . . my mistress, visiting . . . friends.' Again, there was just the slightest hesitation in her words. Gilan frowned slightly, noticing it.

'Your mistress is a noble lady, I take it? A knight's wife, or perhaps a lord's wife?'

Evanlyn nodded. 'She is daughter to . . . Lord and Lady Caramorn of Greenfield Fief,' she said quickly. But again there was that fleeting hesitation. Gilan pursed his lips thoughtfully.

'I've heard the name,' he said. 'Can't say I know them.'

'Anyway, she was here visiting a lady of King Swyddned's court — an old friend — when Morgarath's force attacked.'

Gilan frowned once more. 'How did they accomplish that?' he wanted to know. 'The cliffs and the Fissure are impassable. You couldn't get an army down the cliffs, let alone across the Fissure.'

The cliffs rose from the far side of the Fissure to form the boundary between Celtica and the Mountains of Rain and Night. They were sheer granite, several hundred metres in height. There were no passes, no way up or down — certainly not for large numbers of troops.

'Halt says no place is ever really impassable,' Will put in. 'Particularly if you don't mind losing lives in the attempt.'

'We ran into a small party of Celts escaping to the south,' the girl said. 'They told us how the Wargals managed it. They used ropes and scaling ladders and came down the cliffs by night, in small numbers. They found a few narrow ledges, then used the scaling ladders to cross the Fissure.

'They picked the most remote spot they could find, so they went undetected. During the day, those already across the Fissure hid among the rocks and valleys until they had the entire force assembled. They wouldn't have needed many. King Swyddned didn't keep a large standing army.'

Gilan made a disapproving sound and caught Will's eye.

'He should have. The treaty obliged him to. But remember what we said about people growing complacent? Celts would rather dig in their ground than defend it.' He gestured for the girl to continue.

'The Wargals overran the countryside, concentrating on the mines in particular. For some reason, they wanted the miners alive. They killed anyone else.

Gilan rubbed his chin thoughtfully. 'Pordellath and Gwyntaleth are both totally deserted,' he said. ' Any idea where the people might have gone?'

'A lot of the people in the towns got away in time,' she told him. 'They'll have headed south. The Wargals seem to be driving them that way.'

'Makes sense, I suppose,' Gilan commented. 'Keeping them bottled up in the south would prevent word getting out to Araluen.'

'That's what the captain of our escort said,' Evanlyn agreed. 'King Swyddned and most of his surviving army retreated to the south-west coast to form a defensive line. Any Celts who managed to get away from the Wargals have joined him there.'

'And what about you?' Gilan wanted to know.

'We were trying to escape back to the border when we were cut off by a war party,' she told them. 'Our men held them off while my lady and I escaped. We were almost clear but her horse stumbled and they caught her. I wanted to go back for her but she screamed at me to get away. I couldn't . . . I wanted to help her but . . . I just . . .'

Tears began to cascade down her cheeks once more. She didn't seem to notice, making no attempt to wipe them away, just staring silently into the fire as the horror of it all came back to her. When she spoke once more, her voice was almost inaudible.

'I got clear and I turned back to watch. They were . . . they were . . . I could see them . . .' Her voice died away. Gilan reached forward and took her hand.

'Don't think about it,' he said gently and she looked up at him, gratitude in her eyes. 'I take it that after . . . that . . . you got away into the hills?'

She nodded several times, her thoughts still vivid with the terrible scenes she had witnessed. Will and Horace sat in silence. Will glanced at his friend and a look of understanding passed between them. Evanlyn had been lucky to escape.

'I've been hiding ever since,' she said quietly. 'My horse went lame about ten days back and I turned him loose. Since then, I've kept moving back towards the north by night and hiding by day.' She indicated Bart and Carney, sitting trussed like two captive chickens on the far side of the clearing. 'I saw those two a few times, and others like them. I didn't make myself known to them. I didn't think I could trust them.'

Carney assumed a hurt look. Bart was still too dizzy from the crack Horace had given him with the flat of his sword to be taking any interest in proceedings.

'Then I saw you three earlier today from across a valley and I recognised you as King's Rangers — well, two of you, anyway,' she amended. 'All I could think was "Thank God".'

Gilan looked up at her at that, a small frown of concentration creasing his forehead. She didn't notice the reaction as she went on.

'It took me most of the day to reach you. It wasn't far as the crow flies, but there was no way across the valley that separated us. I had to go the long way around. Then down and up again. I was terrified that you'd be gone by the time I got here. But luckily, you weren't,' she added, unnecessarily.

Will was leaning forward, elbow on his knee and hand propped under his chin, trying to piece together all she'd told them.

'Why would Morgarath want miners?' he asked of nobody in particular. 'He doesn't have mines, so it doesn't make sense.'

'Maybe he's found some?' Horace suggested. Maybe he's found gold up there in the Mountains of Rain and Night and he needs slaves to dig it out.'

Gilan gnawed thoughtfully at a thumbnail as he considered what Horace had said. 'That could be,' he said at last. 'He's going to need gold to pay off the Skandians. Maybe he's mining his own.'

Evanlyn had sat up a little straighter at the mention of the sea wolves.

'Skandians?' she asked. 'Are they in league with Morgarath now?'

Gilan nodded. 'They've got something cooking,' he

told her. 'The entire Kingdom's on alert. We were bringing despatches to King Swyddned from Duncan.'

'You'll have to go south-west to find him,' Evanlyn replied. Will noticed that she had started a little at the mention of King Duncan's name. 'But I doubt he'll leave his defensive positions there.'

Gilan was already shaking his head. 'I think this is more important than taking despatches to Swyddned. After all, the main thrust of them was to tell him that Morgarath was on the move. I guess he knows that by now.'

He stood up, stretching and yawning. It was already full dark.

'I suggest we get a good night's sleep,' he said, 'and start back north in the morning. I'll take first watch, so you can keep my cloak, Evanlyn. I'll take Will's when he relieves me.'

'Thank you,' Evanlyn said simply and all three of them knew she was talking about more than just the use of the cloak. Will and Horace moved to douse the fire as Gilan took his longbow and moved to a rock outcrop that gave him a good view of the track leading to and from their camp site.

As Will was helping Evanlyn arrange a sleeping spot, he heard Carney's whining voice once more.

'Sir, please, could you loosen these ropes a little for the night? They're awful tight, like.'

And he heard Gilan's uncaring, 'Of course not,' as he climbed up onto the rocks to take the first watch.

Fourteen

The following morning, of course, they were faced with the problem of what to do with Bart and Carney.

The two bandits had spent a supremely uncomfortable night, tied back to back and forced to sit upright on the stony ground. As each watch changed, Gilan had loosened their bonds for a few minutes to give their cramped muscles a brief respite. He even eventually relented and allowed them a small amount of the party's food and water. But it was still a very unpleasant experience for them, made even more so because they had no idea what he planned to do with them in the morning.

And, truth be told, neither did Gilan. He had no wish to take them along as prisoners. As it was, they had only four horses, counting the pack horse that had been carrying their camping supplies and would now have to carry Evanlyn as well. He felt that the news of Morgarath's puzzling foray into Celtica should be taken back to King

Duncan as soon as possible, and dragging two prisoners along on foot would slow them down immeasurably. In addition, he was already considering the idea that he might push on ahead at top speed, allowing the other three to follow at their own pace. He knew the clumsy pack pony would never keep up with Blaze's mile-eating lope.

So, faced with these two problems, he frowned to himself as he ate breakfast, allowing himself the luxury of a second cup of coffee from their dwindling supply. After all, he thought, if he did go on ahead, it was the last coffee he'd see for some days. After a while he glanced up, caught Will's eye and beckoned him over.

'I'm thinking of pushing on ahead,' he said quietly. Instantly he saw the look of alarm in Will's eyes.

'You mean alone?' Will asked and Gilan nodded.

'This is vital news, Will, and I need to get it to King Duncan as soon as possible. Aside from anything else, it means that there'll be no reinforcements coming from Celtica. He needs to know that.'

'But . . .' Will hesitated. He looked around the little camp site as if searching for some argument against Gilan's idea. The tall Ranger was a comforting presence. Like Halt, he always seemed to know the right thing to do. Now, the thought that he was planning to leave them created a sense of near-panic in Will's mind. Gilan recognised the self-doubt that was racking the boy. He stood and placed a hand on his shoulder.

'Let's walk a little,' he said and they began to pace away from the camp site. Blaze and Tug glanced up curiously as they passed then, realising they weren't required, went back to cropping the sparse vegetation.

'I know you're worried about what happened with those four Wargals,' Gilan said. Will stopped walking and looked up at him.

'Halt told you?' he said. There was a note of doubt in his voice. He wondered what Halt had said about his behaviour. Gilan nodded gravely.

'Of course he told me. Will, you have nothing to be ashamed of, believe me.'

'But, Gil, I panicked. I forgot all my training and I . . .'

Gilan held up a hand to stop the torrent of self-recrimination that he sensed was about to pour out.

'Halt says you stood your ground,' he said firmly. Will shuffled his feet.

'Well . . . I suppose so. But . . .'

'You were scared but you didn't run. Will, that's not cowardice. That's courage. That's the highest form of courage. Weren't you scared when you killed the Kalkara?'

'Of course,' Will said. 'But that was different. It was forty metres away and attacking Sir Rodney.'

'Whereas,' Gilan finished for him, 'the Wargal was ten metres away and coming straight at you. Big difference.'

Will wasn't convinced. 'It was Tug who saved me,' he said. Gilan allowed himself a grin.

'Maybe he thought you were worth saving. He's a smart horse. And while Halt and I aren't nearly as smart as Tug, we think you've got what it takes, too.'

'Well, I've been beginning to doubt it,' Will said. But for the first time in some weeks, he felt his confidence lift a little.

'Then don't!' Gilan said forcefully. 'Self doubt is a disease. And if it gets out of control, it becomes self fulfilling. You have to learn from what happened with those Wargals. Use the experience to make you stronger.'

Will thought about Gilan's words for a few seconds. Then he took a deep breath and squared his shoulders.

'All right,' he said. 'What do you want me to do?'

Gilan studied him for a moment. There was a new-found determination in the boy's stance.

'I'm going to leave you in command,' he said. 'There's no point now continuing on with the mission, so follow on behind me to Araluen as quickly as you can.'

'To Redmont?' Will asked and Gilan shook his head.

'By now, the army will be on the move to the Plains of Uthal. That's where I'm heading and that's where Halt will be. We'll go over the map before I leave and plan the best route for you.'

'What about the girl?' Will asked. 'Should I bring her along or leave her somewhere safe once we're back in Araluen?'

Gilan considered the point for a moment. 'Bring her. The King and his advisers may want to question her some more. She'll be in the middle of the Araluan army, so she'll be as safe as anywhere else.'

He hesitated, then decided to share his suspicions with Will. 'There's something else about her, Will,' he began.

'You think her story isn't quite right?' Will interrupted. 'She keeps hesitating and stopping, as if she's afraid to tell us something.' Another thought struck him and he lowered his voice instinctively, even though the camp site was well out of earshot. 'You don't think she's a spy, do you?'

Gilan shook his head. 'Nothing so dramatic. But remember when she said she saw us and thought, "Thank

God they're Rangers"? Ordinary people don't think that way about us. Only the nobles are comfortable around Rangers.'

Will frowned. 'So you think . . .' He hesitated. He wasn't sure what Gilan thought.

'I think she may be the lady and she's assumed her maid's identity.'

'So on the one hand, she sees Rangers and is glad, then she doesn't trust us enough to tell us the truth? It doesn't make sense, Gil!' Will said. Gilan shrugged.

'It may not be that she doesn't trust us. She may have other reasons for not saying who she really is. I don't think it's a problem for you. I just think you should be aware of it.'

They turned and began to walk back to the camp

'I don't like to leave you in the lurch,' Gilan said. 'But you're not exactly unarmed. You've got your bow and your knives, and of course, there's Horace.'

Will glanced across to where the muscular apprentice was sharing a joke with Evanlyn. As she threw back her head and laughed, he felt a small pang of jealousy. Then he realised that he should be glad to have Horace along with him.

'He's not bad with that sword of his, is he?' he said.

Gilan shook his head in admiration. 'I'd never tell him, because it doesn't do a swordsman any good to have an inflated opinion of himself, but he's a lot better than not bad.' He looked down at Will. 'That's not to say you should go looking for trouble. There may still be Wargals between here and the border, so travel by night and hide up in the rocks by day.'

'Gil,' Will said, as an awkward thought struck him. 'What are we going to do about those two?' He jerked a thumb towards the two bandits, still tied back to back, still trying to doze off and still jerking each other awake as they did so.

'That's the question, isn't it?' said the Ranger. 'I suppose I could hang them. I do have the authority. After all, they did try to interfere with officers on the King's business. And they're looting in time of war. They're both capital offences.'

He cast his gaze around the rocky hills surrounding them. 'The question is whether I can actually do that here,' he murmured.

'You mean,' said Will, not liking the way his friend was thinking, 'you may not have the authority to hang them now that we're not in the Kingdom itself?'

Gilan grinned at him. 'I hadn't considered that. I was actually thinking that it'd be a bit difficult when there isn't a tree over a metre high within a hundred kilometres.'

Will heaved a small inner sigh of relief as he realised Gilan hadn't been serious. Then the Ranger's grin faded and he said warningly:

'The one thing I do know is that we don't want them coming after you three again. So make no mention of my plans until we've got rid of them, all right?'

In the end, the solution was a simple one. First, Gilan had Horace break the blade of Carney's sword by levering it sharply between two rocks. Then he hurled Bart's cudgel into the ravine by the road's edge. They heard it clattering and bouncing off the rocky slope for several seconds.

Once that was done, Gilan forced the two men to strip to their underwear.

'You needn't watch this,' he told Evanlyn. 'It won't be a pretty sight.'

Smiling to herself, the girl retreated inside the tent while the two men stripped down to their ragged underpants. They were shivering now in the cold mountain air.

'And your boots,' Gilan ordered and the two men sat awkwardly on the stony ground and removed their boots. Gilan nudged the piles of clothing with one toe.

'Now bundle 'em up and tie them in a ball with your belts,' he ordered and watched as Bart and Carney complied. When all was ready, he called Horace over and jerked a thumb at the two bundles of clothes and boots.

'Send 'em after the cudgel, Horace,' he ordered. Horace grinned as he began to understand. Bart and Carney understood too and started a chorus of protest. It stopped as Gilan swung an icy stare upon them.

'You're getting off lightly,' he told them in a cold voice. 'As I mentioned to Will earlier, I could hang you if I chose to.'

Bart and Carney instantly went quiet, then Gilan gestured for Horace to tie them up again. Meekly, they submitted, and in a few minutes they were back to back again, shivering in the keen wind that circled and dipped around the hills. Gilan considered them for a moment or two.

'Throw a blanket over them,' he said reluctantly. 'A horse blanket.'

Will obliged, grinning. He took care not to use Tug's blanket, but used the one belonging to the sturdy pack pony.

Gilan began to saddle Blaze, speaking to the others over his shoulder. 'I'm going to scout around Gwyntaleth. There may be someone there who can shed a little more light on what Morgarath is up to.' He looked meaningfully at Will and the apprentice realised that Gilan was saying this to throw the two bandits off. He gave a slight nod.

'I should be back about sunset,' Gilan continued loudly. 'Try to have something hot waiting for me then.'

He swung up into the saddle and beckoned Will closer. Leaning down, he whispered:

'Leave those two tied up and head off at sunset. They'll eventually get themselves loose but then they'll have to retrieve their boots and clothes. They won't go anywhere in these mountains without them. It will give you a day's start over them and that should take you clear.'

Will nodded. 'I understand. Ride safely, Gilan.' The Ranger nodded. He seemed to hesitate for a moment, then came to a decision.

'Will,' he said quietly. 'We're in uncertain times and none of us know what might be around the corner. It might be a good idea if you told Horace Tug's code word.'

Will frowned. The code word was a jealously guarded secret and he was reluctant to let anyone know it, even a trusted comrade like Horace. Seeing his hesitation, Gilan continued.

'You never know what might happen. You could be injured or incapacitated and, without the code word, Horace won't be able to make Tug obey him. It's just a precaution,' he added. Will saw the sense in the idea and nodded.

'I'll tell him tonight,' he said. 'Take care, Gilan.'

The tall Ranger leaned down and gripped his hand tightly.

'One other thing. You're in command here, and the others will take the lead from you. Don't give them any sign that you're not sure of yourself. Believe in yourself and they'll believe in you too.'

He nudged Blaze with his knee and the bay swung round towards the road. Gilan raised a hand in farewell to Horace and Evanlyn and cantered away. The dust of his passage was quickly dispersed by the keening wind.

And then Will felt very small. And very alone.

Fifteen

They rode as hard as they could that night, held back somewhat by the docile pace that was all the pack pony could manage.

The rain came back during the night to make them more miserable. But then, an hour before dawn, it cleared, so that the first streaks of light in the east painted the sky a dull pearl colour. With the gathering light, Will began to look for a place to make camp.

Horace noticed him looking around. 'Why don't we keep going for a couple more hours?' he suggested. 'The horses aren't really tired yet.'

Will hesitated. They'd seen no sign of anyone else during the night, and certainly no evidence of any Wargals in the area. But he didn't like to go against Gilan's advice. In the past, he'd found that advice given by senior Rangers usually turned out to be worth following. Finally, the decision was made for him when they rounded a bend in the road and saw a thicket of shrubs set back about thirty metres from the road. The bushes, while not more than three metres high at their tallest point, offered a thick screen, providing shelter from both the wind and any unfriendly eyes that might chance to come along.

'We'll camp here,' Will said, indicating the bushes. 'That's the first decent-looking camp site we've passed in hours. Who knows when we'll see another?'

Horace shrugged. He was quite content to let Will make the decisions. He had only been making a suggestion, not trying to usurp the Ranger apprentice's authority in any way. Horace was essentially a simple soul. He reacted well to commands and to other people making decisions. Ride now. Stop here. Fight there. As long as he trusted the person making the decisions, he was happy to abide by them.

And he trusted Will's judgement. He had a hazy idea that Ranger training somehow made people more decisive and intelligent. And of course, in that he was right, to a large degree.

As they dismounted and led their horses through the thick bushes into a clearing beyond, Will gave a small sigh of relief. He was stiffer than he'd realised after a full night in the saddle with only a few brief rests. Several good hours' sleep seemed like a capital idea right now. He helped Evanlyn down from the pack pony — riding on the pack saddle as she had to, it was a little awkward for her to dismount. Then he began unstrapping their packs of food supplies and the rolled canvas length that they used as a weather shelter.

Evanlyn, with barely a word to him, stretched, then walked a few paces away to sit down on a flat rock.

Will, his forehead creased in a frown, tossed one of the food packs onto the sand at her feet.

'You can start getting a meal ready,' he said, more abruptly than he'd really intended. He was annoyed that the girl would sit down and make herself comfortable, leaving the work to him and Horace. She glanced down at the pack and flushed angrily.

'I'm not particularly hungry,' she told him. Horace started forward from where he was unsaddling his horse.

'I'll do it,' he said, keen to avoid any conflict between the other two. But Will held up a hand to stop him.

'No,' he said. 'I'd like you to rig the shelter. Evanlyn can get the food out.'

His eyes locked with hers. They were both angry but she realised she was in the wrong. She shrugged faintly and reached for the pack. 'If it means so much to you,' she muttered, then asked: 'Is it all right if Horace makes the fire for me? He can do it a lot quicker than I.'

Will considered the idea, screwing up his face thought-fully. He was reluctant to light a fire while they were still in Celtica. It hardly seemed logical to travel by night to avoid being seen, then light a fire whose smoke might be visible in daylight. Besides, there was another consideration that Gilan had pointed out to him the previous day.

'No fire,' he said decisively and Evanlyn tossed the food pack down sulkily.

'Not cold food again!' she snapped. Will regarded her evenly.

'Not so long ago, you would have happily eaten anything — hot or cold — as long as it was food,' he reminded her and she dropped her eyes from his. 'Look,' he added, in a more reasoning tone, 'Gilan knows more about these things than any of us and he told us to make sure we aren't spotted. All right?'

She muttered something. Horace was watching the two of them, his honest face troubled by the conflict between them. He offered a compromise.

'I could just make a small fire for cooking,' he suggested. 'If we built it in under these bushes, the smoke should be pretty hard to see by the time it filters through.'

'It's not just that,' Will explained, slinging their water bags over one shoulder and taking his bow from the saddle scabbard. 'Gil says the Wargals have an amazingly keen sense of smell. If we did light a fire, the smell of the smoke would hang around for hours after we'd put it out.'

Horace nodded, conceding the point. Before anyone could raise any more objections, Will headed towards the jumble of rocks behind the camp site.

'I'm going to scout around,' he announced. 'I'll see if there's any water in the area. And I'll just make sure we're alone.'

Ignoring the girl's 'As if we're not,' which was muttered just loud enough for him to hear it, he began to scramble up the rocks. He made a careful circuit of the area, staying low and out of sight, moving from cover to scant cover as carefully as he could. *Whenever you're scouting,* Halt had once said to him, *move as if there's somebody there to see you. Never assume that you're on your own.*

He found no sign of Wargals or of Celts. But he did come across a small, clear stream that sluiced cold water over a bed of rocks. It was running fast enough to look safe for drinking, so he tested it and, satisfied that it wasn't polluted, filled their water bags to the brim. The cold fresh water tasted particularly good after the leathery-tasting supply from the bags. Once water had been in a water bag for more than a few hours, it began to taste more like the bag and less like water.

Back at the camp site, Horace and Evanlyn were waiting for his return. Evanlyn had set out a plate of dried meat and the hard biscuit they had been eating in place of bread for some time now. He was grateful that she'd also put a small amount of pickle on the meat. Any addition to the tasteless meal was welcome. He noticed as they were eating that there was none on her plate.

'Don't you like pickles?' he asked, through a mouthful of meat and biscuit. She shook her head, not meeting his eyes.

'Not really,' she replied.

But Horace wasn't prepared to let it rest at that. 'She gave you the last of them,' he told Will.

For a moment, Will hesitated, embarrassed. He'd just mopped up the last small mouthful of the tangy yellow pickles on a corner of biscuit, and popped it into his mouth. There was no way now he could offer to share it.

'Oh,' he mumbled, realising this was her way of making the peace between them. 'Um . . . well, thanks, Evanlyn.'

She tossed her head. With her close cropped hair, the effect was a little wasted and the thought struck him that she was probably used to making that gesture with long blonde locks that would accentuate the movement.

'I told you,' she said. 'I don't like pickles.' But now there was a hint of a grin in her voice, and the earlier bad humour was gone. He looked up at her and grinned in reply.

'I'll take the first watch,' he said. It seemed as good a way as any of letting her know he didn't hold a grudge.

'If you take the second watch as well, you can have my pickles too,' offered Horace, and they all laughed. The atmosphere in the little camp site lightened considerably as Horace and Evanlyn busied themselves shaking out blankets and cloaks and gathering some of the leafier branches from the bushes around them to shape into beds.

For his part, Will took one of the water bottles and his cloak and climbed up onto one of the larger rocks surrounding their camp. He settled himself as comfortably as possible, with a clear view of the rocky hills behind them in one direction, and over the bushes that screened them from the road in the other. Mindful as ever of Halt's teaching, he settled himself among a jumble of rocks that formed a more or less natural nest, allowing him to peer between them on either side, without raising his head above the horizon level. He wriggled himself around for a few minutes, wishing there were not so many sharp stones to dig into him. Then he shrugged, deciding that at least they'd stop him from dozing off during his watch.

He donned his cloak and raised the hood. As he sat there, unmoving among the grey rocks, he seemed to blend into the background until he was almost invisible.

It was the sound that first alerted him. It came and went vaguely with the breeze. As the breeze grew stronger, so did the sound. Then, as the breeze faded, he could no longer hear anything, so that at first he thought he was imagining things.

Then it came again. A deep, rhythmic sound. Voices, perhaps, but not like any he'd heard. It could have been singing, he thought, then, as the breeze blew a little harder, he heard it again. Not singing. There was no melody to it. Just a rhythm. A constant, unvarying rhythm.

Again the breeze died and the sound with it. Will felt the hairs on the back of his neck rising. There was something unhealthy about that sound. Something dangerous. He sensed it in every fibre of his body.

There it was again! And this time, he had it. Chanting. Deep voices chanting in unison. A tuneless chanting that had an unmistakable menace to it.

The breeze was from the south-west, so the sound was coming from the road where they had already travelled. He raised himself slowly and carefully, peering under one hand in the direction of the breeze. From this point he could make out various curves and bends in the road, although some of it disappeared behind the rocks and hills. He estimated that he could see sections of the road for perhaps a kilometre and there was no sign of movement.

Quickly, he scrambled down from the rocks and hurried to wake the others.

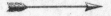

The chanting was closer now. It no longer died away as the breeze came and went. It was growing louder and more defined. Will, Horace and Evanlyn crouched among the bushes, listening as the voices came closer.

'Maybe you two should move back a little,' Will

suggested. He knew that, wrapped in his Ranger cloak, with his face concealed deep within the cowl, he would be virtually invisible. He wasn't so sure about the others. Without any reluctance, they squirmed back, deeper into the cover of the thick shrubs. Horace's reaction was a mixture of curiosity and nervousness. Evanlyn, Will noted, was pale with fear.

Just in case the chanters had scouts deployed, Will had quickly struck their camp, obliterating any traces that they may have left. He'd led the horses a hundred metres back into the rocks and tethered them there, leaving the camping equipment with them. Then, with Horace and Evanlyn, he had sought the cover of the thick scrub, hiding deep within the bushes but leaving himself a relatively clear view of the road.

'Who are they?' Horace breathed as the chanting grew louder still. Will estimated that it was coming from somewhere around the nearest bend in the road, a mere hundred metres away.

'Don't you know?' Evanlyn replied, her voice strained with terror. 'They're Wargals.'

Sixteen

ill and Horace both turned quickly to look at her.

'Wargals? How do you know?' Will asked.

'I've heard them before,' she said in a small voice, biting her lip. 'They make that chanting sound as they march.'

Will frowned. The four Wargals he and Halt had tracked had made no chanting sound. But then he realised that they had been tracking their own quarry at the time. Out of the corner of his eye, Will saw a movement at the bend in the road.

'Get down!' he hissed urgently. 'Keep your faces down!' And both Horace and Evanlyn dropped their faces into the sand. He reached up and pulled the shadowing depths of his cowl further over his own face, then held a forearm draped in the folds of his cloak to obscure everything but his eyes.

The chant, he saw now, was a form of cadence, designed to keep the Wargals moving at the same pace — in the same way a sergeant might call the step for a troop of infantry. He counted perhaps thirty in the group. Big, heavy-set figures, dressed in dark metal-studded jackets and breeches of some heavy material. They ran at a steady jog, chanting the guttural, wordless rhythm — which, he realised now, was nothing more than a series of grunts.

They were all armed, with an assortment of short spears, maces and battleaxes, which they carried ready for use.

As yet, he couldn't make out their features. They ran with a shambling movement in two files. Then he realised that they were escorting another group between the two files: prisoners.

Now the group was closer, he realised that the prisoners — about a dozen of them — were staggering along, trying desperately to keep pace with the chanting Wargals. He recognised them as Celts — miners, judging by the leather aprons and skull caps they wore. They were exhausted and as he watched, he could see the Wargals using short whips to urge them along.

The chanting grew louder.

'What's happening?' Horace whispered and Will could have cheerfully choked him.

'Shut up!' he shot back. 'Not another word!'

Now the Wargals were closer and he could make out their faces. He felt the hairs on the back of his neck begin to rise as he saw the thick, heavy jowls and noses that had lengthened and thickened almost to the size of muzzles. The eyes were small and savage and seemed to glow with a red hatred as they lashed their whips at the Celts. Once, as one of them snarled at a stumbling prisoner, Will caught a quick glimpse of yellow fangs. He was tempted to shrink down further. But he knew any movement now would risk discovery. He had to trust to the shelter of his cloak. He wanted to close his eyes to those animal-like faces, but somehow, he couldn't. He stared in fascinated horror as the terrible Wargals, creatures from a nightmare, chanting incessantly, jogged past the spot where he lay.

The Celt miner couldn't have lost his footing at a worse place.

Lashed by one of the Wargals, he stumbled, staggered, then crashed over in the road, bringing down the prisoners on either side of him. Will could see now that they were roped together with a thick rawhide leash.

As the column came to a confused stop, the chanting broke up into a series of snarls and growls from the Wargals. The two prisoners who had been brought down struggled to their feet, under a rain of lashes from their captors. The miner who had caused the fall lay still, in spite of the vicious whipping from one of the Wargals.

Finally another joined the first, and began beating at the still figure with the butt of his heavy, steel-shod spear. There was no reaction from the miner. Watching in horror, Will realised that the man was dead. Eventually, that same realisation came to the Wargals. At an incomprehensible command from one who must have been in charge, the two stopped beating the dead man and cut the bonds that attached him to the central leash. Then they picked up the limp body and threw it clear, hurling it towards the thicket where Will and the others sheltered.

The body crashed into the bushes closest to the road and Will heard Evanlyn utter a small cry of fear. Face down, not knowing what was happening, the sudden crashing in the bushes had obviously been too much for her to bear. She bit the noise off almost as soon as it started, but she was just a little too late.

The leader of the Wargals seemed to have heard something. He turned now and stared hard at the spot where the body lay, wondering if the noise had come from the miner. Obviously, he was suspicious that the dead man might be merely foxing, in an effort to escape. He pointed and shouted an order and the Wargal with the spear stepped forward and ran it casually through the dead body.

Still the commander's suspicions weren't satisfied. For a long moment, he stared into the bushes, looking straight at the spot where Will lay, wrapped in the protective camouflage of his Ranger cloak. The apprentice found himself staring deep into the angry red eyes of the savage thing out on the road. He wanted to drop his eyes away from that gaze, convinced that the creature could see him. But all of Halt's training over the past year told him that any movement now would be fatal, and he knew that dropping his eyes could lead to a tiny, involuntary movement of his head. The true value of the camouflaged cloaks lay not in magic as so many people believed, but in the wearer's ability to remain unmoving under close scrutiny.

Forcing himself to believe, Will remained motionless, staring at the Wargal. His mouth was dry. His heart pounded at what seemed like twice its normal rate. He could hear the heavy, rasping breathing of the bear-like figure, see the nostrils twitching slightly as it sampled the light breeze, testing for unknown scents.

Finally, the Wargal turned away. Then, in an instant, it whipped back again to stare once more. Fortunately, Will's training had covered that particular trick as well. He made no movement. This time, the Wargal grunted, then called an order to the group.

Chanting once more, they moved out, leaving the dead miner on the roadside.

As the sound receded and they disappeared round the next bend in the road, Will felt Horace moving behind him.

'Stay still!' he whispered fiercely. It was possible that the Wargals had a sweeper following – a silent-moving rear scout who might catch unwary fugitives who thought the danger was past.

He forced himself to count to one hundred before he allowed the others to move, crawling clear of the bushes and stretching their stiff and aching limbs.

Signalling to Horace to take Evanlyn back to the camp site, Will stepped cautiously into the road to check the Celt. As he had suspected, the man was dead. He had obviously been beaten many times over the past few days. His face was bruised and cut by the whips and fists of the Wargals.

There was nothing he could do for the man so he left him where he lay and went to rejoin the others.

Evanlyn was sitting crying. As he approached, she looked up at him, her face streaked with tears and her shoulders heaving with the great sobs that shook her. Horace stood by, a helpless expression on his face, making useless little movements with his hands.

'I'm sorry,' Evanlyn finally managed to gasp. 'It's just

that . . . chanting . . . those voices . . . I could remember everything when they . . .'

'It's all right,' Will told her quietly. 'My God, they're horrible creatures!' he added, shaking his head at Horace. The warrior apprentice swallowed once or twice. He hadn't seen the Wargals. He'd lain there throughout the entire encounter with his face pressed hard into the sandy ground. In a way, thought Will, that must have been just as terrifying.

'What are they like?' Horace asked in a small voice. Will shook his head again. It was almost impossible to describe.

'Like beasts,' he said. 'Like bears . . . or a cross between a bear and a dog. But they walk upright like men.'

Evanlyn gave another shuddering cry. 'They're vile!' she said bitterly. 'Vile, horrible creatures. Oh God, I hope I never see them again!'

Will moved to her and patted her shoulder awkwardly.

'They're gone now,' he said quietly, as if soothing a small child. 'They're gone and they can't hurt you.'

She made an enormous effort and gathered her courage. She looked up at him, a frightened smile on her face. She reached up and took his hand in her own, taking comfort from the mere contact.

He let her hold his hand for a while. He wondered how he was going to tell them what he had decided to do.

Seventeen

'Follow them? Are you out of your mind?'

Horace stared at the small, determined figure, unable to believe what he was hearing. Will didn't say anything, so Horace tried again.

'Will, we've just spent half an hour hiding behind a bush hoping those things wouldn't see us. Now you want to follow them and give them another chance?'

Will glanced around to make sure that Evanlyn was still out of earshot. He didn't want to alarm the girl unnecessarily.

'Keep your voice down,' he warned Horace, and his friend spoke more softly, but no less vehemently.

'Why?' he asked. 'What can we possibly gain by following them?'

Will shifted uneasily from one foot to the other. Frankly, the idea of following the Wargals was already frightening him. He could feel his pulse rate was running higher than normal. They were terrifying creatures, and obviously totally devoid of any feelings of mercy or pity, as the fate of the prisoner had shown. Still, he could see that this was an opportunity that shouldn't be wasted.

'Look,' he said quietly. 'Halt always told me that knowing why your enemy is doing something is just as important as knowing what he's doing. Sometimes more important, in fact.'

Horace shook his head stubbornly. 'I don't get it,' he said. To him this idea of Will's was a crazy, irresponsible and terrifyingly dangerous impulse.

To be truthful, Will wasn't absolutely sure that he was right either. But Gilan's parting words about not showing uncertainty rang in his ears and his instincts, honed by Halt's training, told him this was an opportunity he shouldn't miss.

'We know that the Wargals are capturing Celtic miners and carrying them off,' he said. 'And we know Morgarath doesn't do anything without a reason. This might be a chance to find out what he's up to.'

Horace shrugged. 'He wants slaves,' he said and Will shook his head quickly.

'But why? And why only miners? Evanlyn said they were only interested in the miners. Why? Can't you see?' he appealed to the bigger boy. 'This could be important. Halt says that wars often turn on the smallest piece of information.'

Horace pursed his lips, thinking over what Will had said. Finally, he nodded slowly.

'Okay,' he agreed. 'I guess you may be right.' Horace wasn't a fast thinker, or an original one. But he was methodical and, in his own way, logical. Will had instinctively seen the necessity for following the Wargals.

Horace had to work his way through it. Now that he had, he could see Will wasn't acting on some wild adventurous impulse. He trusted the Ranger apprentice's line of reasoning. 'Well, if we're going to follow them, we'd better get moving,' he added and Will looked at him in surprise, shaking his head.

'We?' he said. 'Who said anything about "we"? I plan to follow them alone. Your job is to get Evanlyn back safely.'

'Says who?' asked the bigger boy, with some belligerence. 'My job, as it was explained to me by Gilan, was to stay with you and keep you out of trouble.'

'Well, I'm changing your orders,' Will told him. But this time Horace laughed.

'So who died and left you the boss?' he scoffed. 'You can't change my orders. Gilan gave me those orders and he outranks you.'

'And what about the girl?' Will challenged him. For a moment, Horace was stuck for an answer.

'We'll give her food and supplies and the pack horse,' he said. 'She can make her own way back.'

'That's very gallant of you,' Will said sarcastically. Horace merely shook his head again, refusing to be baited into an argument on that score.

'You're the one who said this is so darned important,' he replied. 'Well, I'm afraid I think you're right. So Evanlyn will simply have to take her chances, just like us. We're close to the border now anyway and one more night's riding will see her out of Celtica.'

In truth, Horace didn't like the thought of leaving Evanlyn to her own devices. He'd grown genuinely fond of the girl. She was bright and amusing and good company.

But his time in Battleschool had given him a strong sense of duty, and personal feelings came second.

Will tried one more time. 'I can move a lot faster without you,' he pointed out but Horace cut him off immediately.

'So what? We won't need speed if we're following the Wargals. We've got horses. We'll have no trouble keeping up with them, particularly as they have to drag those prisoners along.' He found he was rather enjoying the experience of arguing with Will and coming up with winning points. Maybe, he decided, spending time with Rangers had done him more good than he'd realised.

'Besides, what if we find out something really important? And what if you want to keep following them and we still have to get a message back to the Baron? If there are two of us, we can split up. I can take a message back while you keep following the Wargals.'

Will considered the idea. Horace had a point, he had to concede. It would make sense to have someone else along with him, now that he thought about it.

'All right,' he said finally. 'But we're going to have to tell Evanlyn.'

'Tell me what?' the girl asked. Unnoticed by either of them, she'd approached to within a few metres of where they had been standing, arguing in lowered voices. The two boys now looked guiltily at each other.

'Uh . . . Will had this idea, you see . . .' Horace began, then stopped, looking at Will to see if his friend was going to continue. But, as it turned out, there was no need.

'You're planning to follow the Wargals,' the girl said flatly and the two apprentices exchanged looks, before Will answered.

'You were listening?' he accused her. She shook her head.

'No. It's the obvious thing to do, isn't it? This is our chance to find out what they're up to and why they're kidnapping the miners.'

For the second time in a few minutes, Will found himself picking up on the use of the plural. 'Our chance?' he asked her. 'What exactly do you mean by "our" chance?'

Evanlyn shrugged. 'Obviously, if you two are following them, I'm coming along with you. You're not leaving me out here on my own in the middle of nowhere.'

'But . . .' Horace began and she turned to look calmly at him. 'These are Wargals,' he said.

'I had gathered that.'

Horace cast a hopeless glance at Will. The apprentice Ranger shrugged, so Horace tried again. 'It'll be dangerous. And you . . .'

He hesitated. He didn't want to remind her of her fear of the Wargals, and the reasons for it. Evanlyn realised his predicament and she smiled wanly at him.

'Look, I'm scared of those things,' she said. 'But I assume you're planning to follow them, not join up with them.'

'That was the general idea,' Will said and she turned her level gaze on him.

'Well, with the noise they make, we shouldn't have to get too close to them,' she told him. 'And besides, this might be a chance to spoil whatever plans they have. I think I'd enjoy that.'

Will regarded her with a new respect. She had every reason to fear the Wargals, more than he or Horace. Yet she was willing to put that fear aside in order to strike a blow against Morgarath.

'You're sure?' he said finally and she shook her head.

'No. I'm not sure at all. I feel decidedly queasy at the prospect of getting within earshot of those things again. But equally, I don't like the idea of being abandoned here on my own.'

'We weren't abandoning you . . .' Horace began and she turned back to him.

'Then what would you call it?' she asked him, smiling faintly to take the sting out of her words. He hesitated.

'Abandoning you, I guess,' he admitted.

'Exactly,' she said. 'So, given the choice of running into another group of Wargals, or more bandits, or following some Wargals with you two, I'll choose the latter.'

'We're only a day from the border,' Will pointed out to her. 'Once you're across that, you'll be relatively safe.'

But she shook her head decisively.

'I feel more secure with you two,' she said. 'Besides, it might be handy for you to have someone else along. It'll be one more person to keep watch at night. That means you'll get more sleep.'

'That's the first sensible reason I've heard for her coming along so far,' said Horace. Like Will, he realised that she'd made her mind up. And both boys somehow knew that when Evanlyn did that, there was no way on earth they were going to make her change it. She grinned at him.

'Well,' she said, 'are we going to stand here all day nattering? Those Wargals aren't getting any closer while we're doing it.'

And, turning on her heel, she led the way to where the horses were tethered.

Eighteen

Following the Wargals was easier than they expected. The creatures were single minded, concentrating only on the task in hand, which was to take the Celt miners to their end destination. They feared no attack in these parts, having already driven the occupants out, so they posted no forward scouts or sweepers. Their constant chanting, ominous as it might sound at first, also served to mask any sounds that might have been made by their pursuers.

At night, they simply camped wherever they might find themselves to be. The miners remained chained together and sentries were posted to keep watch over them while the rest of the group slept.

By the beginning of the second day, Will began to have an idea of the direction the Wargals were heading. He had been riding some thirty metres in the lead, relying on Tug to sense any danger ahead. Now he dropped back a little, waiting for Horace and Evanlyn to come level with him.

'We seem to be heading for the Fissure,' he said, more than a little puzzled.

Already, in the distance, they could make out the high, brooding cliffs that towered over the massive split in the earth. Celtica itself was a mountainous country, but Morgarath's domain reared hundreds of metres above it.

'I wouldn't care to come down those cliffs on ropes and scaling ladders,' Horace said, nodding towards them.

'Even if you did, you'd have to find a level space on the other side to cross from,' Will agreed. 'And apparently, there are precious few of them. For the most part, the cliffs go right down to the bottom.'

Evanlyn looked from one to the other. 'Yet Morgarath has done it once,' she said. 'Maybe he's planning to attack Araluen the same way.'

Horace brought his horse to a halt, considering what she'd said. Will and Evanlyn stopped beside him. He chewed his lip for a few seconds as he thought back over the lessons that Sir Rodney's instructors had dinned into him. Then he shook his head.

'It's a different situation,' he said finally. 'The attack on Celtica was more of a raid than an invasion. He wouldn't have needed more than five hundred men for that and they could travel light. To attack Araluen, he'll need an army — and he wouldn't get an army down those cliffs and across with a few ladders and rope bridges.'

Will regarded him with interest. This was a side of Horace that was new to him. Apparently, Horace's learning curve in the past seven or eight months had gone beyond his mere skill with the sword.

'But surely, if he had enough time . . .?' he began but

Horace shook his head again, more decisively this time.

'Men, yes, or Wargals in this case. Given enough time, you could get them down and across. It would take months but you could manage it. Although the longer it took, the more chance word would get out about what you were doing. 'But an army needs equipment – heavy weapons, supply wagons, provisions, tents, spare weapons and blacksmith's equipment to repair them. Horses and oxen to pull the wagons. You'd never get all that down cliffs like those. And even if you did, how would you get it across? It's just not feasible. Sir Karel used to say that . . .'

He realised the others were regarding him with a certain amount of respect and he flushed. 'Didn't mean to go on and on,' he mumbled, and urged his horse forward again.

But as Will followed, he was shaking his head, impressed by his friend's grasp of the subject. 'Not at all,' he said. 'You're making good sense.'

'Which still leaves us the question, what is he up to?' Evanlyn said.

Will shrugged. 'I suppose we'll find out soon enough,' he said, and urged Tug forward to take up the point position once more.

They found out the following evening.

As before, the first hint as to what was taking place came by sound: the ring and thud of hammers striking stone or wood. Then they heard a thinner sound as they drew closer. A constant but irregular cracking sound. Will signalled for the others to stop and, dismounting, he proceeded carefully along the road to the final bend.

Shrouded in his cloak, and moving carefully from one patch of cover to the next, he moved off the road and cut across country to find a vantage point from which to view the next stretch of road. Almost immediately, he saw the top of the massive wooden structure that was being constructed: four wooden towers, linked by heavy rope cables and a timber framework. His heart sinking, he already knew what he was looking at. But he moved closer to make sure.

It was as he feared. An immense wooden bridge was in the final stages of construction. On the far side of the Fissure, Morgarath had discovered one of the few places where a narrow ledge ran, almost level with the Celtic side. The natural ledge had been dug out and widened until there was a sizeable piece of level ground there. The four towers stood, two either side of the Fissure, linked by massive rope cables. Supported by them, a wooden roadway was half completed — capable of taking six men abreast across the dizzying depths of the Fissure.

Figures recognisable as Celt prisoners swarmed over the structure, hammering and sawing. The cracking sound was made by the whips used by the Wargal overseers.

Beyond them, the sound of hammers on stone came from the mouth of a tunnel that opened onto the ledge some fifty metres south of the bridge. It was little more than a crack in the cliff face — only a little wider than a man's shoulders — but as he watched, the Celt prisoners were hard at work at its entrance, gouging at the hard rock, widening and enlarging the small opening.

Will glanced up at the dark cliffs towering on the other side. There was no sign of ropes or ladders leading down to the ledge. The Wargals and their prisoners must access it via the narrow crack in the rock, he reasoned.

The party they had been following was crossing the Fissure now. The final fifteen metres of roadway was yet to be constructed, and only a temporary timber footway was in place. It was barely wide enough for the Celts to cross, tethered in pairs as they were, but the miners of Celtica were used to awkward footing and dizzy drops and they crossed without incident.

He'd seen enough for the time being, he thought. It was time to get back. He wriggled his way backwards into the cover of the broken rocks. Then, bending almost double, he ran back to where the others were waiting.

When he reached them, he slumped down, leaning back against the rocks. The tension of the last two days was beginning to tell on him, along with the strain of being in command. He was a little surprised to realise that he was physically exhausted. He had no idea that mental tension could sap a person's strength so thoroughly.

'So what's going on? Did you see anything?' Horace said. Will looked up at him, wearily.

'A bridge,' he told him. 'They're building a huge bridge.'

Horace frowned, puzzled by it all. 'Why would Morgarath want a bridge?'

'It's a huge bridge, I said. Big enough to bring an army across. Here we've been discussing how Morgarath couldn't move an army and all its equipment down the cliffs and across the Fissure, and all the time, he's been building a bridge to do it.'

Evanlyn picked at a loose thread on her jacket. 'That's why he wanted the Celts,' she said. When both boys looked at her, she elaborated. 'They're expert builders and tunnellers. His Wargals wouldn't have the skill for an undertaking like this.'

'They're tunnelling too,' Will said. 'There's a narrow crack — sort of a cave mouth — in the far side that they're widening.'

'Where does it lead to?' Horace asked and Will shrugged.

'I don't know. It might be important to find out. After all, the plateau on the other side is still hundreds of feet above this point. But there must be some access between the two because there's no sign of ropes or ladders.'

Horace stood and began to pace back and forth as he considered this new information. His face was screwed up in thought.

'I don't get it,' he said finally.

'It's not that hard to "get", Horace,' Will told him, with some asperity. 'There's a barking great bridge being built over the Fissure — big enough for Morgarath and all his Wargals *and* their supply wagons *and* their blacksmiths *and* their oxen and Uncle Tom Cobbley and all to come waltzing over.'

Horace waited until Will had finished his tirade. Then he cocked his head to one side.

'Finished?' he said mildly and Will, realising that he'd been a little excessive, made a vaguely apologetic gesture for Horace to continue.

'What I don't get,' Horace said, enunciating very carefully, 'is why it was never mentioned in those plans you captured.'

Evanlyn looked up curiously. 'Plans?' she said. 'What plans?'

But Will, realising that Horace had made a vital point, gestured for her to wait for an explanation.

'You're right,' he said softly. 'The plans never mentioned a bridge across the Fissure.'

'And it's not as if it's a small undertaking. You'd think it would be in there somewhere.' Horace said. Will nodded agreement. Evanlyn, her curiosity thoroughly piqued by now, repeated her question.

'What are these plans you keep talking about?'

Horace took pity on her, realising how frustrating their conversation must be for her.

'Will and Halt — his Craftmaster — captured a copy of Morgarath's battle plans a couple of weeks ago. There was a lot of detail about how his forces are going to break out of the Mountains via Three Step Pass. There was even the date on which they were going to do it and how Skandian mercenaries were going to help them. Only there was no mention of this bridge.'

'Why not?' Evanlyn asked. But Will was beginning to see what Morgarath had in mind, and his horror was growing by the second.

'Unless,' he said, 'Morgarath *wanted* us to capture those plans.'

'That's crazy,' Horace said instantly. 'After all, one of his men died as a result.'

Will met his gaze evenly. 'Would that stop Morgarath? He doesn't care about other people's lives. Let's think it through. Halt has a saying: *When you can't see the reason for something, look for the possible result — and ask yourself who might benefit from it.*'

'So,' said Evanlyn, 'what's the result of your finding those plans?'

'King Duncan has moved the army to the Plains of Uthal to block Three Step Pass,' said Horace promptly. Evanlyn nodded and continued with the second part of the equation.

'And who might benefit from that?'

Will looked up at her. He could see she'd reached the same conclusion he had. Very slowly, he said:

'Morgarath. If those plans were false.'

Evanlyn nodded agreement. Horace was not quite so quick to see the point.

'False? What do you mean?'

'I mean,' said Will, 'Morgarath wanted us to find those plans. He wanted the Araluan army assembled at the Plains of Uthal — the whole army. Because Three Step Pass isn't where the real attack will come from. The real attack will come from here — a surprise attack from behind. And our army will be trapped and destroyed.'

Horace's eyes widened in horror. He could envisage the result of a massive attack from the rear. The Araluans would be caught between the Skandians and Wargals in front of them and another army of Wargals in their rear. It was a recipe for disaster — the kind of disaster every general feared.

'Then we've got to tell them,' he said. 'Right away.'

Will nodded. 'We've got to tell them. But there's one more thing I want to see. That tunnel they're digging. We don't know if it's finished, or half finished, or where it goes. I want to take a look at it tonight.'

But Horace was shaking his head before he even finished. 'Will, we've got to go *now*,' he said. 'We can't hang around here just to satisfy your curiosity.'

It was Evanlyn who solved the argument. 'You're right,

Horace,' she said. 'The King must know about this as soon as possible. But we have to be sure that we're not taking him another red herring. The tunnel Will's talking about could be weeks away from completion. Or it could lead to a dead end. This whole thing could be yet another ruse to convince the army to divert forces to protect their rear. We have to find out as much as possible. If that means waiting a few more hours, then I say we wait.'

Will glanced at the girl curiously. She certainly seemed to have more of an air of authority and decision than one would expect from a lady's maid. He decided that Gilan's theory was correct.

'It'll be dark in an hour, Horace. We'll go across tonight and take a closer look.'

Horace looked from one of his companions to the other. He wasn't happy. His instinct was to ride now, as fast as he could, and spread the word of this bridge. But he was outvoted. And he still believed Will's powers of deduction were better than his own. He was trained for action, not this sort of tortuous thinking. Reluctantly, he allowed himself to be convinced.

'All right,' he said. 'We'll look tonight. But tomorrow, we leave.'

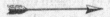

Wrapped in his cloak and moving carefully, Will returned to his former vantage point. He studied the bridge carefully, thinking that Halt would expect him to be able to draw an accurate plan of the structure.

He hadn't been in position for more than ten minutes when a horn blast rang out.

He froze, terrified. For a moment, he thought it was an alarm and that an alert sentry had spotted him moving among the rocks. Then he heard more cracking of whips and the grunting cries of the Wargals and, as he raised his head, he saw that they were driving the Celts off the bridge and back towards the half-finished tunnel. The prisoners, as they went, downed their tools in stacks. Wargals began re-shackling them to a central leash.

Glancing up to the west, Will saw the last curve of the sun dropping behind the hills and he realised that the horn had simply been sounding the end of the working day. Now the prisoners were being returned to wherever it was that they were kept.

There was one brief altercation, a few metres from the tunnel mouth, as two of the Celt prisoners stopped to try to lift a prone figure that lay there. Angrily, the Wargal guards surged forward, beating the miners away with their whips and forcing them to leave the still figure where it lay.

Then, one after the other, they filed through the narrow entrance of the tunnel and disappeared.

The shadows of the huge bridge lengthened across the hillside. Will remained unmoving for another ten minutes, waiting to see if any Wargals re-emerged from the tunnel. But there was no sound, no sign of anyone returning. Only the still form lying by the tunnel mouth remained. In the rapidly worsening light, Will couldn't make it out clearly. It looked like the body of a miner. But he couldn't be sure.

Then the figure moved and he realised that, whoever it was, he was still alive.

Nineteen

Treading carefully, Will and Horace made their way across the narrow plank path that bridged the last fifteen metres of the Fissure. Will, with his excellent head for heights, could have run lightly across it without a problem. But he went slowly out of regard for his bigger, less nimble, friend.

When they finally made it to the finished roadway, Horace heaved a sigh of relief. Now they took a moment to examine the structure. It was built with all the thoroughness that Celts were famous for. As a nation, they'd developed the art of tunnelling and bridging over the centuries and this was a typical sturdy structure.

The smell of fresh sawn pine planking filled the cold night air and, overlaid on that, there was another sweetish, aromatic smell. They looked at each other, puzzled, for a moment. Then Horace recognised it.

'Tar,' he said and they looked around to see that the massive rope cables and support ropes were thick with the stuff. Will touched a hand on one and it came away sticky.

'I guess it prevents the ropes fraying and rotting,' he said carefully, noticing that the main cables were constructed of three heavy ropes twisted and plaited together, then thickly coated with the tar to protect them. Also, as the tar hardened, it would bind the three together more permanently.

Horace glanced around. 'No guards?' he commented. There was a disapproving note in his voice.

'They're either very confident or very careless,' Will agreed.

It was full night now and the moon was yet to rise. Will moved towards the eastern bank of the Fissure. Loosening his sword in its scabbard, Horace followed him.

The figure by the tunnel mouth lay as Will had last seen it. There had been no further sign of movement. The two boys approached him carefully now and knelt beside him — for now they could see that it was a Celt miner. His chest rose and fell — barely moving.

'He's still alive,' Will whispered.

'Only just,' Horace replied. He placed his forefinger to the Celt's neck to gauge the pulse there. At the touch, the man's eyes slowly opened and he gazed up at the two of them, uncomprehending.

'Who . . . you?' he managed to croak. Will unslung the water bottle from his shoulder and moistened the man's lips with a little of the liquid. The tongue moved greedily across the wetness and the man croaked again, trying to rise on one elbow.

'More.'

Gently, Will stopped him moving, and gave him a little more water.

'Rest easy, friend,' he said softly. 'We're not going to harm you.'

It was obvious that somebody had done him harm — and plenty of it. His face was matted with the dried blood that had welled from a dozen whip cuts. His leather jerkin was shredded and torn and his bare torso underneath showed signs of more whipping — recent and from long ago.

'Who are you?' Will asked softly.

'Glendyss,' the man sighed, seeming to wonder at the sound of his own name. Then he coughed, a racking, rattling cough that shook his chest. Will and Horace exchanged sad glances. Glendyss didn't have long, they both realised.

'When did you come here?' Will asked the man, gently allowing more water to trickle through the dried, cracked lips.

'Months...' Glendyss replied in a voice they could barely hear. 'Months and months I've been here... working on the tunnel.'

Again, the two boys looked at one another. Maybe the man's mind was wandering.

'Months?' Will pressed him. 'But the Wargal attacks only started a month ago, surely?'

But Glendyss was shaking his head. He tried to speak, coughed and subsided, gathering his fading strength. Then he spoke, so softly that Will and Horace had to lean close to hear him.

'They took us almost a year ago... from all over. Secretly... a man here, two men there... fifty of us in all. Most of the others . . . dead . . . by now. Me soon.' He stopped, gasping for breath again. The effort of speaking was almost too much for him. Will and Horace looked at each other, puzzling over this new information.

'How was it that nobody knew this was happening?' Horace asked his friend. 'I mean, fifty people go missing and nobody says anything?'

But Will shook his head. 'He said they took them from villages all over Celtica. So one or two men go missing — people might talk about it locally, but nobody could see the entire picture.'

'Still,' said Horace, 'why do it? And why are they so open about it now?'

Will shrugged. 'Maybe we'll get an idea on that if we take a look around,' he said.

They hesitated uncertainly, not sure what they could do for the crumpled, battered form beside them. As they waited, the moon rose, soaring over the hills and flooding the bridge and the bank with soft pale light. It touched on Glendyss's face and his eyes opened. Then he tried weakly to raise an arm to ward off the light. Gently, Will leaned forward to shield him.

'I'm dying,' said the miner, with a sudden clarity and a sense of peace. Will hesitated, then answered simply.

'Yes.' It would have been no kindness to lie to him, to try to cheer him along and protest that he would be all right. He was dying and they all knew it. Better to let him prepare, to let him face death with dignity and calm. The hand clutched feebly at Will's sleeve and he took it in his own, pressing it gently, letting the Celt feel the contact with another person.

'Boys,' he said weakly. 'Don't let me die out here . . . in the light.'

Again, Horace and Will exchanged glances.

'I want the peace of the Out of Light,' he continued softly, and Will suddenly understood.

'I guess Celts like the darkness. They spend most of their lives in tunnels and mines, after all. Maybe that's what he wants.'

Horace leaned forward. 'Glendyss?' he said. 'Do you want us to carry you into the tunnel?'

The miner's head had swivelled to Horace as the boy spoke. Now he nodded, faintly. Just enough for them to make out the action.

'Please,' he whispered. 'Take me to the Out of Light.'

Horace nodded to him, then slipped his arms under the Celt's shoulders and knees to lift him. Glendyss was only small and the weeks he had spent in captivity had obviously been a time of starvation for him. He was an easy burden for Horace to lift.

As the warrior apprentice stood straight with Glendyss cradled in his arms, Will motioned for him to wait. He sensed that once Glendyss was in the peace of the dark tunnel, he would let go the faint thread that held him to life. And there was one more question Will needed answered.

'Glendyss,' he said softly. 'How long do we have?'

The miner looked at him wearily, uncomprehending. Will tried again.

'How long before they finish the bridge?' he asked. This time, he could see a light of understanding in the Celt's eyes. Glendyss thought for a second or two.

'Five days,' he replied. 'Maybe four. More workers came today . . . so maybe four.'

Then his eyes closed, as if the effort had been too much. For a second, they thought he had died. But then his chest heaved with a massive shudder and he continued to breathe.

'Let's get him into the tunnel,' Will said.

They squeezed through the narrow opening. For the first ten metres, the walls of the tunnel were close enough to touch. Then they began to widen, as the results of the Celts' labour became evident. It was a dark confined place, lit only by the dim flames of torches set in brackets every ten to twelve metres. Some of these were guttering now, and provided only a fitful, uncertain light. Horace looked around uneasily. He didn't like heights and he definitely didn't like confined spaces.

'Here's the answer,' Will said. 'Morgarath needed those first fifty miners to do this work. Now that the tunnel is nearly finished, he needs more men to get the bridge built as quickly as possible.'

Horace nodded. 'You're right,' he agreed. 'The tunnelling would take months, but nobody would see it was going on. Once they started building the bridge, the risk of discovery would be much higher.'

In the wider reaches of the tunnel, they found a small sandy patch, almost a grotto, off to one side. They laid Glendyss in it. Will realised that this must have been what the two Celts had been trying to do for their countryman when the stop work horn had sounded.

He hesitated. 'I wonder what the Wargals will think when they find him here tomorrow?'

Horace merely shrugged. 'Maybe they'll think he crawled in here by himself,' he suggested. Will thought about it doubtfully. But then he looked at the peaceful expression on the dying miner's face in the gloomy light and he couldn't bring himself to take the man back outside once more.

'Just put him a little further in, as far out of sight as you can,' he said.

There was a small elbow of rock and Horace gently placed the miner behind it. He was now visible only if you looked carefully and Will decided that was good enough. Horace stepped back into the main tunnel. Will noticed that he was still glancing uneasily around.

'What do we do now?' Horace asked. Will came to a decision.

'You can wait here for me,' he said. 'I'm going to see where this leads.'

Horace didn't argue. The thought of going further into that dark, winding tunnel didn't appeal to him at all. He found a place to sit, close to one of the brighter torches.

'Just make sure you come back,' he said. 'I don't want to have to come looking for you.'

Twenty

The tunnel, level at first, began to angle steeply upwards as Will went on, leaving Horace behind him. The walls and floor showed evidence of the Celts' picks and drills as they had torn and gouged at the rock to widen the path.

Will guessed that the original narrow tunnel had been nothing more than a natural fault in the rock — a mere crevice. But as he went on, he saw how much it had been widened, until there was room for four or five men to walk abreast. And still it climbed up into the heart of the mountains.

A circle of light showed the end of the tunnel. He estimated that he'd travelled maybe three hundred metres in total and the end was another forty away. The light that he could see seemed to be stronger than simple moonlight and, as he carefully emerged from the tunnel, he saw why.

Here, the hills separated, forming a large valley about two hundred metres across and half a kilometre long. To one side, the moonlight showed him massive wooden structures leading up to the higher reaches of the plateau. Staircases, he realised after a few moments' study. The floor of the valley was lit with camp fires and there were hundreds of figures moving in the flickering orange light. Will guessed that this would be the assembly area for Morgarath's army. At the moment, it was where the Wargals kept their Celt prisoners at night.

He paused, trying to form a picture of the overall situation. The plateau that formed the greater part of Morgarath's domain was still at least fifty metres above this point. But the staircases and the less formidable slope of the surrounding hills would provide relatively easy access down to this valley. The valley itself must be some thirty metres above the level where the bridge stood. The sloping tunnel would take troops down to the bridge from here. Once again, Halt's words echoed in his ear: *nowhere is really impassable.*

He moved to the left of the tunnel mouth and found cover in a jumble of rocks and boulders while he took stock of the situation. There was a rough stockade in the centre of the valley. Inside the wooden fencing, he could see a large number of small fires, each with a group of figures seated or sprawled around it. This was the prisoner's compound, he guessed.

Large fires outside the compound marked the places where the Wargals were camped. He could see the hulking, shambling forms clearly against the firelight as they moved around. Yet there was one fire close to him that seemed different. The figures seemed more upright, more humanoid in the way they stood and carried themselves.

Curiously, he worked his way closer to it, sliding through the night with barely a sound, moving quickly from one patch of cover to the next, until he was just at the outer ring of light thrown by the fire — a spot where he knew the darkness, by contrast, would seem more intense to those sitting around the fire.

There was a haunch of some kind of meat roasting slowly over the fire and the smell of it set his mouth watering. He'd been travelling for days on cold rations and the meat filled the air with a delicious fragrance. He felt his stomach begin to rumble and fear stabbed through him. It would be unthinkably bad luck to be betrayed by a rumbling stomach, he thought. The fear did the trick, killing his appetite. His digestion more or less under control, he edged his face around a boulder, low to the ground, to get a better look at the figures eating by the fire.

As he did so, one of them leaned forward to slice off a chunk of the meat, juggling the hot, greasy food in his hand as he took it. The movement let the firelight shine clearly on him and Will could see that these were not Wargals. From their rough sheepskin vests, woollen legging bound with tapes and heavy seal fur boots, he recognised them as Skandians.

Further study showed him their horned helmets, round wooden shields and battle axes piled to one side of the camp site. He wondered what they were doing here, so far from the ocean.

The man who had moved finished his meat and wiped his hands on his sheepskin vest. He belched, then settled himself in a more comfortable spot by the fire.

'Be domned glod when Olvak's men get 'ere,' he said in the thick, almost indecipherable accent of Skandia. Will knew that Skandians spoke the same tongue as the Kingdom. Hearing it now for the first time, though, he barely recognised it.

The other sea wolves growled their agreement. There were four of them round the fire. Will edged forward a little to hear them more clearly, then froze, horrified, as he saw the unmistakable shambling form of a Wargal moving directly towards him from the other side of the fire.

The Skandians heard him coming and looked up warily. With an immense feeling of relief, Will realised that the creature was not coming towards him but was approaching the Skandians' fire.

''Ullo,' said one of the Skandians in a low voice. ''Ere comes one of Morgarath's beauties.'

The Wargal had stopped on the far side of the fire. He grunted something unintelligible at the group of sea raiders. The one who had just spoken shrugged.

'Sorry, 'andsome. Didn't catch that,' he said. There was an obvious note of hostility in his voice. The Wargal seemed to sense it. He repeated his statement, growing angry now. Again, the circle of Skandian warriors shrugged at him.

The Wargal grunted again, growing angrier by the minute. He gestured at the meat hanging over the fire, then at himself. He shouted at the Skandians now, making eating gestures.

'Ugly brute wants our venison,' said one of the Skandians. There was a low growl of dissent from the group.

'Let 'im catch 'is own,' said the first man. The Wargal stepped inside the circle now. He had stopped shouting. He simply pointed to the meat, then turned his red, glaring eyes on the speaker. Somehow, the silence was more menacing than his shouting had been.

'Careful, Erak,' warned one of the Skandians, 'we're outnumbered here at the moment.'

Erak scowled at the Wargal for a second, then seemed to realise the wisdom of his friend's advice. He gestured angrily at the meat.

'Go on then. Take it,' he said curtly. The Wargal stepped forward and snatched the wooden spit from the fire, taking a huge bite at the meat and tearing a large chunk loose. Even from where he was lying, scarcely daring to breathe, Will could see the ugly light of triumph in the red, animal eyes. Then the Wargal turned abruptly and bounded out of the circle, forcing several of the Skandians to move hurriedly aside to avoid being trampled on. They heard its guttural laugh as it faded into the darkness.

'Damn things give me the heebies,' muttered Erak. 'Don't know why we have to have anything to do with them.'

''Cause Horth don't trust Morgarath,' one of the others told him. 'If we're not along, these damn bear-men will keep all the plunder for themselves and all we'll get is the hard fighting at the Plains of Uthal.'

'And hard marching too,' put in another. 'Wouldn't be any fun with Horth's men, either, working their way round Thorntree Forest to take the enemy in the rear. That's rough going, all right.'

Will frowned as he heard that. Obviously, Morgarath and Horth, who, Will assumed, was a Skandian war leader, were planning another treacherous surprise for the Kingdom's forces. He tried to picture a map of the countryside around the Plains of Uthal, but his memory was sketchy. He wished he'd paid more attention to the geography lessons Halt had taught him.

'Why is geography so important?' he remembered asking his teacher.

'Because maps are important if you want to know where your enemy is and where he's going,' had been the reply. Glumly, Will realised now how right he had been. Halt had shaken his head at him then, in that mock serious way he had. Suddenly, thinking of his wise and capable teacher, Will felt very lonely and more than a little out of his depth.

'Anyway,' Erak was saying, 'things'll be different when Olvak's men get 'ere. Although they seem to be taking their damned time about it.'

'Relax,' said the other speaker. 'It'll take a few days to get five 'undred men up them South Cliffs. Think 'ow long it took us.'

'Yeah,' said another. 'But we were blazing a trail. All they 'ave to do is follow it.'

'Well, they can't get 'ere too soon for me,' said Erak, rising and stretching. 'Well, I'm for sleep, lads, just as soon as I've done the necessaries.'

'Well, don't do 'em 'ere by the fire,' said one of the others irritably. 'Go up behind them rocks there.'

Horrified, Will realised that the Skandian had gestured towards the rocks where he was hiding. And now Erak, laughing at the other man, was turning and heading his way. It was definitely time to go. He scuttled backwards a few metres, then, crawling rapidly on his stomach, used all his training and natural skill to blend with the available cover.

He'd gone perhaps twenty metres when he heard a splashing sound from the spot where he'd been eaves-dropping. Then he heard a contented sigh and, looking back, saw the shaggy-haired form of Erak silhouetted against the glow of the hundred or so camp fires in the valley.

Realising that the Skandian was intent on what he was doing, Will slipped through the darkness and back into the tunnel. He went carefully for the first few metres, allowing his eyes to become accustomed to the dim light of the torches Then he began to run, his soft hide boots making barely a noise on the sandy floor.

Twenty-one

He had found Horace waiting for him, his hand ready on his sword hilt, where he had left him in the tunnel.

'Did you find out anything?' the apprentice warrior whispered hoarsely. Will let go a pent-up breath, realising that he'd been holding it for some time now.

'Plenty,' he said. 'All of it bad.'

He held up a hand to forestall Horace's further questions.

'Let's get back across the bridge,' he said. 'I'll tell you then.' He glanced into the side tunnel where they had left the Celt miner.

'Have you heard anything more from Glendyss?' he asked. Horace shrugged sadly.

'He started moaning about an hour ago. Then he went quiet. I think he's dead. At least he died the way he wanted to,' he said, then he followed Will back through the dimly lit tunnel to the bridge.

They made their way across the planking again, to where Evanlyn waited with the horses, well back from the bridge and out of sight. When they were close, Will called her name softly, so as to avoid startling her. Horace had left his dagger with Evanlyn and Will thought an armed Evanlyn would not be a person to approach unexpectedly.

As he described the scene at the other end of the tunnel, he hastily scratched a map in the sand for them.

'Somehow, we're going to have to find a way to delay Morgarath's forces,' he said.

The other two looked at him curiously. Delay them? How could two apprentices and a girl delay five hundred Skandians and several thousand relentless Wargals?

'I thought you said we should get word to the King,' Evanlyn said.

'We don't have time any more,' Will said simply. 'Look.'

They leaned forward, as he smoothed over the diagram he had drawn in the sand and hastily sketched out a new one. He wasn't sure that it was totally accurate, but at least it included the most important features of the Kingdom, as well as the Southern Plateau, where Morgarath ruled.

'They said they have more Skandians coming up the cliffs on the south coast — to join with the Wargals we've already seen. They'll cross the Fissure here, where we are, and move north to attack the barons in the rear, while they wait for Morgarath to try to break out of Three Step Pass.'

'Yes,' said Horace. 'We know that. We guessed it as soon as we saw the bridge.'

Will looked up at him and Horace fell silent. He realised the Ranger apprentice had something else to say.

'But,' said Will, emphasising the word and pausing for a moment, 'I also heard them saying something about Horth and his men marching around Thorntree Forest. That's up here to the north of the Plains of Uthal.'

Evanlyn grasped the point immediately. 'Which would bring the Skandians north-west of the King's army. They'd be trapped between the Wargals and Skandians who have crossed the bridge and the other force from the north.'

'Exactly,' said Will, meeting her gaze. They could both appreciate how dangerous that situation would be for the assembled barons. Expecting a Skandian attack through the fenlands, to the east, they'd be taken by surprise from not one, but two different directions, caught between the arms of a pincer and crushed.

'Then we'd better warn the King, surely!' insisted Horace.

'Horace,' said Will patiently. 'It would take us four days to reach the Plains.'

'Even more reason to get going. We haven't a moment to waste!' said the young warrior.

'And then,' put in Evanlyn, seeing Will's point, 'it would take at least another four days for any sort of force to get back here and hold the bridge. Maybe more.'

'That's eight days all told,' said Will. 'Remember what that poor miner said? The bridge will be ready in four days. The Wargals and Skandians will have plenty of time to cross the Fissure, assemble in battle formation and attack the King's army.'

'But . . .' Horace began and Will interrupted him.

'Horace, even if we get warning to the King and the barons, they'll be badly outnumbered and they'll be caught between two forces — with no way to retreat. The swamps of the fenlands will be behind them. Now I know we have to get a warning to them. But we can also do something here to even the numbers.'

'Plus,' Evanlyn put in, and Horace turned to face her, 'if we can do something to stop the Wargals and Skandians crossing here, the King will have the advantage over this northern force of Skandians.'

Horace nodded. 'They won't be outnumbered, I guess,' he said.

Evanlyn nodded, but then added, 'That's part of it. But those Skandians will be expecting reinforcements to attack the King from the rear — reinforcements that will never arrive.'

Understanding dawned in Horace's eyes. He nodded slowly, several times. Then the frown returned. 'But what can we do to stop the Wargals here?' he asked.

Will and Evanlyn exchanged a glance. He could see they'd come to the same conclusion. They both spoke at the same time.

'Burn the bridge,' they said.

Twenty-two

Blaze's head hung low as he trotted slowly into the outskirts of the King's camp on the Plains of Uthal. Gilan swayed wearily in the saddle. He had barely slept in the past three days, snatching only brief rests once every four hours.

Two guards stepped forward to query his progress and the young Ranger fumbled inside his shirt for the silver amulet in the form of an oak leaf – the Rangers' badge of office. At the sight of it, the guards stepped back hurriedly to clear the way. In times like these, nobody delayed a Ranger – not if he knew what was good for him.

Gilan rubbed his gritty eyes. 'Where is the War Council tent?'

One of the guards pointed with his spear to a larger than normal tent, set up on a knoll overlooking the rest of the camp. There were more guards there, and a large number of people coming and going, as one would expect at the nerve centre of an army.

'There, sir. On that small rise.'

Gilan nodded. He'd come so far, so fast, finishing the four-day journey in just over three days. Now, these few hundred metres seemed like miles to him. He leaned forward and whispered in Blaze's ear.

'Not much farther, my friend. One more effort, please.'

The exhausted horse's ears twitched and his head came up a little. At Gilan's gentle urging, he managed to raise a slow trot and they passed through the camp.

Dust drifting on the breeze, the smell of woodsmoke, noise and confusion: the camp was like any army camp anywhere in the world. Orders being shouted. The clang and rattle of arms being repaired or sharpened. Laughter from tents, where men lay back relaxing with no duties to be performed — until their sergeants found them and discovered jobs for them to be doing. Gilan smiled tiredly at the thought. Sergeants seemed to be totally averse to seeing their men having an easy time of it.

Blaze came to a halt once more and Gilan realised, with a jerk, that he'd actually nodded off in the saddle. Before him, two more guards barred the way to the War Council compound. He looked at them blearily.

'King's Ranger,' he croaked, through a dry throat. 'Message for the Council.'

The guards hesitated. This dust-covered, half-asleep man, seated on a lathered, exhausted bay horse, might well be a Ranger. He was certainly dressed like a Ranger, as far as they could tell. Yet the guards knew most of the senior Rangers by sight, and they had never seen this young man before. And he showed no sign of identification.

What's more, they noticed, he carried a sword, which

was definitely not a Ranger's weapon, so they were reluctant to admit him to the carefully guarded War Council compound. Irritably, Gilan realised that he had neglected to leave the silver oakleaf device hanging outside his shirt. The effort of finding it again suddenly became intense. He fumbled blindly at his collar. Then a familiar, and very welcome, voice cut through his consciousness.

'Gilan! What's happened? Are you all right?'

That was the voice that had meant comfort and security to him throughout his five years as an apprentice. The voice of courage and capability and wisdom. The voice that knew exactly what action should be taken at any point in time.

'Halt,' he murmured, and realised that he was swaying, then falling from the saddle. Halt caught him before he hit the ground. He glared at the two sentries, who were standing by, not sure whether to help or not.

'Give me a hand!' he ordered and they leapt forward, dropping their spears with a clatter, to support the semi-conscious young Ranger.

'Let's get you somewhere to rest,' Halt said. 'You're all in.'

But Gilan summoned some last reserves of energy and, pushing clear of the soldiers, steadied himself on his own feet. 'Important news,' he said to Halt. 'Must see the Council. There's something bad going on in Celtica.'

Halt felt a cold hand of premonition clutch his heart. He cast his gaze around, looking back down the path where Gilan had come. Bad news from Celtica. And Gilan apparently alone.

'Where's Will?' he asked quickly. 'Is he all right?'

His heart lifted as Gilan nodded, a shadow of his normal grin showing through the bone-weariness.

'He's all right,' Gilan told the grizzled Ranger. 'I came on ahead.'

As they had been talking, they had begun to move towards the central pavilion. There were more guards on duty here but they moved out of the way at the sight of the senior Ranger. He was a familiar figure round the War Council. He put out a hand now to steady his former apprentice and they entered the cool shade of the Council pavilion.

A group of half a dozen men were clustered round a sand map — a large table with the main features of the Plains and Mountains modelled in sand. They turned now at the sound of the new arrivals and one of them hurried forward, concern written on his face.

'Gilan!' he cried. He was a tall man, and his greying hair showed him to be in his late fifties. But he still moved with the speed and grace of an athlete, or a warrior. Gilan gave that tired smile again.

'Morning, Father,' he said, for the tall grey-haired man was none other than Sir David, Battlemaster of Caraway Fief and field commander of the King's army. The Battlemaster looked quickly to Halt and caught the quick nod of reassurance there. Gilan was all right, he realised, just exhausted. Then, his sense of duty caught up with his fatherly reaction.

'Greet your King properly,' he said softly, and Gilan looked up to the group of men, all their attention now focused on him.

He recognised Crowley, the Ranger Corps Commandant, and Baron Arald and two other senior Barons of the realm — Thorn of Drayden and Fergus of Caraway. But the figure in the centre took his attention. A tall blonde man in his late thirties, with a short beard and piercing green eyes. He was broad-shouldered and muscular, because Duncan was not a king who let other men do all his fighting for him. He had trained with sword and lance since he was a boy and he was regarded as one of the most capable knights in his own Kingdom.

Gilan attempted to sink to one knee. His joints screamed in protest and tried to lock up on him. The pressure of Halt's hand under his arm was all that stopped him falling once again.

'My lord . . .' he began apologetically, but Duncan had already stepped forward, seizing his hand to steady him. Gilan heard Halt's introduction.

'Ranger Gilan, my lord, attached to Meric Fief. With messages from Celtica.'

Suddenly, the King was galvanised with interest. 'Celtica?' he repeated, studying Gilan more closely. 'What's happening there?'

The other Council members had moved from the sand map to group around Gilan. Baron Arald spoke: 'Gilan was carrying your messages to King Swyddned, my lord,' he said. 'Invoking our mutual defence treaty and requesting that Swyddned send troops to join us —'

'They won't be coming,' Gilan interrupted. He realised he had to tell the King his news before he collapsed from exhaustion. 'Morgarath has them bottled up on the south-west peninsula.'

There was a stunned silence in the Council tent. Finally, it was Gilan's father who broke it. 'Morgarath?' he said, incredulously. 'How? How could he get any sort of army into Celtica?'

Gilan shook his head, suppressing a huge need to yawn. 'They sent small numbers down the cliffs, until they had enough troops to catch the Celts by surprise. As you know, Swyddned keeps only a small standing army . . .'

Baron Arald nodded, anger showing on his face. 'I warned Swyddned, my lord,' he put in. 'But those damned Celts have always been more interested in digging than protecting their own land.'

Duncan made a small, pacifying gesture with one hand. 'No time now for recriminations, Arald,' he said softly. 'What's done is done, I'm afraid.'

'I should imagine Morgarath has been watching them for years, waiting for their greed to overcome their good sense,' Baron Thorn said bitterly. The other men nodded quietly. Morgarath's ability to maintain a network of spies was all too well known to them.

'So Celtica has been defeated by Morgarath? Is this what you're telling us?' Duncan asked. This time, as Gilan shook his head, there were relieved glances around the tent.

'The Celts are holding out in the south-west, my lord. They're not defeated yet. But the strange business of it all is that Wargal raiding parties have been carrying off the Celt miners.'

'What?' This time it was Crowley who interrupted. 'What earthly use has Morgarath for miners?'

Gilan shrugged in reply. 'I've no idea, sir,' he told his

chief. 'But I thought I'd better get here with the news of it as soon as possible.'

'You saw this happening, then, Gilan?' Halt asked, frowning darkly as he puzzled over what the young Ranger had just told them.

'Not exactly,' Gilan admitted. 'We saw the empty mining towns and the deserted border posts. We were heading deeper into Celtica when we met a young girl who told us about the raids.'

'A young girl?' the King said. 'A Celt?'

'No, my lord. She was Araluan. A lady's maid whose mistress was visiting Swyddned's court. Unfortunately, they ran into a Wargal war party. Evanlyn was the only one to escape.'

'Evanlyn?' Duncan said, his voice the merest whisper. The others turned to him as he spoke. The King's face had turned a chalky white and his eyes were wide with horror.

'That was her name, my lord,' said Gilan, puzzled by the King's reaction. But Duncan wasn't listening. He had turned away and moved blindly to a canvas chair set by his small reading table. He dropped into the chair, his head sunk in his hands. The members of his War Council moved towards him, alarmed at his reaction.

'My lord,' said Sir David of Caraway. 'What is it?'

Duncan slowly raised his eyes to meet the Battle-master's.

'Evanlyn . . .' he said, his voice breaking with emotion. 'Evanlyn was my daughter's maid.'

Twenty-three

There was no time to put the plan into action that night — dawn was less than an hour away. At one stage, Will had suggested that Horace and Evanlyn should leave him behind to burn the bridge, while they rode to take the news to Araluen. But Horace had refused.

'If we go now, we won't know if you've succeeded or not, so what do we tell the King? There might be a bridge or there might not be?' he said, in another example of the solid commonsense that had become part of his thinking. 'And besides, destroying a bridge this size might be a little more than you can manage alone — even a famous Ranger like yourself.'

He smiled as he said the last words, to let Will know he meant no insult. Will conceded the point. Secretly, he was glad they would be with him. He shared Horace's doubt that he might not be able to handle the task alone.

They slept fitfully until dawn, finally woken by the sounds of shouting and whips as the Wargals drove the miners back to their task of finishing the bridge. Through-out the day, they watched with alarm as the completed footway crept closer and closer to the side of the ravine where they lay hidden. With a sinking feeling, Will realised that the estimate given them by the dying miner was not to be relied upon. Perhaps the extra numbers of slaves were the reason, but it was obvious that the bridge would be all but completed by the end of the following day.

'We'll have to do it tonight.'

He breathed the words in Evanlyn's ear. The two of them lay prone on the rocks, overlooking the building site. Horace was a few metres away, dozing quietly in the cold morning sun. The girl shifted her position so that her mouth was closer to his ear and whispered back.

'I've been thinking, how will we get this fire started? There's barely enough wood around here for a decent camp fire.'

The same question had been taxing Will's brain throughout the night. Then the answer had come to him. He smiled quietly as he watched a group of Celt miners hammering pine boards onto the bridge framework to form the roadway.

'There's plenty of good firewood here,' he replied. 'If you know where to look for it.'

Evanlyn glanced at him, puzzled, then followed the line of his gaze. The frown on her forehead disappeared and she smiled slowly.

As dusk fell, the Wargals herded their weary, starving slaves back from the bridge and into the tunnel. Will noticed that by the end of the afternoon, the work of enlarging the tunnel seemed to have been completed. They waited an hour longer, until full darkness. During that time, there had been no sign of any activity from the tunnel. Now that they knew to look for it, they could see the loom of the firelight from the valley at the other end of the tunnel, reflecting on the low, scudding clouds.

'I hope it doesn't rain,' said Horace suddenly. 'That'd put paid to our idea all right.'

Will stopped in his tracks and looked up at him quickly. That unpleasant thought hadn't occurred to him. 'It isn't going to rain,' he said firmly, and hoped he was right. He continued on then, leading Tug gently to the unfinished end of the bridge. The little horse stopped there, ears pricked and nostrils twitching to the scents of the night air.

'Alert,' said Will softly to the horse, the command word that told him to give warning if he sensed approaching danger. Tug tossed his head once, signifying that he understood. Then Will led the way across the framework of the bridge to where the footway was completed, stepping lightly as he crossed the narrow beams above the dizzying drop. Horace and Evanlyn followed, more carefully. But this night, to Horace's relief, there was less distance to travel before they reached the firm and comforting surface of the completed bridge. He realised that Will was right. Another day would see the bridge completed.

Will unslung his bow and quiver and laid them on the planking. Then he drew his saxe knife from its scabbard and, dropping to his knees, began to prise up one of the nearest planks from the bridge walkway. The wood was soft pine, roughly sawn, and perfect firewood. Horace drew his dagger and began prising up the planks in the next row. As they loosened them, Evanlyn moved them to one side, stacking them in a pile. When she had six planks, each over a metre long, she gathered them up and ran lightly to the far side of the bridge, stacking them on the far bank of the fissure, close to where the massive, tarred cables were fastened to wooden pylons. By the time she returned, Will and Horace were well on the way to removing another six. These she took to the other cable. Will had explained his plan to them earlier in the day. To make sure there was no remaining structure on the far side, they would need to burn through both cables and pylons at that end, letting the bridge fall into the depths of the Fissure. The Wargals might be able to span the Fissure with a small, temporary rope affair, but nothing substantial enough to permit large numbers of troops to cross in a short time.

Once they had burnt the bridge, they would ride full speed to alert the King's army to the threat in the south. Any small numbers of Wargals who might cross the Fissure could then be easily dealt with by the Kingdom's troops.

The two boys continued levering the planks free and setting them to one side for Evanlyn. In her turn, she maintained her constant ferrying back and forth across the bridge, until the stacks by each pylon were piled high. In spite of the cold night, both boys were sweating freely with the effort. Finally, Evanlyn laid a hand on Will's shoulder as he prised up one board and began immediately on another.

'I think it's enough,' she said simply and he stopped, rocking back on his heels and wiping his forehead with the back of his left hand. She gestured towards the other end of the bridge, where there were at least twenty planks piled up on either side of the road. He eased the cramps out of his neck, rolling his head from side to side, then stood up.

'You're right,' he told her. 'That should be enough to get the rest of it burning.'

Gesturing for the others to follow, he picked up his bow and quiver and led the way to the far side of the bridge. He looked critically at the two piles of wood for a moment or two.

'We'll need kindling,' he said, glancing around to see if there were any small trees or bushes in the vicinity where they might find light wood to help them start their fire. Of course, there were none. Horace held out his hand for Will's saxe knife.

'Lend me that for a moment,' he asked and Will handed it to him. Horace tested the balance of the heavy knife for a moment. Then, taking one of the long planks, Horace stood it on end and, in a bewilderingly fast series of flashing strokes, sliced it into a dozen thin lengths.

'It's not quite sword practice,' he grinned at them. 'But it's close enough.'

As Will and Evanlyn began forming the thin pine strips into two small pyres, Horace took another plank and whittled more carefully, carving off thin curls from the pine to catch the first sparks from the flint and steel they would use to light the fire. Will glanced once to see what Evanlyn was doing. Satisfied that she knew what she was about, he turned back to his own task, accepting the shaved pine from Horace as the other boy passed it to him in handfuls and stacking it around the base of the kindling.

As Will moved across to Evanlyn's side to do the same with her fire, Horace split a few more planks in halves, then snapped the thinner lengths in two. Will looked up nervously at the noise.

'Keep it down,' he warned the apprentice warrior. 'Those Wargals aren't exactly deaf, you know, and the sound might carry through the tunnel.'

Horace shrugged. 'I'm finished now anyway,' he said.

Will paused and studied both pyres. Satisfied that they had the right combination of kindling and light wood to get them going, he motioned the others to cross back to the other side.

'You two get going,' he told them. 'I'll start the fires and follow you.'

Horace needed no second invitation. He didn't want to have to run across the bare beams of the bridge with the fire licking around the cables behind him. He wanted plenty of time to negotiate the gap. Evanlyn hesitated for a moment, then saw the sense in what Will had said.

They crossed carefully, trying not to look down into the agonising depths below the bridge as they negotiated the last ten metres. There was a wider gap now, of course, as they'd removed some of the boards that formed the road surface. Safe on the other side, they turned and waved to Will. They saw him, a crouched, indistinct figure in the shadows beside the right-hand bridge support. There was a bright flash as he struck his flint and steel together. Then another. And this time, a small yellow glow of light formed at the base of the piled wood as the pine shavings caught fire and the flame grew.

Will blew on it gently and watched the eager little yellow tongues spread out, licking at the rough pine, feeding on the flammable resin that filled the grain of the wood and growing larger and more voracious by the second. He saw the first of the thin stakes take fire, then the flames shot up, licking greedily around the rope balustrade of the bridge and beginning to reach for the heavy cable. The tar began sizzling. Drops melted and fell into the flames, flaring up with a bright blue flash each time.

Satisfied that the first fire was well under way, Will ran to the opposite side and went to work with his flint and steel once more. Again, the watchers saw the bright flashes, then the small, rapidly growing pool of yellow.

Will, now silhouetted clearly by the light of the two fires, stood erect and stepped back, watching to make sure that they were both properly alight. Already, the right-hand pylon and cable were beginning to smoke in the heat of the fire. Satisfied at last, Will gathered his bow and quiver and ran back across the bridge, barely slowing when he reached the narrow beams.

Reaching their side, he turned to look back at his handiwork. The right-hand cable was now blazing fiercely. A sudden gust of wind sent a shower of sparks high into the air above it. The left-hand fire didn't seem to be burning nearly as well. Perhaps it was a trick or an eddy of the wind that stopped the flames reaching the tar-soaked rope on that side. Perhaps the wood they had used was damp. But as they watched, the fire beneath the left-hand cable slowly died away to a red glow of embers.

Twenty-four

Gilan dropped his eyes from the tortured gaze of his King. Everyone in the tent could see the pain there as Duncan realised that his daughter had been killed by Morgarath's Wargals. Gilan looked around the other men, seeking some form of support from them. None of them, he saw, could bring themselves to meet their monarch's eyes.

Duncan rose from the chair and walked to the doorway of the tent, looking to the south-west as if he could somehow see his daughter across the distance.

'Cassandra left to visit Celtica eight weeks ago,' he said. 'She's a good friend of Princess Madelydd. When all this business with Morgarath started, I thought she'd be safe there. I saw no reason to bring her back.' He turned away from the door and his gaze held Gilan's. 'Tell me. Tell me everything you know . . .'

'My lord . . .' Gilan stopped, gathering his thoughts. He knew he had to tell the King as much as possible. But he also wanted to avoid causing him unnecessary pain. 'The girl saw us and came to us. She recognised Will and myself as Rangers. Apparently, she had managed to escape when the Wargals attacked their party. She said the others were . . .'

He hesitated. He couldn't go on.

'Continue,' Duncan said. His voice was firm. He was in control once more.

'She said the Wargals had killed them, my lord. All of them,' Gilan finished in a rush. Somehow, he felt it might be easier if he said it quickly. 'She didn't tell us details. She wasn't up to it. She was exhausted — mentally and physically.'

Duncan nodded. 'Poor girl. It must have been a terrible thing to witness. She's a good servant — more of a friend to Cassandra, in fact,' he added softly.

Gilan felt the need to keep talking to the King, to give the King whatever detail he could about the loss of his daughter. 'At first, we almost mistook her for a boy,' he said, remembering the moment when Evanlyn had walked into their camp. Duncan looked up, confusion on his face.

'A boy?' he said. 'With that mass of red hair?'

Gilan shrugged. 'She'd cut it short. Probably to conceal her appearance. The Celtic foothills are full of bandits and robbers at the moment, as well as Wargals.'

Something was wrong, he sensed. He was bone-weary, aching for sleep, and his brain wasn't functioning as it should. But the King had said something that wasn't right. Something that . . .

He shook his head, trying to clear it, and swayed on his feet, glad of Halt's ready arm to steady him. Seeing the movement, Duncan was instantly apologetic.

'Ranger Gilan,' he said, stepping forward and seizing his hand. 'Forgive me. You're exhausted and I've kept you here because of my own personal sorrow. Please, Halt, see that Gilan has food and rest.'

'Blaze . . .' Gilan started to say, remembering his dust-covered, weary horse outside the tent. Halt replied gently.

'It's all right. I'll look after Blaze.' He glanced at the King once more, nodding his head towards Gilan. 'With your majesty's permission?'

Duncan waved the two of them out.

'Yes, please, Halt. Look after your comrade. He's served us well.'

As the two Rangers left the tent, Duncan turned to his remaining advisers. 'Now, gentlemen, let's see if we can put some reason to this latest move by Morgarath.'

Baron Thorn cast a quick glance at the others, seeking and gaining their assent to act as spokesman. 'My lord,' he said awkwardly, 'perhaps we should give you some time to come to terms with this news . . .' The other councillors all mumbled their agreement to the idea but Duncan shook his head firmly.

'I'm the King,' he said simply. 'And for the King, private matters come last. Matters of the Kingdom come first.'

'It's gone out!' said Horace, in an agony of disappointment.

The three of them looked, desperately hoping that he was wrong, that their eyes were somehow deceiving them. But he was right. The fire under the left-hand pylon had died away to a small, glowing heap of embers.

By contrast, the other side was well and truly alight, with the fire running fiercely up the tarred rope side rails to the massive cable supporting the right side of the bridge. Indeed, as they watched, one of the three ropes forming the cable burned through and the right-hand side of the bridge creaked alarmingly.

'Maybe one side will be enough?' Evanlyn suggested hopefully, but Will shook his head in frustration, willing the second fire to flare up again.

'The right-hand pylon is damaged, but it's still useable,' he pointed out. 'If the left-hand side survives, they can still get across to this side. And if they can do that, they might be able to repair the whole thing before we can get warning to King Duncan.'

Resolutely, he hitched his bow over his shoulder and started across the bridge once more.

'Where are you going?' Horace asked him, eyeing the structure with distrust. The bridge had taken a definite lean to one side now that part of the right-hand cable had burned through. As he put the question, the structure trembled again, settling a little further towards the bottom of the abyss.

Will paused, balanced on the bare beam that stretched across the gap.

'I'll have to relight it,' he said. 'We've got to make sure there's nothing left on that side for them to salvage.'

And, so saying, he ran to the far side. Horace felt queasy watching him move so quickly across that massive drop, with nothing but a narrow beam beneath him. Then he and Evanlyn watched in a fever of impatience as Will crouched by the embers. He began fanning them, then leaned down and blew on them until a small tongue of flame flickered inside the pile of unburnt kindling.

'He's done it!' Evanlyn cried, then the triumph in her voice died as the flicker faded. Once again, Will leaned down and began to blow gently on the embers. Something else gave on the right-hand side cable and the bridge lurched, sinking further to that side.

'Come on! Come on!' Horace said over and over to himself, his hands clenching and unclenching as he watched his friend.

Then Tug gave a quiet whinny.

Both Horace and Evanlyn turned to look at the small horse. If it had been either of their own mounts, they wouldn't have reacted. But they knew Tug was trained to remain silent, unless . . .

Unless! Horace looked to where Will was crouched over the remains of the fire. Obviously, he hadn't heard Tug's warning. Evanlyn seized Horace's arm and pointed.

'Look!' she said and he followed her pointing finger to the mouth of the tunnel, where a glimmer of light was showing. Someone was coming! Tug pawed the ground and whinnied again, a little louder this time, but Will, close to the noise of the burning right-hand cable, didn't hear. Evanlyn came to a decision.

'Stay here!' she told Horace, and started out across the wooden beam framework. She inched her way carefully, her heart in her mouth as the weakened bridge structure lurched and swayed. Below her was blackness, and, at the very bottom, the silver glimmer of the river that ran wildly through the base of the Fissure. She swayed, recovered, then went on. The roadway was only eight metres away now. Now five. Now three.

The bridge swayed again and she hung there for an awful moment, arms spread to hold her balance, teetering over that horrific drop. Behind her, she heard Horace's warning cry. Taking a deep breath, she lunged for the safety of the boardwalk, falling full length on the rough pine floor of the bridge.

Heart pounding with the reaction of her near miss, she came to her feet and raced across the bridge. As she drew closer, Will sensed her movement and looked up. Breathlessly, she pointed to the mouth of the tunnel.

'They're coming!' she cried. And now, the reflected glow of light from within the tunnel was revealed to be the flare of several burning torches as a small group of figures emerged. They paused at the tunnel mouth, pointing and shouting as they saw the flames reaching high above the bridge. She counted six of them, and from their shambling, clumsy gait, she recognised them as Wargals.

The Wargals began to run towards the bridge. They were just over fifty metres away, but covering the ground quickly. And she knew there must be more behind them.

'Let's get out of here!' she said, grabbing at Will's sleeve. But he shook her hand off, grim-faced. He was already scooping up his bow and quiver, slinging the quiver over his shoulder and checking that the bowstring was firmly anchored.

'You get back!' he told her. 'I'll stay and hold them off.'

Almost as he spoke, he nocked an arrow to the string and, barely seeming to aim, sent it hissing towards the lead

Wargal. The arrow took in the chest and it fell, crying out once, then lay silent.

His companions halted in their tracks, seeing the arrow. They looked warily around them, trying to see where it had come from. Perhaps this was a trap, their primitive, single track minds told them. As yet, they couldn't see the small figure at the end of the bridge. And even as they looked, another three arrows came hissing out of the darkness. The steel heads of two of the arrows struck sparks as they smashed into the rocks. The third took one of the Wargals at the rear of the party in the lower arm. He cried out in pain and fell to his knees.

The Wargals hesitated uncertainly. Seeing the light and smoke of the fire above the hill that separated their camp area from the bridge, they had come to investigate. Now unseen archers were firing at them. Coming to a decision, and with no one to order them forward, they retreated quickly to the shelter of the tunnel mouth.

'They're going back!' Evanlyn told Will. But he'd already seen the movement and he was on his knees again, trying to frantically rebuild the fire.

'We'll have to reset the whole thing!' he muttered. Evanlyn dropped to her knees beside him and began shaping the half-burnt strips and heavier pieces into a conical pyre.

'You watch the Wargals!' she said. 'I'll look after this.'

Will hesitated. After all, this was the fire she had set in the first place. He had a moment of doubt as he wondered if she'd done the job correctly. Then he looked up to the tunnel mouth, saw movement there once again and realised she was right. Grabbing his bow, he started to move towards the cover of some rocks nearby, but she stopped him.

'Your knife!' she said. 'Leave it with me.'

He didn't ask why. He slid the saxe from its scabbard and dropped it onto the planking beside her. Then he moved to the rocks. As he left the bridge, he felt it tremble again as the right-hand cable gave a little more. Silently, he cursed the caprice of wind that had fanned one fire and extinguished the other.

Encouraged by the lack of arrows whistling around their ears in the past few minutes, the four remaining Wargals had emerged from the tunnel again and were moving cautiously forward. Without any real intelligent leadership, and with a false sense of their own superiority, they stayed grouped together, an easy target. Will fired three times, carefully aimed shots.

Each one found its mark. The surviving Wargal looked at his fallen comrades, then lumbered into the cover of the rocks. Will sent another arrow skating off the granite directly above his head, to encourage him to stay where he was.

He checked his quiver. There were sixteen arrows left. Not a lot if the Wargals had sent for reinforcements. He glanced at Evanlyn. She seemed to be maddeningly slow with her efforts to rebuild the fire. He wanted to yell at her to hurry, but realised he would only distract her and slow her down if he did. He looked back to the tunnel, his fingers clenching and unclenching on the bow.

Four more figures emerged, running fast and fanning out so that they weren't grouped together. Will brought the bow up, sighted quickly and released at the one furthest to the right. He let go a little cry of exasperation as the arrow flew behind the running figure. Then he was obscured by the rocks.

Blessing the weeks and months of practice that Halt had insisted on, Will had another arrow out of the quiver and ready nocked, without even looking at it. But the other three runners had gone to ground as well.

Now one of them rose in the middle of the line and darted forward. Will's snapshot cleaved the air above his head as he dived for cover. Then another was moving on the left, dropping into cover before Will could fire. His heart was beating rapidly as they made their quick rushes and he forced himself to breathe deeply and think calmly. The time to shoot would be in the last thirty metres, where there was less cover and where the arrows, with a shorter distance to cover, would be travelling faster and so be harder to dodge. Will's heart hammered inside his ribs. He was remembering the last time – only a few weeks ago – when fear had made his shots go wide. His face hardened as he determined that it would not happen again.

'Stay calm,' he told himself, trying to hear Halt's voice saying the words. Another of the figures made a short rush and this time, as the firelight illuminated him more clearly, Will held his fire as his eyes confirmed what he had begun to suspect.

The newcomers weren't Wargals. They were Skandians.

Twenty-five

Gilan slept like a log for six hours, totally exhausted, in the tent where Halt had taken him. Throughout that time, he didn't stir once. His mind and body were shut down, drawing new strength from total rest.

Then, after those six hours, his subconscious mind stirred and began to function, and he began to dream. He dreamt of Will and Horace and the girl Evanlyn. But the dream was wild and confused and he saw them as captives of the Wargals, tied together while the two robbers Bart and Carney stood by and laughed.

Gilan rolled onto one side, muttering in his sleep. Halt, sitting nearby repairing the fletching on his arrows, glanced up. He saw that the young Ranger was still asleep and went back to his routine task. Gilan muttered again, then fell silent.

In his dream, he saw the servant Evanlyn as the King had described her — with her hair long and uncropped, masses of it flowing down her back, thick and lustrous and red.

And then he sat up, wide awake.

'My God!' he said to a startled Halt. 'It's not her!'

Halt swore as he spilled the thick, viscous glue that he was using to attach the goose feather vanes to the arrow shaft. Gilan's sudden movement had caught him by surprise. Now he mopped up the sticky liquid and turned with some irritation to his friend.

'Could you give a bit of warning when you're going to start shouting like that?' he said peevishly. But Gilan was already out of the camp bed and hauling on his breeches and shirt.

'I've got to see the King!' he said urgently. Halt stood warily, not altogether sure that Gilan wasn't sleepwalking. The young Ranger shoved past him, dashing out into the night, and tucking his shirt into his trousers as he went. Reluctantly, Halt followed him.

There was a slight delay as they reached the King's pavilion. The guard had changed several hours before and the new sentries didn't know Gilan by sight. Halt smoothed things over, but not before Gilan had convinced him that it was vital for him to see King Duncan, even if it meant waking him from a well-deserved sleep.

As it turned out, in spite of the late hour, the King wasn't sleeping. He and his supreme army commander were discussing possible reasons for the raids into Celtica when Gilan, barefoot, rumple-haired and with several buttons still askew on his shirt front, was allowed into the pavilion. Sir David looked up in alarm at the sight his son presented.

'Gilan! What on earth are you doing here?' he demanded, but Gilan held up a hand to stop him.

'Just a moment, Father,' he said. Then, he continued, facing the King, 'Sir, when you described the maid Evanlyn earlier, did you say "red" hair?'

Sir David looked to Halt for an explanation. The older Ranger shrugged and Sir David turned back to his son, anger clearly showing on his face.

'What difference does that make?' he began. But again Gilan cut him off, still addressing the King.

'The girl who called herself Evanlyn was blonde, sir,' he said simply. This time, it was King Duncan who held out a hand to silence his angry Battlemaster.

'Blonde?' he asked.

'Blonde, sir. She'd cut it short, as I said, but it was blonde, like your own. And she had green eyes,' Gilan told him, watching Duncan carefully, and sensing the importance of what he was telling him. The King hesitated a moment, covering his face with one hand. Then he spoke, the hope growing in his voice.

'And her build? Slight, was she? Small of stature?'

Gilan nodded eagerly. 'As I said, sir, for a moment, we could have taken her for a boy. She must have used her maid's identity because she thought it was safer if she remained incognito.' Now, he understood those slight hesitations in Evanlyn's speech, and why she had a broader grasp of politics and strategy than most servants would be expected to have.

Slowly, Halt and Sir David began to realise the import of what was being said. The King looked from Gilan to Halt to David, then back to Gilan again.

'My daughter is alive,' he said quietly. There was a long silence. It was finally broken by Sir David.

'Gilan, how far behind you were the two apprentices and the girl?'

Gilan hesitated. 'Possibly two days' ride, Father,' he estimated, following his father to the map table and indicating the furthest point that he thought Will and the others might have reached by now. Sir David took instant charge, sending messengers running to rouse the commander of the cavalry wing and have him prepare a company of light cavalry to leave camp immediately.

'We'll send a company of the Fifth Lancers to bring them in, sir,' he told the King. 'If they leave within the hour and ride through the night, they should make contact sometime around noon tomorrow.'

'I'll guide them,' Gilan offered immediately and his father nodded assent.

'I'd hoped you'd say that.' He seized the King's arm, smiling with genuine pleasure at the relief on the tall man's face. 'I can't tell you how pleased I am for you, sir,' he said. The King looked at him, a little bemused. So recently, he had been privately mourning the loss of his beloved daughter Cassandra. Now, miraculously, she had been restored to life.

'My daughter is alive,' he said once more. 'She's safe.'

Evanlyn crouched over the pile of wood beside the bridge railing. From time to time, she heard the dull thrum of Will's bow as he fired at the approaching enemy, but she forced herself not to look up, concentrating on the job in hand. She knew they had one last chance to get the fire going properly. If she got it wrong this time, it would mean disaster for the Kingdom. So she carefully stacked and placed the wood, making sure there was sufficient air space between the pieces to allow a good draft. She had none of the shavings left to use for tinder this time, but only a few metres away, she had a perfect source of fire. The right-hand cable was still blazing fiercely.

Satisfied that the wood was stacked properly, she took Will's saxe and cut several one-metre lengths of tarred rope from the bridge railing — thinner lengths, not the massive cable itself. It would have been almost impossible to hack through that in time.

Taking the rope lengths, she came to her feet and darted across the bridge to the blazing fire on the other side. It was a simple matter to get the lengths of tarred rope burning, then she ran back to her fire pile and draped the burning rope around the base, trailing it through the gaps she had left in the wood. The flames licked at her fingers as she pushed the rope in between pieces of wood. She bit her lip, ignoring the pain as she made sure the fire was burning freely.

The tar-fed flames crackled at the wood, flickered, then took. She fanned them for a few seconds as they became established, until the lighter kindling strips were burning fiercely, then the heavier planks began to take fire as well. The handrail caught in several places and now tongues of flame were shooting up to the cable, beginning to lick at it, feeding on the tar, then running up to where it joined the wooden pylon structure.

Only now did she take the time to glance up at Will. Her eyes were dazzled by the fire and she could see him only as a dull blur, five metres away, behind a rock outcrop.

As she looked, he rose to a standing position and fired an arrow. She looked into the surrounding darkness but could see no sign of their attackers.

The bridge gave another convulsive jerk beneath her feet and the roadway tilted to an alarming degree as the second of the three strands of the right-hand cable burnt through and the structure sagged further to that side. They wouldn't have much time to get back across to where Horace and Tug waited. She had to warn Will.

Saxe knife in hand, she ran full pelt to where he crouched behind the rocks, his eyes searching the darkness for movement. He glanced quickly at her as she arrived.

'The other side's burning,' she said. 'Let's get out of here.'

Grimly, he shook his head, then pointed with his chin to a jumble of rocks barely thirty metres from where they crouched.

'Can't risk it,' he told her. 'One of them has got behind those rocks. If we go now, he might have time to save the bridge.'

Out of the corner of her eye, she saw a quick, darting movement to their left and pointed quickly.

'There's one!' she said. Will nodded.

'I see him,' he replied evenly. 'He's trying to draw my fire. As soon as I shoot at him, the one closer to us will have a chance. I have to wait for him to show himself before I can shoot.'

She looked at him, horrified, as she realised the significance of what he was saying. 'But that means the others can close in on us,' she said. This time, Will said nothing. The incipient panic he had felt was now replaced by a calm sense of resolution. Deep in his heart, a part of him was glad — glad that he hadn't failed Halt and glad that he had repaid the faith that the older Ranger had placed in him when he chose him as an apprentice.

He glanced at Evanlyn for a long moment and she realised he was willing to be captured if it kept the enemy away from the bridge just a few minutes longer.

Captured or killed, she amended.

Behind them, there was a groaning crash and she turned to see the first cable finally give way in a shower of flame and sparks. It took the burnt-through upper half of its pylon with it. That was the result they had wanted. They had discussed the idea of simply cutting the main cables, but that would have left the major structure of the bridge untouched. The pylons themselves had to be destroyed. Now the entire bridge was hanging, suspended by the left-hand cable, and flames were already eating their way through that. In a few more minutes, she knew, the bridge would be gone. The Fissure would be impassable once more.

Will tried to give her a reassuring smile. It wasn't a very successful attempt. 'You can't do much more here,' he told her. 'Get across the bridge while you've still got time.'

She hesitated, desperately wanting to go but unwilling to leave him on his own. He was only a boy, she realised, but he was willing to sacrifice himself for her and the rest of the Kingdom.

'Go!' he said, turning to her and shoving at her. And now she thought she could see the glitter of tears in his eyes. Her own eyes filled and she couldn't see him clearly. She blinked to clear her vision, just in time to see a jagged rock curving down out of the firelit night.

'Will!' she shouted, but she was too late. The rock took him in the side of the head and he grunted in surprise, then his eyes rolled up and he fell at her feet, dark blood already welling from his scalp. She heard a rush of feet from several directions and she tossed the saxe knife aside and scrabbled in the dirt for Will's bow. Then she found it and was trying to nock an arrow when rough hands grabbed her, knocking the bow from her grasp and pinning her arms to her sides. The Skandian held her in a bear hug, her face pressed into the rough sheepskin of his vest, smelling of grease and smoke and sweat and all but suffocating her. She kicked out, lashing with her feet and tossing her head, trying to butt the man who was holding her, but to no avail.

Beside her, Will lay unmoving in the dust. She began to sob in frustration and anger and sadness and she heard the Skandians laughing. Then another sound came and they stopped. The arms holding her released a little and she was able to see.

It was a drawn out, creaking groan and it came from the bridge. The right-hand support was gone, and the left-hand side, already weakened by the fire, was now holding the entire structure. It was never meant for such a load, even in perfect condition. With a final sharp SNAP! the pylon shattered at its halfway point and, cables and all, the bridge collapsed slowly into the depths of the Fissure, trailing a bright shower of sparks behind it in the darkness.

Twenty-six

Gilan watched impatiently as the company of cavalrymen remounted after a fifteen-minute break. He was itching to be away, but he knew that both horses and men needed rest if they were to continue at the killing pace he had set them. They had been travelling for half a day and he estimated that they should meet Will's party sometime in the early afternoon.

Checking that all the troopers were mounted, he turned to the captain beside him.

'All right, Captain,' he said. 'Let's get them moving.'

The captain had actually drawn breath to bellow his command when there was a call from the lead troop.

'Horseman coming!'

An expectant buzz ran through the cavalrymen. Most of them had no idea what their mission was about. They'd been roused out of bed in the early dawn and told to mount and ride. Gilan stood in his stirrups, shading his eyes against the midday glare, and peered in the direction the trooper had indicated.

They hadn't reached the Celtic border yet, and here the terrain was open grasslands, with occasional thickets of trees. To the south-west, Gilan's keen eyes could make out a small cloud of dust, with a galloping figure at the head of it.

'Whoever he is, he's in a hurry,' the captain observed. Then the forward scout called more information.

'Three horsemen!' came the shout. But already Gilan could see that the report wasn't quite correct. There were three horses, but only one rider. He experienced a sinking feeling in the pit of his stomach.

'Should we send out an intercept party, sir?' the captain asked him. In times like these, it wasn't always wise to let a stranger ride full pelt into the middle of a group. But now that the rider was closer, Gilan could recognise him. More to the point, he could recognise one of the horses he was riding: small, shaggy, barrel-chested. It was Will's horse, Tug. But it wasn't Will riding him.

The lead troop had already fanned out to stop the rider's progress. Gilan said quietly to the captain: 'Tell them to let him through.'

The captain repeated the order with considerably more volume and the troopers separated, leaving a path for Horace. He saw the small group of officers around the company banner and headed for them, bringing the shaggy little Ranger horse to a halt in front of them. The other horses, which Gilan now recognised as Horace's and the pack pony that Evanlyn had ridden, were following behind Tug on a rope rein.

'They've got Will!' the boy shouted hoarsely, recognising Gilan among the group of officers. 'They've got Will and Evanlyn!'

Gilan closed his eyes briefly, feeling a lance of pain in his heart. Then, knowing the answer before he asked, he said: 'Wargals?'

'Skandians!' he replied. 'They took them at the bridge. They . . .'

Gilan flinched in surprise at the word. Surprise and horror.

'Bridge?' he said urgently. 'What bridge?'

Horace was breathing heavily from his exertions. He'd alternated between the three horses, switching from one to the other, but not resting himself at any stage. He paused now to get his breath, realising he should start from the beginning.

'Across the Fissure,' he said. 'That's why Morgarath took the Celts. They were building a huge bridge for him to bring his army across. They'd almost got it finished when we got there.'

The captain beside Gilan had turned pale. 'You mean there's a bridge across the Fissure?' he asked. The implications of such a fact were horrendous.

'Not anymore,' Horace replied, his breathing steadier and his voice a little more under control now. 'Will burnt it. Will and Evanlyn. But they stayed on the other side to keep the Skandians back and —'

'Skandians!' said Gilan. 'What the devil are Skandians doing on the plateau?' Horace made an impatient gesture at his interruption.

'They were the advance party for a force that's coming

up the southern cliffs. The Skandians were going to join forces with the Wargals, cross the bridge and attack the army in the rear.'

The group of cavalry officers exchanged looks. Professional soldiers, all of them could imagine how disastrous that could have been for the royal forces.

'As well the bridge is gone then,' said a lieutenant. Horace swung his tormented gaze on the officer — a young man barely a few years older than himself.

'But they've got Will!' he cried, his eyes welling with tears as he thought of how he had stood by and watched helplessly as his friend was knocked out, then carried away.

'And the girl,' added Gilan, but Horace dismissed her.

'Yes! Of course they got her!' he said. 'And I'm sorry she's been caught. But Will was my friend!'

'You're sorry she's been caught? Do you know who . . .' the captain interrupted indignantly, for he was one of the few who knew the true nature of their task. But Gilan stopped him before he could say more.

'That's enough, Captain!' he said crisply. The officer looked at him angrily and Gilan leaned forward, speaking so that only he could hear.

'The fewer people who know the girl's name now, the better,' he said, and understanding dawned in the officer's eyes. If Morgarath knew that his men held the King's daughter hostage, he would have a powerful tool to bargain with. He looked back to Horace. 'Horace, is there any way they might be able to repair this bridge?' he asked and the muscular youth shook his head vehemently. He was devastated at the loss of his friend but his pride in Will's accomplishment was obvious as he described it.

'No way at all,' he replied. 'It's gone, well and truly. Will made sure that nothing remained on the far side. That's why he was caught. He wanted to make sure.' He paused and added: 'They might get a small rope bridge across, of course.'

That decided Gilan. He turned to the captain.

'Captain, you'll continue with the company and make sure no bridge of any kind is thrown across the Fissure. We don't want any of Morgarath's forces, no matter how small, coming across. Get Horace to show you the location on a map. Hold the west side of the Fissure until you're relieved, and send out patrols to locate any other possible crossing points. There won't be many of those,' he added. 'Horace, you'll come with me and report to the King. Now.' He stopped abruptly as he realised that Horace was waiting for a chance to say something. He nodded for the apprentice to go ahead.

'The Skandians,' said Horace. 'They're not just on the plateau. They're sending a force north of the Thorntree Forest as well.'

There was another buzz of comment from the officers as they realised how close their army had come to disaster. Two unexpected forces, attacking from the rear, would have left the King's men very hard-pressed indeed.

'You're sure of this?' Gilan asked and Horace nodded several times.

'Will overheard them talking about it,' he said. 'Their forces on the beach and in the fens are a feint. The real attack was always going to come from behind.'

'Then we don't have a moment to waste,' said Gilan. 'That force in the north-west could still be a big problem if the King doesn't know about it.' He turned to the company commander. 'Captain, you have your orders. Get your men to the Fissure as soon as you can.'

The captain saluted briefly and issued a few crisp orders to his officers. They galloped off to their troops and, after a quick conference while Horace pointed out the site of the fallen bridge on a map of the area, the entire company was on the move, heading at a brisk canter for the Fissure.

Gilan turned to Horace. 'Let's go,' he said simply. Wearily, the young warrior nodded, then turned back to mount his own horse. Tug hesitated, pawing the ground as he watched the cavalry ride away — back towards where he had last seen his master. He trotted a few uncertain paces after the troop then, at a word from Gilan, he reluctantly fell in behind the tall Ranger.

Twenty-seven

Will's head ached abominably. He could feel a constant, rhythmic thudding that pounded through his skull, setting flashes off behind his tight closed eyes.

He forced his eyes open and found himself staring at close range at a sheepskin vest and the back of a pair of leather-bound woollen leggings. The world was upside down and he realised he was being carried over someone's shoulder. The thudding was the thud of the man's feet as he jogged along. Will wished he would walk.

He groaned aloud and the jogging stopped.

'Erak!' the man carrying him called. ''E's awake.'

And so saying, the Skandian lowered him to the ground. Will tried to take a pace, but his knees gave out and he sank to his haunches. Erak, the leader of the group, leaned down now and examined him. One thick thumb caught hold of his eyelid and he felt his eye being opened wide. The man wasn't cruel. But he was none too gentle either. Will recognised him now as the Skandian who had come so close to discovering him when he was eavesdropping by their camp fire in the valley.

'Hmmm,' he said thoughtfully. 'Concussed, most likely. That was a good throw with that rock, Nordel,' he said to one of the others. The Skandian he'd spoken to, a giant of a man with his blond hair in two tightly plaited braids that were greased so they swept upwards like horns, smiled at the praise.

'Grew up hunting seals and penguins that way, I did,' he said, with some satisfaction.

Erak released Will's eyelid and moved away. Now Will felt a gentler touch on his face and, opening his eyes again, found himself looking into Evanlyn's eyes. She stroked his forehead gently, trying to clean away the dried, matted blood there.

'Are you all right?' she said and he nodded, then realised that was not a good idea.

'Fine,' he managed, fighting back a wave of nausea. 'They got you as well?' he added, unnecessarily, and she nodded. 'Horace?' he said softly and she put a finger to her lips.

'He got away,' she said softly. 'I saw him running when the bridge collapsed.'

Will sighed with relief. 'We did it then? We got the bridge?'

This time it was Evanlyn's turn to nod. A smile even touched her lips at the memory of the bridge crashing into the depths of the Fissure.

'It's gone,' she said. 'Well and truly.'

Erak heard the last few words. He shook his head at them.

'And no thanks you'll get from Morgarath for that,' he told them. Will felt a small chill of fear at the mention of the Lord of Rain and Night's name. Here on the plateau, it seemed somehow more ominous, more dangerous, altogether more malevolent. The Skandian glanced at the sun.

'We'll take a break,' he said. 'Maybe our friend here will be up to walking in an hour or so.'

The Skandians opened their packs and produced food and drink. They tossed a water bottle and a small loaf of bread to Will and Evanlyn and the two ate hungrily. Evanlyn began to say something but Will raised a hand to hush her. He was listening to the Skandians' conversation.

'So what do we do now?' asked the one called Nordel. Erak chewed a piece of dried cod, washed it down with a gulp of the fiery liquor he carried in a leather bottle and shrugged.

'For mine, we get out of here as fast as we can,' he said. 'We only came for the booty and there's going to be precious little of that now the bridge is gone.'

'Morgarath won't like it if we pull out,' warned a short, heavily built member of the party. Erak simply shrugged.

'Horak, I'm not here to help Morgarath take over Araluen,' he replied. 'Neither are you. We fight for profit, and when there's no profit to be had, I say we go.'

Horak looked down at the ground between his feet and scratched in the dust with his fingers. He didn't look up when he spoke again. 'What about those two?' he said, and Will heard a sharp intake of breath from Evanlyn as she realised the Skandian meant her and Will.

'We take 'em with us,' said Erak and this time Horak looked up from the dust, where he was drawing senseless patterns.

'What good are they to us? Why shouldn't we just hand 'em over to the Wargals?' he asked, and the others mumbled their agreement. It was obviously a question which had been on their minds. They'd simply been waiting for someone else to bring it up.

'I'll tell you,' said Erak. 'I'll tell you what good they are to us. First and foremost, they're hostages, aren't they?'

'Hostages!' snorted the fourth member of the group, the one who so far hadn't spoken. Erak rounded upon him.

'That's right, Svengal,' he told him. 'They're hostages. Now I've been on more raids and in more campaigns than any of you and I don't like the way this one's shaping up. Seems to me like Morgarath's been getting too clever for his own good. All this leaking false plans and building secret tunnels and planning surprise attacks with Horth and his men coming around Thorntree Forest — it's too complicated. And complicated isn't the way to go when you're facing people like the Araluans.'

'Horth can still attack around the Thorntree,' said Svengal stubbornly, but Erak was shaking his head.

'He can. But he won't know that the bridge is gone, will he? He'll be expecting support that will never come. I'll wager Morgarath won't hurry to tell him. He knows Horth would give it all away if he found out. Let me tell you, it'll be the toss of a coin to see which way that battle goes. That's the problem with these clever-clever plans! You take away one element and the whole thing can come crashing down.'

There was a short silence while the other Skandians thought about what he had said. A few heads nodded in agreement and Erak continued.

'I'll tell you, boys, I don't like the way things are shaping and I say we should take the chance to get to Horth's ships through the fens.'

'Why not go back the way we came?' asked Svengal, but his leader shook his head emphatically.

'And try to get down those cliffs again, with Morgarath after us?' he asked. 'No thank you. I don't think he'd take too kindly to deserters. We'll go along with him as far as Three Step Pass, then once we're in the open, we'll head east for the coast.' He paused to let this sink in. 'And we'll have these two as hostages in case the Araluans try to stop us,' he added.

'They're kids!' said Nordel derisively. 'What use are they as hostages?'

'Didn't you see that oakleaf amulet the boy was wearing?' Erak asked and, instinctively, Will's hand went to the oak leaf on the thong around his neck.

'That's the Rangers' symbol,' Erak continued. 'He's one of them. Maybe some kind of trainee. And they look after their own.'

'What about the girl?' said Svengal. 'She's no Ranger.'

'That's right,' Erak agreed. 'She's just a girl. But I'm not handing any girl over to the Wargals. You've seen what they're like. They're worse than animals, that lot. No. She comes with us.'

There was another moment's silence as the others considered his words. Then Horak spoke. 'Fair enough,' he agreed. Erak looked around the others, and saw that

Horak had spoken for them all. The Skandians were warriors, and hard men. But they weren't totally ruthless.

'Good,' he said. 'Now let's get on the road again.'

He rose and moved towards Will and Evanlyn while the other Skandians repacked the remains of the brief meal.

'Can you walk?' he asked Will. 'Or does Nordel have to carry you again?'

Will flushed angrily and rose quickly to his feet. Instantly he wished he hadn't. The ground heaved and his head swam. He staggered and only Evanlyn's firm hand on his arm prevented him from falling. But he was determined not to show weakness in front of his captors. He steadied himself, then glared defiantly at Erak.

'I'll walk,' he managed to say and the big Skandian studied him for a moment, an appraising look in his eye.

'Yes,' he said finally. 'I daresay you will.'

Twenty-eight

Battlemaster David chewed the ends of his moustache as he frowned at the plan outlined on the sand table. 'I don't know, Halt,' he said doubtfully. 'It's very risky. One of the first principles of warfare is never to split your forces.'

Halt nodded. He knew the knight's criticism was intended to be constructive, not simply negative thinking. It was Sir David's role to find any faults in the plan and weigh them against its possible advantages.

'That's true,' the Ranger replied. 'But it's also true that surprise is a powerful weapon.'

Baron Tyler walked around the table, considering the plan from another viewpoint. He pointed with his dagger at the mass of green that represented the Thorntree Forest.

'You're sure you and Gilan can guide a large cavalry force through the Thorntree? I thought nobody could get through there,' he asked dubiously, and Halt nodded.

'The Rangers have charted and surveyed every inch of the Kingdom for years, my lord,' he told the Baron. 'Especially the parts people think there's no way through. We can surprise this northern force. Then Morgarath will be caught out as well, when no Skandians turn up behind us.'

Tyler continued to pace around the table, staring intently at the designs drawn there and the markers set in place in the sand map.

'All the same,' he said, 'we'll be in a pretty scrape if the Skandians defeat Halt and the cavalry over here in the north. After all, you'll be outnumbered almost two to one.'

Halt nodded agreement again. 'That's true. But we'll catch them in open country, so we'll have the advantage. And don't forget we'll be taking two hundred archer units as well. They should even the numbers a little.'

An archer unit consisted of two men: one archer and one accompanying pikeman, mutually supporting each other. Against lightly armoured infantry, they were a deadly combination. The archers could cut down large numbers of the enemy at a distance. Once the battle got to close quarters, the pikemen took over, allowing the archers to withdraw to safety.

'But,' insisted Baron Tyler, 'let's assume that the Skandians do manage to win through. Then the tables will be turned. We'll be fighting a real enemy in the north-west, with our rear exposed to Morgarath's Wargals coming out of the Pass.'

Arald managed to suppress a sigh. As a strategist, Tyler was notoriously cautious. 'On the other hand,' he said, doing his best to keep the impatience out of his voice, 'if Halt succeeds, it will be his force that Morgarath sees coming round from the north-west. He'll assume it's the Skandians attacking us from that direction and he'll bring his forces out onto the Plains to attack us from behind. And then we'll have him — once and for all.'

The prospect seemed to appeal to him.

'It's still a risk,' Tyler said stubbornly. Halt and Arald exchanged a glance and the Baron's shoulders lifted slightly in a shrug.

Halt said, in a dry tone, 'All warfare has a risk attached to it, sir. Otherwise it would be easy.'

Baron Tyler looked up angrily at him. Halt met his gaze evenly. As the Baron opened his mouth to say something, Sir David forestalled him, smacking one gauntlet into his palm in a decisive gesture.

'All right, Halt,' he said. 'I'll put your plan to the King.'

At the mention of the King, Halt's face softened slightly.

'How is his majesty taking the news?' he asked and Sir David shrugged unhappily.

'Personally, he's devastated, of course. It was the cruellest possible blow to have his hopes raised and then shattered again. But he manages somehow to put his personal life to one side and continue to perform his duties as King. He says he'll mourn later, when this is all over.'

'There may be no need for mourning,' Arald put in, and David smiled sadly at him.

'I've told him that, of course. He says he'd prefer not to have false hopes raised once more.'

There was an awkward silence in the tent. Tyler, Fergus and Sir David felt deep sorrow for their King. Duncan was a popular and just monarch. Halt and Baron Arald, on the other hand, both felt the loss of Will deeply. In a remarkably short time, Will had become an integral part of Castle Redmont. Finally, it was Sir David who broke the silence.

'Gentlemen, perhaps you might begin preparing your orders. I'll take this plan to the King.'

And as he turned away to the inner sections of the pavilion, the barons and Halt left the large tent. Arald, Fergus and Tyler walked quickly away, to prepare movement orders for the army. Halt, seeing a dejected figure in Ranger green and grey waiting by the sentry post, moved down the small hill to talk to his former apprentice.

'I want leave to go across the Fissure after them,' said Gilan.

Halt knew how deeply he felt the hurt of Will's loss. Gilan blamed himself for leaving Will alone in the hills of Celtica. No matter how many times Halt and the other Rangers told him that he had taken the right course, he refused to believe it. Now, Halt knew, it would hurt him even more to be refused. Nevertheless, as Rangers, their first duty was to the Kingdom. He shook his head and answered curtly.

'Not granted. You're needed here. We're to lead a force through the Thorntree to cut off Horth's men. Go to Crowley's tent and get hold of the charts showing the secret ways for this part of the country.'

Gilan hesitated, his jaw set. 'But . . .' he began to protest, and then something in Halt's eyes stopped him as the older Ranger leaned forward.

'Gilan, do you think for one moment that I don't want to tear that plateau apart stone by stone until I find Will?

But you and I took an oath when they gave us these silver oak leaves, and now we have to live up to it.'

Gilan dropped his eyes and nodded. His shoulders slumped as he gave in.

'All right,' he said in a broken voice, and Halt thought he saw traces of tears in his eyes. He turned away hurriedly before Gilan could see the moisture in his own.

'Get the charts,' he said briefly.

Twenty-nine

The four Skandians and their prisoners had trudged across the bleak, windswept plateau for the rest of the day and into the evening. It wasn't until several hours after dark that Erak called a halt, and Will and Evanlyn sank gratefully to the rocky ground. The ache in Will's head had receded somewhat through the day, but it still throbbed dully in the background. The dried blood on the wound where the jagged rock had hit him itched abominably, but he knew that if he scratched at the irritation, he would only open the wound and set the blood flowing once more.

At least, thought Will, Erak hadn't kept them tied or restrained in any way. As the Skandian leader put it, there was nowhere for the two prisoners to run.

'This plateau is full of Wargals,' he'd told them roughly. 'You can take your chances with them if you choose.'

So they'd kept their position in the middle of the party, passing bands of Wargals throughout the day, and heading constantly to the north-east, and Three Step Pass. Now, the four Skandians eased their heavy packs to the ground and Nordel began to gather wood for a fire. Svengal tossed a large copper pot at Evanlyn's feet and gestured towards a stream that bubbled through the rocks close by.

'Get some water,' he told her gruffly. For a moment, the girl hesitated, then she shrugged, took up the pot and rose, groaning softly as her tired muscles and joints were called upon once more to take her weight.

'Come on then, Will,' she said casually. 'You can give me a hand.'

Erak was rummaging in his open pack. His head snapped round as she spoke.

'No!' he said sharply, and the entire group turned to look at him. He pointed one blunt forefinger at Evanlyn.

'You, I don't mind wandering off,' he said. 'Because I know you'll come back. But as for that Ranger, he might just take it into his head to make a run for it, in spite of things.'

Will, who had been thinking of doing just that, tried to look surprised.

'I'm no Ranger,' he said. 'I'm just an apprentice.'

Erak gave a short snort of laughter. 'You may say so,' he replied. 'But you dropped them Wargals at the bridge as well as any Ranger might. You stay where I can keep an eye on you.'

Will shrugged, smiled wanly at Evanlyn and sat down again, sighing as he leaned his back against a rock. In a few moments, he knew, it would become hard and knobbly and uncomfortable. But right now, it was bliss.

The Skandians went ahead making camp. In short order, they had a good fire going, and when Evanlyn returned with the pot full of water, Erak and Svengal produced dried provisions which they added to the water as it heated to make a stew. The meal was plain and fairly tasteless, but it was hot and it filled their bellies. Will thought ruefully for a few minutes of the pre-prepared food that came from Master Chubb's kitchen. Sadly, he realised that such thoughts of Master Chubb's kitchen and his times in the forest with Halt were no more than memories now. Images sprang into his mind, unbidden: of Tug, and Gilan and Horace. Of Castle Redmont, seen in the last rays of the setting sun, with its ironstone walls glowing dull red, seeming to hold an inner light. Tears formed behind his eyes, stinging and aching for release. Surreptitiously, he tried to wipe them away with the back of his hand. The meal was suddenly even more tasteless than before.

Evanlyn seemed to sense his deepening sadness. He felt her warm, small hand cover his and he knew she was looking at him. But he couldn't meet those vivid green eyes with his own, feeling the tears welling up in them.

'It'll be all right,' she whispered. He tried to talk, but couldn't form the words. Silently, he shook his head, his eyes downcast, staring intently at the scratched surface of the wooden bowl the Skandians had given him to use.

They were camped some metres from the side of the road, at the top of a slight rise. Erak had stated that he liked to see anyone who might choose to approach. Now, rounding a bend in the road several hundred metres away, came a large group of horsemen, followed by a troop of Wargals, running to keep up with the horses' trot. The sound of the Wargals' chant came to them on the breeze once more and Will felt the hairs on the back of his neck rising.

Erak turned swiftly to the two of them, gesturing them back into the cover of the rocks behind their camp site.

'Quick, you two! Behind them rocks if you value your lives! That's Morgarath himself on the white horse! Nordel, Horak, move into the light to screen them!'

Will and Evanlyn needed no second bidding. Staying low, they scrambled into the cover provided by the rocks. As Erak had commanded, two of the Skandians stood and moved into the glare of the firelight, drawing the attention of the approaching riders away from the two small figures in the half light.

The chant, mingled with the clatter of hooves and the chink of harness and weapons, came closer as Will lay on his stomach, one arm covering Evanlyn in the darkness. As he had done before, he scooped the hood of his cloak over his head, to leave his face in deep shadow. There was a tiny gap between two of the rocks and, knowing he was taking a terrible risk but unable to resist, he pressed his eye to it.

The view was restricted to a few metres of space. Erak stood on the far side of the fire, facing the approaching riders. Will realised that by doing so, he had placed the glare of the firelight between the new arrivals and the spot where he and Evanlyn lay hidden. If any of the Wargals looked in their direction, they would be staring straight into the bright firelight. It was a lesson in tactics he filed away for future reference.

The sounds of horses and men stopped. The Wargal

chant died abruptly. For a second or two, there was silence. Then a voice spoke. A low voice, with a slight, snake-like sibilance to it.

'Captain Erak, where are you bound?'

Will glued his eye to the crack in the rocks, straining to see the speaker. Without a doubt, that cold, malevolent voice had to belong to Morgarath. The sound of it was the sound of ice and hatred. The sound of nails scraping on tile. The blood ran cold to hear it. The hairs on the back of his neck stood up and, beneath his hand, he felt Evanlyn shiver.

If it had a similar effect on Erak, however, he showed no sign of it.

'My correct title is "Jarl", Lord Morgarath,' he said evenly, 'not "Captain".'

'Well then,' replied the cold voice, 'I must try to remember that, in case it is ever of the slightest interest to me. Now . . . Captain,' he said, laying stress on the title this time, 'I repeat, where are you bound?'

There was a jingle of harness and, through the crack in the rocks, Will saw a white horse move forward. Not a glossy-coated, shining white horse such as a gallant knight might ride, but a pale horse without sheen or life to its coat. It was huge, dead white and with wild, rolling eyes. He craned slightly to one side and managed to make out a black gloved hand holding the reins loosely. He could see no more of the rider.

'We thought we'd join your forces at Three Step Pass, my lord,' Erak was saying. 'I assume you will still go ahead with your attack, even though the bridge is down.'

Morgarath swore horribly at the mention of the bridge. Sensing his fury, the white horse sidestepped a few paces and now Will could see the rider.

Immensely tall, but thin, he was dressed all in black. He stooped in the saddle to talk down to the Skandians and the hunched shoulders and his black cloak gave him the look of a vulture.

The face was thin, with a beak of a nose and high cheekbones. The skin on the face was white and pallid, like the horse. The hair above it was long, set to frame a receding hairline, and white-blond in colour. By contrast, the eyes were black pools. He was clean-shaven and his mouth was a thin red slit in the pallor of his face. As Will looked, the Lord of Rain and Night seemed to sense his presence. He looked up, casting his gaze beyond Erak and his three companions, searching into the darkness behind them. Will froze, barely daring to breathe as those black eyes searched the night. But the light of the fire defeated Morgarath and he returned his gaze to Erak.

'Yes,' he replied. 'The attack will go ahead. Now that Duncan has his own forces deployed and in what he thinks is a strong defensive position, he'll allow us to come out onto the Plains before attacking.'

'At which point, Horth will take him in the rear,' Erak put in, with a chuckle, and Morgarath stared at him, head slightly to one side as he considered him. Again, the bird-like pose made Will think of a vulture.

'Exactly,' he agreed. 'It would be preferable if there were two flanking forces as I'd planned originally, but one should be enough.'

'My thoughts too, my lord,' Erak agreed and there was a long moment of silence. Obviously, Morgarath had no interest in whether Erak agreed with him or not.

'Things would be easier if your other countryman had not abandoned us,' Morgarath said eventually. 'I've been told that your compatriot Ovlak has sailed back to Skandia with his men. I had planned that they should come up the southern cliffs to reinforce us.'

Erak shrugged, refusing to take blame for something outside his sphere of influence. 'Ovlak is a mercenary,' he said. 'You can't trust mercenaries. They fight only for profit.'

'And you . . . don't?' the toneless voice said with scorn. Erak squared his shoulders.

'I'll honour any undertaking I've made,' he said stiffly. Morgarath stared at him again for a long, silent moment. The Skandian met his gaze and, finally, it was Morgarath who looked away.

'Chirath told me you took a prisoner at the bridge – a mighty warrior, he said. I don't see him.' Again, Morgarath tried to look through the light into the further gloom. Erak laughed harshly.

'If Chirath was the leader of your Wargals, neither did he,' he replied sarcastically. 'He spent most of his time at the bridge cowering behind a rock and dodging arrows.'

'And the prisoner?' Morgarath asked.

'Dead,' Erak replied. 'We killed him and threw him over the edge.'

'A fact that displeases me intensely,' Morgarath said and Will felt his flesh crawling. 'I would have preferred to make him suffer for interfering in my plans. You should have brought him to me alive.'

'Well, we would have preferred it if he hadn't been whipping arrows around our ears. He could shoot, that's for sure. The only way to take him was to kill him.'

Another silence as Morgarath considered the reply. Apparently, it was not satisfactory to him. 'Be warned for the future. I did not approve of your actions.'

This time, it was Erak who let the silence stretch. He shrugged his shoulders slightly, as if Morgarath's displeasure was a matter of absolutely no interest to him. Eventually, the Lord of Rain and Night gathered his reins and shook them, heeling his horse savagely to turn it away from the camp fire.

'I'll see you at Three Step Pass, Captain,' he said. Then, almost as an afterthought, he turned his horse back. 'And Captain, don't get any ideas about deserting. You'll fight with us to the end.'

Erak nodded. 'I told you, my lord, I'll honour any bargain I've made.'

This time, Morgarath smiled, a thin movement of the red lips in the lifeless white face. 'Be sure of it, Captain,' he said softly.

Then he shook the reins and his horse turned away, springing to a gallop. The Wargals followed, the chant starting up again and ringing through the night. Will realised that, behind the rocks, he'd been holding a giant breath. He let it go now, and heard a corresponding sigh of relief from the Skandians.

'My god of battles,' said Erak, 'he doesn't half give me the creeps, that one.'

'Looks like he's already died and gone to hell,' put in Svengal, and the others nodded. Erak walked round the fire now and stood over where Will and Evanlyn were still crouched behind the rocks.

'You heard that?' he said and Will nodded. Evanlyn remained crouching, face down, behind the rock. Erak stirred her with the toe of his boot.

'And you, missy,' he said. 'You heard too?'

Now she looked up, tears of terror staining tracks in the dust on her face. Wordlessly, she nodded. Erak glanced away, in the direction where Morgarath and his Wargals had gone.

'Then remember it if you plan to escape,' he said. 'That's all that awaits you if you get away from us.'

Thirty

The Plains of Uthal formed a wide open space of rolling grasslands. The grass was rich and green. There were few trees, although occasional knolls and low hills served to break the monotony. Some distance behind the position occupied by the Araluan army, the Plains began to rise gradually, to a low ridgeline.

Closer to the fens, where the Wargals were forming up, a creek wound its way. Normally a mere trickle, it had been swollen by the recent spring rains so that the ground ahead of the Wargals was soft and boggy, precluding any possible attack by the Araluan heavy cavalry.

Baron Fergus of Caraway shaded his eyes against the bright noon sun and peered across the Plains to the entrance to Three Step Pass.

'There are a lot of them,' he said mildly.

'And more coming,' Arald of Redmont replied, easing his broadsword a little in its scabbard.

The two barons were slowly walking their battlehorses

across the front of Duncan's drawn-up army. It was good for morale, Arald believed, for the men to see their leaders relaxed and engaging in casual conversation as they watched their enemies emerging from the narrow mountain pass and fanning out onto the Plains. Dimly, they could hear the ominous, rhythmic chant of the Wargals as they jogged into position.

'Damned noise is quite unnerving,' Fergus muttered and Arald nodded agreement. Seemingly casual, he cast his glance over the men behind them. The army was in position, but Battlemaster David had told them to remain at rest. Consequently, the cavalry were dismounted and the infantry and archers were sitting on the grassy slope.

'No sense in wearing them out standing at attention in the sun,' David had said and the others had agreed. By the same token, he had set the various Kitchenmasters the task of keeping the men supplied with cool drinks and fruit. The white-clad servers moved among the army now, carrying baskets and water skins. Arald glanced down and smiled at the portly form of Master Chubb, his chef from Redmont Castle, supervising a group of hapless apprentices as they handed out apples and peaches to the men. As ever, his ladle rose and fell with alarming frequency on the heads of any apprentice he deemed to be moving too slowly.

'Give that Kitchenmaster of yours a mace and he could rout Morgarath's army single-handed,' commented Fergus, and Arald smiled thoughtfully. The men around Chubb and his apprentices, distracted by the fat cook's antics, were taking no notice of the chanting from across the Plains. In other areas, he could see signs of restlessness and evidence that the men were becoming increasingly ill at ease.

Looking around, Arald's eye fell on an infantry captain seated with his company. Their minimal armour, plaid cloaks and two-handed broadswords marked them as belonging to one of the northern fiefs. He beckoned the man over and leaned down from the saddle as he saluted.

'Good morning, Captain,' he said easily.

'Morning, my lord,' replied the officer, his heavy northern accent making the words almost unrecognisable.

'Tell me, Captain, do you have pipers among your men?' the Baron asked, smiling. The officer answered immediately, in a very serious manner.

'Aye, sir. The McDuig and the McForn are with us. And always so when we go to war.'

'Then perhaps you might prevail upon them to give us a reel or two?' the Baron suggested. 'It might be an altogether more pleasant sound than that tuneless grunting from over yonder.'

He inclined his head towards the Wargal forces and now a slow smile spread over the captain's face. He nodded readily.

'Aye, sir. I'll see to it. There's nothing like a skirl or two on the pipes to get a man's blood prancing!' Saluting hurriedly, he turned away towards his men, shouting as he ran: 'McDuig! McForn! Gather your wind and set to the pipes, men! Let's hear "The Feather Crested Bonnet" from ye!'

As the two barons rode on, they heard behind them the preliminary moaning of bagpipes coming to full volume. Fergus winced and Arald grinned at him.

'Nothing like the skirl of the pipes to get the blood prancing,' he quoted.

'In my case, it gets the teeth grinding,' replied his companion, surreptitiously nudging his horse with his heel to move them a little further away from the wild sound of the pipes. But, when he looked at the men behind them, he had to agree that Arald's idea had worked. The pipes were successfully drowning out the dull chanting and, as the two pipers marched and countermarched in front of the army, they held the attention of all the men in their immediate vicinity.

'Good idea,' he said to Arald, then added, 'I can't help wondering if that's an equally good one.'

He gestured across the plain to where the Wargals were emerging from the Pass and taking up their positions. 'All my instincts say we should be hitting them before they have a chance to form up.'

Arald shrugged. This point had been hotly debated by the War Council for the past few days.

'If we hit them as they come out, we simply contain them,' he said. 'If we want to destroy Morgarath's power once and for all, we have to let him commit his forces in the open.'

'And hope that Halt has been successful in stopping Horth's army,' Fergus said. 'I'm getting a nasty crick in my neck from looking over my shoulder to make sure there's no one behind us.'

'Halt has never let us down before,' Arald said mildly.

Fergus nodded unhappily. 'I know that. He's a remarkable man. But there are so many things that could have gone wrong. He could have missed Horth's army altogether. He may still be fighting his way through the Thorntree. Or, worse yet, Horth may have defeated his archers and cavalry.'

'There's nothing we can do about it but wait,' Arald pointed out.

'And keep an eye to the north-west, hoping we don't see battleaxes and horned helmets coming over those hills.'

'There's a comforting thought,' said Arald, trying to make light of the moment. Yet he couldn't resist the temptation to turn in his saddle and peer anxiously towards the hills in the north.

Erak had waited till the last few hundred Wargals were moving down Three Step Pass to the Plains, then forced his small group into the middle of the jogging creatures. There were a few snarls and scowls as the Skandians shoved their way into the living stream that was flowing through the narrow, twisting confines of the Pass, but the heavily armed sea raiders snarled back and handled their double-sided battleaxes with such easy familiarity that the angry Wargals soon backed off and left them alone.

Evanlyn and Will were in the centre of the group, surrounded by the burly Skandians. Will's easily recognisable Ranger cloak had been hidden away in one of the packs and both he and Evanlyn wore sheepskin half capes that were too large for them. Evanlyn's short hair was covered by a woollen cap. So far, none of the Wargals had taken any notice of them, assuming them to be servants or slaves to the small band of sea raiders.

'Just keep your mouths shut and your eyes down!' Erak had told them as they shoved their way into the crowd of jogging Wargals. The narrow confines of the Pass echoed to the tuneless chanting that the Wargals used as a cadence. The sound ebbed and flowed about them as they half-ran with the stream. Erak's plan was to move eastwards as soon as they had cleared the Pass, ostensibly with the purpose of taking up a position on the right flank of the Wargal army. As soon as an opportunity presented itself, the Skandians would break off and escape into the swampy wilderness of the fenlands, travelling through the bogs and grassy islands to the beaches where Horth's fleet lay at anchor.

They shuffled along, twisting and turning with the convolutions of the Pass. The narrow trail led down through the sheer mountains for at least five kilometres and Will could understand why it had always been a barrier to both sides. Morgarath's men couldn't move out in any large numbers unless Duncan held back and allowed them to. Similarly, the King's army couldn't penetrate the Pass to attack Morgarath on the plateau.

Black walls of sheer, glistening-wet rock towered above them on either side. The Pass saw sunlight for less than an hour each day, right on high noon. At any other time, it was cold and damp and shrouded in shadow. All of which served to help conceal the presence of the two younger members of the party from prying eyes.

Will felt the ground beneath his feet beginning to level out and realised they must be in the last extremities of the Pass — down at the level of the Plains. There was no way he could even see the ground ahead of him, trapped in the seething, jostling crowd. They rounded a final bend and a lance of sunlight stabbed into the Pass, forcing him to throw up a hand to shield his eyes. They had reached the entrance, he realised. He felt a shove from his left.

'Get over to the right!' Erak told them and the four Skandians formed a human wedge, forcing their way through the crowd until they were on the extreme right-hand side of the Pass. There were growls and angry grunts from the Wargals they shoved, several of them being sent sprawling and then trampled before they could regain their feet. But the Skandians gave as good as they got in terms of threats and abuse.

The sunlight hit them like a physical barrier as they emerged from the darkness of the Pass and, for a moment, Will and Evanlyn hesitated. Erak shoved them on again, more anxious now as he could hear a familiar voice calling commands for the Wargals to deploy.

Morgarath was here, directing operations.

'Curse him!' muttered Erak. 'I'd hoped he'd be out with the vanguard of the army. Keep moving, you two!' He shoved Will and Evanlyn along a little faster. Will glanced back. Above the heads of the Wargals, he could see the tall, thin form of the Lord of Rain and Night, now clad entirely in black mail armour and surcoat, still seated on his white horse and calling instructions to the milling, chanting Wargals.

Gradually, they were moving into ordered formations, then taking their position with the main army. As Will looked back, the pale face turned towards the group of hurrying Skandians and Morgarath urged his horse towards them, unmindful of the fact that he was trampling through his own men to reach them.

'Captain Erak!' he called. The voice wasn't loud, but it carried, thin and cutting, through the chanting of the Wargals.

'Keep going!' Erak ordered them in a low voice. 'Keep moving.'

'Stop!' Now the voice was raised and the cold anger in it instantly silenced and stilled the Wargals. As they froze in place around them, the Skandians reluctantly did the same, Erak turning to face Morgarath.

The Lord of Rain and Night spurred his horse through the throng, Wargals falling back to make way for him, or being buffeted out of the way if they failed to do so. Slowly, his eyes locked on those of Erak, he dismounted. Even on foot, he towered over the bulky Skandian leader.

'And where might you and your men be bound today, Captain?' he asked in a silky tone. Erak gestured to the right.

'It's normal for me and my men to fight on the right wing,' he said, as casually as he could manage. 'But I'll go wherever you need me if that doesn't suit.'

'Will you?' replied Morgarath with withering sarcasm. 'Will you indeed? How terribly kind of you. You . . .' He broke off, his gaze on the two smaller figures whom the other Skandians had been trying, unsuccessfully, to shield from his gaze.

'Who are they?' he demanded. Erak shrugged.

'Celts,' he said easily. 'We took them prisoner in Celtica and I'm planning to sell them to Oberjarl Ragnak as slaves.'

'Celtica is mine, Captain. Slaves from Celtica are mine as well. They're not for you to take and sell to your barbarian of a king.'

The Skandians surrounding Will and Evanlyn stirred angrily at his words. Morgarath turned his cold eyes on them, then looked away at the thousands of Wargals who surrounded them — every one ready to obey any command of his without question. The message was clear.

Erak tried to bluff his way through the situation.

'Our agreement was we fought for booty and that includes slaves,' he insisted, but Morgarath cut him off.

'If you fought!' he shouted furiously. '*If!* Not if you stood by and let my bridge be destroyed.'

'It was your man Chirath who was in command at the bridge,' Erak flashed back at him. 'It was he who decided no guard was to be left on it. We were the ones who tried to save it while he was hiding behind rocks!'

Morgarath's gaze locked with Erak's once more and now his voice dropped to a low, almost inaudible level.

'I am not spoken to in that fashion, *Captain* Erak,' he spat. 'You will apologise to me at once. And then . . .'

He stopped in mid-sentence. He seemed to possess almost unnatural peripheral senses. Although he had been staring, unblinkingly, into Erak's eyes, he had apparently sensed something off to one side. Those black eyes now turned and trained on Will. One white, bony finger was raised, pointing at the boy's throat.

'What is that?'

Erak looked and felt a sinking sensation in the pit of his stomach.

There was a dull gleam of bronze visible in the gap of Will's open collar. Then Erak felt himself shoved to one side as Morgarath moved, snake-fast, and snatched at the chain around Will's neck.

Will staggered back, horrified at the implacable fury in those dead eyes, and the slight flare of colour above the cheekbones. Beside him, he heard Evanlyn's intake of breath as Morgarath stared down at the small bronze oak leaf in his hand.

'A Ranger!' he raged. 'This is a Ranger! This is their sign!'

'He's a boy . . .' Erak began, but now Morgarath's fury was turned upon him and he swept his hand in a backhanded blow across the Skandian's cheek.

'He is no boy! He is a Ranger!'

The other three Skandians moved forward at the blow, weapons ready. Morgarath didn't even have to speak. He turned those glittering eyes on them and twenty Wargals moved as well, a warning growl in their throats, clubs and iron spears ready.

Erak signalled for his men to settle. The red mark of Morgarath's blow flared on his cheek.

'You knew,' Morgarath accused him. 'You knew.' Then realisation dawned on him. 'This is the one! Arrows, you said! My Wargals were hiding from arrows as the bridge burnt! Ranger weapons! This is the swine who destroyed my bridge!' The voice rose to a shriek of fury as he spoke.

Will's throat was dry and his heart pounded with terror. He knew of Morgarath's legendary hatred for Rangers — all members of the Corps did. Ironically, it was Halt himself who had triggered that hatred when he led the surprise attack on Morgarath's army at Hackham Heath sixteen years previously.

Erak stood before the raging Black Lord and said nothing.

Will felt a small, warm hand creep into his: Evanlyn.

For a moment, he marvelled at the girl's courage, to bond herself to him like this, in the face of Morgarath's implacable fury and hatred.

Then, another horse forced its way through the crowd. On its back was one of Morgarath's Wargal lieutenants, one of those who had learned basic human speech.

'My lord!' he called, in the peculiar, emotionless tones of all Wargals. 'Enemy advancing!'

Morgarath swung to face him and the Wargal continued.

'Their skirmish line moving towards us, my lord. Battle is beginning!'

The Lord of Rain and Night came to a decision. He swung back into the saddle of his horse, his furious gaze now locked on Will, not Erak.

'We will finish this later,' he said. Then he turned to a Wargal sergeant among those who had surrounded the Skandians.

'Hold these prisoners here until I return. On pain of your life.'

The Wargal saluted, one fist to his left breast, then growled a command to his men. They surrounded the Skandian party. The four sea wolves now formed a small circle, facing out, Will and Evanlyn in the middle. They held their weapons ready. It was a stand-off and they were obviously prepared to sell their lives dearly.

'We'll settle this later, Erak,' Morgarath said. 'Try to escape and my men will cut you to pieces.'

And, wheeling his horse, he galloped through the throng once again, scattering soldiers in his path, trampling those who were too slow to move. They heard the thin, nasal voice calling commands to his forces as he disappeared.

Thirty-one

The first clash of the two armies was inconclusive.

The King's skirmish line, consisting of light infantry accompanied by archers, advanced on Morgarath's left flank in a probing movement, retreating hastily when a battalion of heavy infantry formed up and moved forward to meet them.

The lightly armed skirmishers scampered back to the safety of their own lines, ahead of the slow treading Wargals. Then, as a company of heavy cavalry trotted forward towards the Wargal battalion's left flank, the Wargals re-formed from their column-of-fours marching order into a slower moving, defensive square and withdrew to their own lines.

For the next few hours, that remained the pattern of the battle: small forces would probe the other side's defences. Larger forces would offer to counter and the first attack would melt away. Arald, Fergus and Tyler sat their horses beside the King, on a small knoll in the centre of the royal army. Battlemaster David was with a small group of knights making one of the many forays towards the Wargal army.

'All this toing and froing is getting me down,' Arald said sourly. The King smiled at him. He had one of the most important attributes of a good commander: almost unlimited patience.

'Morgarath is waiting,' he said simply. 'Waiting for Horth's army to show itself in our rear. Then he'll attack, have no doubt.'

'Let's just get on with it ourselves,' growled Fergus, but Duncan shook his head, pointing to the ground immediately to the front of Morgarath's position.

'The land there is soft and boggy,' he said. 'It would reduce the effectiveness of our best weapon — our cavalry. We'll wait till Morgarath comes to us. Then we can fight him on ground that's more to our liking.'

There was an urgent clatter of hooves from the rear, and the royal party turned to watch a courier spurring his horse up the last slope to the knoll where they waited. He hauled on his reins, looked around until he saw the King's blond head, then dug in his spurs again, eventually bringing his horse to a sliding stop beside them. His green surcoat, light mail armour and thin-bladed sword showed him to be a scout.

'Your majesty,' he said breathlessly. 'A report from Sir Vincent.'

Vincent was the leader of the Messenger Corps, a group of soldiers who acted as the King's eyes and ears during a battle, carrying reports and orders to all parts of the battlefield. Duncan nodded acknowledgement, indicating that the man should go ahead and give his message.

The rider swallowed several times and looked anxiously at the King and his three barons. All at once, Arald knew this was not going to be good news.

'Sir,' said the scout hesitantly. 'Sir Vincent's respects, sir, and . . . there appear to be Skandians behind us.'

There were startled exclamations from several of the junior officers surrounding the command group. Fergus swung on them, his brows drawn together in a frown.

'Be quiet!' he stormed and, in an instant, the noise dropped away. The aides looked shamefaced at their lack of discipline.

'Exactly where are these Skandians? And how many are there?' Duncan asked the scout calmly. His unruffled manner seemed to communicate itself to the messenger. This time, he answered with a lot more confidence.

'The first group are visible on the low ridge to the north-west, your majesty. As yet we can see only a hundred or so. Sir Vincent suggests that the best position for you to view the situation would be from the small hill to our left rear.'

The King nodded and turned to one of the younger officers.

'Ranald, perhaps you might ride and advise Sir David of this new development. Tell him we are shifting the command post to the hill Sir Vincent suggested.'

'Yes, my lord!' replied the young knight. He wheeled his horse and set off at a gallop. The King then turned to his companions.

'Gentlemen, let's see about these Skandians, shall we?'

Shading his eyes, Baron Arald peered at the small group of men on the hill behind them. Even at this distance, it was possible to make out the horned helmets and the huge circular shields that the sea raiders carried. A small group had even advanced down the near side of the hill and they were easier to make out.

Just as obvious was their choice of the typical Skandian arrowhead formation as they advanced. He estimated that several hundred of the enemy were now in sight, with who knew how many more hidden on the other side of the hills. He felt a great weight of sadness upon his shoulders. The fact that the Skandians were there meant only one thing: Halt had failed. And knowing Halt as he did, he knew that probably meant that the grizzled Ranger had died in the attempt. He knew Halt would never have surrendered — not when the need to stop the Skandians breaking through to the army's rear was so vital.

Duncan voiced the thoughts of all of them.

'They're Skandians, all right.' He glanced around the hilltop. 'We're going to have to fight a defensive battle, my lords,' he continued. 'I suggest we begin to pull our men into a circle around this hill. It's as good a spot as any to be fighting on both sides.'

They all knew it was only a matter of time now before Morgarath advanced, to crush them between the two jaws of the trap he had set.

'Rider coming!' called one of the aides, pointing. They all turned to face the way he indicated. From a copse of trees at the right-hand end of the ridge, a lone rider burst into sight. Several of the Skandians gave chase, hurling spears and clubs after him. But he was stretched low over his horse's neck, his grey-green cloak streaming behind him in the wind, and he soon outdistanced the pursuit.

'That's Gilan,' Baron Arald muttered, recognising the bay horse he rode. He looked in vain for a second Ranger behind Gilan, hoping against hope that Halt might have somehow survived. But it was not to be. His shoulders sagged a little as he realised that Gilan appeared to be the only survivor of the force that had marched off so boldly into the Thorntree Forest.

Gilan had hit the flat land now and was still riding full pelt towards them. He saw the royal standards flying on the knoll and swerved Blaze towards them. In a few minutes, he drew rein beside them, covered in dust, one sleeve of his tunic ripped and a rough, blood-stained bandage around his head.

'Sir!' he said breathlessly, forgetting the niceties of addressing royalty. 'Halt says can you —'

He got no further as at least four people interrupted him. Baron Fergus's voice, however, was the loudest.

'Halt? He's alive?'

Gilan grinned in reply. 'Oh, yes, sir! Alive and kicking.'

'But the Skandians...?' King Duncan began, indicating the lines of men on the far ridge. Gilan's grin widened even further.

'Beaten, sir. We caught them totally by surprise and cut them to pieces. Those men there are our archers, wearing helmets and shields taken from the enemy. It was Halt's idea...'

'To what purpose?' Arald asked crisply and Gilan turned to face him, with an apologetic nod of his head to the King.

'To deceive Morgarath, my lord,' he replied. 'He's expecting to see Skandians attack you from the rear, and now he will. That's why they even made a pretence of trying to stop me just now.

'Our own cavalry is just beyond the brow of the ridge. Halt proposes that he should advance with the archers, forcing you to turn and face the rear. Then, with any luck, as Morgarath attacks with his Wargals, both the archers and your main army should open a path through the centre, allowing the hidden cavalry to come through and hit Morgarath when he's in the open.'

'By god, it's a great idea!' said Duncan enthusiastically. 'Odds are that we'll stir up so much dust and confusion that he won't see Halt's cavalry until it's right on top of him.'

'Then, my lord, we can deploy the heavy cavalry from either wing to hit the Wargals in the flanks.' The new speaker was Sir David. He had arrived unnoticed as Gilan was explaining Halt's plan.

King Duncan hesitated for a second or two, tugging at his short beard. Then he nodded decisively.

'We'll do it!' he said. 'Gentlemen, you'd better get to your commands straight away. Fergus, Arald, take a section of the heavy cavalry each to the left and right wings, and stand ready. Tyler, command the infantry in the centre. Make sure they know this is a fake attack. And order them to shout and beat their swords on their shields as the "Skandians" approach. We'll make it sound like a battle as well as look like one. Have them ready to split to the sides at three horn blasts.'

'Three horn blasts. Aye, my lord,' said Tyler. He dug his spurs into his battlehorse's side and galloped away to take command of the infantry. Duncan looked to his remaining commanders.

'Get to it, my lords. We don't have much time.'

From behind, one of his aides called out.

'Sir! The Skandians are moving downhill!'

A second or so later, another man echoed the cry:

'And the Wargals are beginning to move forward!'

Duncan smiled grimly at his commanders.

'I think it's time we gave Morgarath a little surprise,' he said.

Thirty-two

From his command position at the centre of his army, Morgarath watched the apparent confusion in the King's forces. Horses were galloping back and forth, men were turning where they stood. Shouts and cries drifted across the plain to the army of Rain and Night.

Morgarath stood in his stirrups. In the far distance, he could see movement on the ridge to the north of the Kingdom's army. Men were forming up and moving forward. He strained his eyes to see more clearly. That was the direction from which he expected Horth to appear, but the rising dust kicked up by all the movement made it difficult to see details.

Although the bulk of Morgarath's forces were the Wargals whose minds and bodies had been enslaved to his own will, the Lord of Rain and Night was surrounded by a small coterie of men whom he had allowed to retain their own powers of thought and decision. Renegades, criminals and outcasts, they came from all over the country. Evil always attracts its own and Morgarath's inner circle were, to a man, pitiless, black-hearted and depraved. All, however, were capable warriors and most were cold-blooded killers.

One of them now rode to Morgarath's side.

'My lord!' he cried, a smile opening on his face, 'the barbarians are behind Duncan's forces! They're attacking now!'

Morgarath smiled back at the young man. His eyes were renowned for their keenness. 'You're sure?' he asked, in his thin, flat voice. The black-clad lieutenant nodded confidently.

'I can make out their ridiculous horned helmets and their round shields, my lord. No other warriors carry them.'

This was the truth. While some of the Kingdom's forces did use round bucklers, the Skandians' shields were enormous affairs, made of hardwood studded with metal. They were over a metre in diameter and only the huge Skandians, heavily muscled from rowing their wolfships across the winter seas, could bear such heavy shields in a battle for any length of time.

'Look, my lord!' the young man continued. 'The enemy are turning to face them!'

And so they appeared to be. The front ranks of the army facing them were now milling in confusion and turning about. The shouting and noise rose in pitch. Morgarath looked to his right, and saw the small hill where the King's standard marked the enemy command post. Mounted figures were pointing, facing the north.

He smiled once more. Even without the forces from across the Fissure bridge, his plan would be successful. He had Duncan's forces trapped between the hammer of the Skandians and the anvil of his own Wargals.

'Advance,' he said softly. Then, as the herald beside him didn't hear the words, he turned, his face expressionless, and whipped the man across the face with his leather-covered steel riding crop.

'Sound the advance,' he repeated, no more loudly than before. The Wargal, ignoring the agony of the whip cut, and the blood which poured down his forehead and into his eye, raised a horn to his lips and blew an ascending scale of four notes.

Along the lines of the Wargal army, company commanders stepped forward, one every hundred metres. They raised their curved swords, and called the first few sounds of the Wargal cadence. Like a mindless machine, the entire army took up the chant immediately – this one set at a slow jog pace – and began to move forward.

Morgarath allowed the first half dozen ranks to pass him, then he and his attendants urged their horses forward and moved with the army.

The Lord of Rain and Night felt his breath coming a little faster, his pulse beginning to accelerate. This was the moment he had planned and waited for over the past fifteen years. High in his windy, rainswept mountains, he had expanded his force of Wargals until they formed an army that no infantry could defeat. Without minds of their own, they were almost without fear. They were inexorable. They would suffer losses no other troops would bear and continue to advance.

They had only one weakness and that was facing cavalry. The high mountains were no place for horses and he had been unable to condition their minds to stand against mounted soldiers. He knew that he would lose many of his own troops to Duncan's cavalry but he cared little about that. In a normal confrontation, the King's cavalry would be a decisive factor in their battle. Now, however, split between the Wargals and the attacking Skandians, their numbers would be insufficient to stop him. He accepted the fact that Duncan's cavalry would cause immense losses among his troops without a qualm. He cared nothing for his army, only for his own desires and plans.

The dust rose from the thousands of jogging feet. The chant surrounded him, a primal rhythm of hatred and implacable evil. He began to laugh. Softly at first, then the laughter became increasingly louder and wilder. This was his day. This was his moment. This was his destiny.

Black-hearted, thoroughly evil and pitiless, he was the Lord of Rain and Night. He was also, unmistakably, insane.

'Faster!' he cried, sliding his huge broadsword from its scabbard and wielding it in gigantic circles over his head. The Wargals didn't need to hear the word. They were bound to him in an unbreakable linkage of minds. The cadence of the chant increased and the black army began to move faster and faster.

In front all was confusion. The enemy, first turning to face the Skandians, now saw the new threat developing at their rear. They hesitated, then, for some unaccountable reason, they responded to three horn blasts by drawing to either side, opening a gap in the heart of their line. Morgarath screamed his triumph. He would drive his army into the gap, separating the left and right wings of the army. Once an army's front line was broken, it lost all cohesion and control and was more than halfway defeated. Now, in their panic, the enemy were presenting him with the perfect opportunity to strike deep into their hearts. They had even left the way open to their own command centre — the small group of horsemen standing under the royal standard on a hill.

'To the right!' Morgarath screamed, pointing his sword towards King Duncan's eagle standard. As before, the Wargals heard the words and his thought in their minds. The army wheeled slightly, heading for the gap. And now, through the chanting, Morgarath heard a dull drumming sound. An unexpected sound.

Hoofbeats.

The sudden doubt in his mind communicated instantly to the minds of his army. The advance faltered for a moment. Then, cursing the Wargals, he drove them forward again. But the hoofbeats were still there and now, peering through the clouds of dust raised by the enemy army, he could see movement. He felt a sudden, overpowering surge of fear and again the Wargal army hesitated.

And this time, before he could mentally flail them forward, the curtains of dust seemed to part and a wedge of charging cavalry burst into sight, less than a hundred metres from his army's front line.

There was no time to form into the sort of defensive square that was infantry's only hope against a cavalry attack. The armoured wedge smashed into the extended front line of the Wargals, collapsing the formation and driving into the heart of Morgarath's army. And the further they penetrated, the wider the gap became, as the wedge shape split and separated the Wargals, just as Morgarath had been planning to do to his enemy. Now Morgarath heard one long rising horn blast in the distance. Standing high in the stirrups, he cast his glance left and right, and saw, from either wing of Duncan's army, more cavalry deploying, driving in on his flanks, smashing his formations. Dimly, he realised that he had exposed his army to the worst possible situation that he could have contrived: caught in the open by the full force of Duncan's cavalry.

The Wargals were facing the only sort of force that could strike fear in their hearts. Morgarath felt the flicker of defeat in their dull mind waves. He tried to force them on mentally, but the barrier of fear was too strongly embedded with them. Screaming his fury, he directed them to retreat. Then he wheeled his horse and, with his remaining henchmen, galloped back through his army, clearing a path with his sword as he went.

At Three Step Pass, there was a hopeless tangle as thousands of the rearguard tried to force their way through the narrow gap in the rocks. There would be no escape for him there — but escape was the last thought on his mind. His only wish now was for revenge against the people who had brought his plans crashing into the dust. He drew his remaining troops into a defensive half circle, their backs to the sheer rocks that barred the way to the high plateau.

Seething in fury and frustration, he tried to make sense of what had just happened. The Skandian attack had melted away as if it were never there. And then he realised that it never had been. The soldiers advancing down from the ridge wore Skandian helmets and carried Skandian shields but it had been a ruse to draw him forward. The fact that they had the helmets and shields meant that, somewhere, Horth's forces had been defeated. That could only have been accomplished if someone had led an intercepting force throughout the impenetrable tangle of the Thorntree Forest.

Someone?

Deep in his mind, Morgarath knew who that someone was. He didn't know how he knew. Or why. He knew it had to be a Ranger and there was only one Ranger who would have done it.

Halt.

Dark, bitter hatred surged in his heart. Because of Halt, his fifteen-year dream was crumbling before his eyes. Because of Halt, fully half of his Wargal soldiers were lying broken in the dust of the battlefield.

The day was lost, he knew. But he would have his revenge on Halt. And he was beginning to see the way. He turned to one of his captains.

'Prepare a flag of truce,' he said.

Thirty-three

The Kingdom's main army advanced slowly across the littered battlefield. The crushing attacks by the cavalry on three sides had given them a decisive victory in the space of a few short minutes.

In the second line of the command party, Horace rode beside Sir Rodney. The Battlemaster had selected Horace as his shield man, riding on his left side, in recognition of his service to the Kingdom. It was a rare honour for someone in his first battle, but Sir Rodney thought the boy had more than deserved it.

Horace viewed the battlefield with mixed emotions. On the one hand, he was vaguely disappointed that, so far, he had not been called upon to play a part. On the other, he felt a profound sense of relief. The reality of battle was far removed from the glamorous dreams he had entertained as a boy. He had pictured a battle like this as a series of carefully co-ordinated, almost choreographed, actions involving skilful warriors performing brave acts of chivalry. Needless to say, in those dreams, the most prominent and chivalrous warrior on the field had been Horace himself.

Instead, he had watched in some horror the stabbing, hacking, shoving brawl of blood and dust and screams that had developed before him. Men and Wargals and horses had all died and their bodies sprawled now in the dust of the Plains of Uthal like so many scattered rag dolls. It had been fast and violent and confused. He glanced now at Sir Rodney. The Battlemaster's grim face told him that it was always this way.

Horace's throat was dry and he tried to ease it by swallowing. He felt a sudden stab of doubt. He wondered, if he were called upon to fight, whether he would simply freeze in fear. For the first time in his life, it had been driven home to him that people actually died in battles. And this time, he could be one of those people. He tried to swallow again. This attempt was no more successful than the last.

Morgarath and his remaining soldiers were in a defensive formation at the base of the cliffs. The soft ground held the cavalry back and there was no option but to take the infantry forward and finish the job in bloody hand-to-hand fighting.

Any normal enemy commander would have seen the inevitable result by now and surrendered to spare the lives of his remaining troops. But this was Morgarath and they knew there would be no negotiating. They steeled themselves for the ugly task ahead of them. It would be a bloody and senseless fight, but there was no alternative. Once and for all, Morgarath's power must be broken.

'Nevertheless,' said Duncan grimly, as his front rank stopped a bare hundred metres from the Wargals' defensive half circle, 'we'll give him the chance to surrender.' He drew breath, about to order his trumpeter to sound the signal for a parley, when there was movement at the front rank of the Wargal army.

'Sir!' said Gilan suddenly. 'They have a flag of truce!'

The Kingdom's leaders looked in surprise as the white flag was unfurled, carried by a Wargal foot soldier. He stepped forward into the clear ground. From deep within the Wargal ranks came a horn signal, five ascending notes — the universal signal that requested a parley. King Duncan made a small gesture of surprise, hesitated, then signalled to his own trumpeter.

'I suppose we'd better hear what he has to say,' he said. 'Give the reply.'

The trumpeter moistened his lips and blew the acceptance in reply — the same notes in reverse order.

'It will be some kind of trick,' said Halt grimly. 'Morgarath will send a herald to talk while he's making his escape. He'll . . .'

His voice tailed off as the Wargal ranks parted once more and a figure rode forward. Immensely tall and thin, clad in black armour and a beaked black helmet, it was, unmistakably, Morgarath himself. Halt's right hand went instinctively to the quiver slung at his back and, within a second, a heavy, armour-piercing arrow was laid on his bowstring.

King Duncan saw the movement.

'Halt,' he said sharply, 'I've agreed to a truce. You'll not cause me to break my word, even to Morgarath.'

The trumpet signal was a pledge of safety and Halt reluctantly returned the arrow to his quiver. Duncan made quick eye contact with Baron Arald, signalling him to keep a close eye on the Ranger. Halt shrugged. If he chose to put an arrow into Morgarath's heart, neither Baron Arald nor anyone else would be quick enough to stop him.

Slowly, the vulturine figure on the white horse paced forward, his Wargal standard bearer before him. A low murmur rose among the Kingdom's army as men saw, for the first time, the man who for the past fifteen years had been a constant threat to their lives and wellbeing. Morgarath stopped a mere thirty metres from their front rank. He could see the royal party where they had moved forward to meet him. His eyes narrowed as he caught sight of the small figure hunched in a grey cloak on a shaggy pony.

'Duncan!' he called, his thin voice carrying through the sudden silence. ' I claim my rights!'

'You have no rights, Morgarath,' the King replied. 'You're a rebel and a traitor and a murderer. Surrender now and your men will be spared. That's the only right I will grant you.'

'I claim the right of trial by single combat!' Morgarath shouted back, ignoring the King's words. Then he continued contemptuously, 'Or are you too cowardly to accept a challenge, Duncan? Will you let thousands more of your men die while you hide behind them? Or will you let fate decide the issue here?'

For a moment, Duncan was caught off guard. Morgarath waited, smiling quietly to himself. He could guess at the thoughts running through the minds of the King and his advisers. He had offered them a course of action that might spare the lives of thousands of their soldiers.

Arald moved his horse alongside the King's and said angrily: 'He has no claim to a knight's privileges. He deserves hanging. Nothing more.' Some of the others muttered agreement.

'And yet . . .' said Halt quietly, and they all turned to look at him. 'This could solve the problem facing us. The Wargals are mind-bound to Morgarath's will. Now that we can't use cavalry, they'll continue to fight as long as he wills them to. And they'll kill thousands of our men in the process. But, if Morgarath were killed in single combat —'

Tyler interrupted, finishing the thought: 'The Wargals would be without direction. Chances are they would simply stop fighting.'

Duncan frowned uncertainly. 'We don't know that . . .' he began.

Sir David of Caraway interrupted. 'Surely, sir, it's worth a try. Morgarath has outsmarted himself here, I think. He knows we can't resist the chance to end this on a single combat. He's thrown the dice today and lost. But he obviously plans to challenge you — to kill you as a final act of revenge.'

'What's your point?' Duncan asked.

'As Royal Battlemaster, I can respond to any challenge made to you, my lord.'

There was a brief murmur at this. Morgarath might be a dangerous opponent, but Sir David was the foremost tournament knight of the Kingdom. Like his son, he had trained with the fabled swordmaster MacNeil, and his skill in single combat was legendary. He continued eagerly.

'Morgarath is using the rules of knighthood to gain a chance to kill you, sir. Obviously, he's overlooked the fact that, as King, you can be represented by a champion. Give him the right to challenge. And then let me accept.'

Duncan considered the idea. He looked to his advisers and saw grudging agreement. Abruptly, he made up his mind.

'All right,' he said finally. 'I'll accept his right to challenge. But nobody, nobody, says anything in acceptance. Only me. Is that clear?'

His council nodded agreement. Once acceptance was made, it was binding. Duncan stood in his stirrups and called to the ominous black figure.

'Morgarath,' Duncan called, 'although we believe you have forfeited any rights you may have had as a knight, go ahead and make your challenge. As you say, let fate decide the issue.'

Now Morgarath allowed the smile to creep over his entire face, no longer trying to conceal it from those who watched him. He felt a quick surge of triumph in his chest, then a cold wash of hatred swept over him as he looked directly at the small, insignificant-looking figure behind the King.

'Then, as is my right before God,' he said carefully, making sure he used the exact, ancient words of challenge, 'and before all here present, I do so make my challenge to prove my cause right and just to . . .' He couldn't help hesitating and savouring the moment for a second. 'Halt the Ranger.'

There was a stunned silence. Then, as Halt urged Abelard forward to respond, Duncan's penetrating cry of 'No!' stopped him. His eyes glittered fiercely.

'I'll take my chance, my lord,' he said grimly. But Duncan threw out an arm to stop him moving forward.

'Halt is not a knight. You cannot challenge him,' he called urgently. Morgarath shrugged.

'Actually, Duncan, I can challenge anyone. And anyone can challenge me. As a knight, I don't have to accept any challenge, unless it is issued by another knight. But I can choose to do so. And I can choose whom I challenge.'

'Halt is forbidden to accept!' Duncan said angrily.

Morgarath laughed thinly. 'Still slinking and hiding then, Halt?' he sneered. 'Like all Rangers. Did I mention that we have one of your Ranger brats as a prisoner?' He knew the Ranger Corps was a close-knit group and he hoped to infuriate Halt with the news that he had captured one of their trainees. 'So small we nearly threw him back. But I've decided to keep him for torture instead. That will make one less sneaking, hiding spy in the future.'

Halt felt the blood draining from his face. There was only one person Morgarath could be talking about. In a fury, he urged Abelard forward.

'You've got Will?' he asked, his voice quiet, but penetrating.

Morgarath felt that shock of triumph again. Even better than he thought! Obviously the Ranger brat was close to Halt. A sudden feeling of elation filled him. Could he possibly be apprenticed to Halt himself? Suddenly, somehow, he knew this was the truth.

'Yes, Will is with us,' he replied. 'But not for long, of course.'

Halt felt a red surge of rage and hatred for the vulture-like figure before him. Hands reached out to stop him but he shoved his horse forward, facing Morgarath.

'Then, Morgarath, yes, I . . .'

'Halt! I command you to stop!' Duncan shouted, drowning him out.

But then all eyes were drawn to a sudden movement from the second rank of the army. A mounted figure burst clear, covering the short distance to Morgarath in a heartbeat. The Lord of Rain and Night reached for his sword, then realised the newcomer's own weapon was sheathed. Instead, his right arm drew back and he hurled his gauntlet into Morgarath's thin face.

'Morgarath!' he yelled, his young voice cracking. 'I challenge you to single combat!'

Then, wheeling his horse a few paces away, Horace waited for Morgarath's reply.

Thirty-four

Will and Evanlyn never learned what it was that caused the wave of uncertainty in the Wargals who surrounded their small group. In fact, it happened at the moment when Morgarath realised he had been tricked into exposing his army to Duncan's cavalry. The sudden frisson of fear that ran through his mind communicated itself instantly to all of his mind slaves.

The two captives, and the four Skandians, all noticed the sudden uneasiness and hesitancy in the twenty or so Wargal warriors who had been left to guard them. Erak glanced quickly at his men, sensing an opportunity. So far, they had not been disarmed. The odds of four against twenty were too much even for Skandians and the Wargals had only been told to detain them, not disarm them.

'Something's happening,' the Skandian jarl muttered. 'Stay ready, everyone.'

Unobtrusively, the small party made sure their weapons were free and ready for action. Then the moment of uncertainty turned to real, palpable fear among the Wargals. Morgarath had just signalled a general retreat and those at the rear didn't distinguish themselves from the front-line troops for whom the order was intended. Over half of the Wargals guarding them simply ran. One sergeant, however, retained a vestige of independent thought and he growled a warning to his section – eight in total. As their companions struggled and fought to make their way into the jam-packed entrance to Three Step Pass, the remaining eight black-clad troops held their position.

But they were distracted and nervous and Erak decided that the opportunity wouldn't get any better than this.

'Now, lads!' he yelled, and swept his double-headed axe in a low horizontal arc at the sergeant. The Wargal tried to bring his iron spear up in defence but he was a fraction too slow. The heavy axe sheared through his armour and he went down.

As Erak sought another opponent, his men fell on the rest of the Wargal troop. They chose the moment when another mind command went out from Morgarath for his men to withdraw and form a defensive position. The confusing orders in their minds made them easy targets for the Skandians and they fell in short order. The others around them, intent on escaping to Three Step Pass, took no notice of the brief and bloody skirmish.

Erak looked around him with some satisfaction, wiping his axe blade clean on a cloth he'd taken from one of the dead Wargals.

'That's better,' he said heartily. 'I've been wanting to do that for days.'

But the Wargals hadn't left their group unscathed. As he spoke, Nordel staggered and sank slowly to one knee. Bright blood stained the corner of his mouth and he looked hopelessly at his leader. Erak moved to his side and dropped to his knees.

'Nordel!' he cried. 'Where are you wounded?'

But Nordel could barely talk. He was grasping his right side, where the sheepskin vest was already heavily stained with his blood. The heavy sword he favoured as a weapon had fallen from his grip. His eyes wide with fear, he tried to reach it, but it was beyond his grasp. Quickly, Horak scooped up the weapon and put it in his hand. Nordel nodded his thanks, and slowly let himself drop to a sitting position. The fear was gone from his eyes now. Will knew that Skandians believed a man must die with his weapon in hand if his soul were not to wander in torment for eternity. Now that he had his sword firmly in his grasp, Nordel was not afraid to die. Weakly, he waved them away.

'Go!' he said, finally finding his voice. 'I'm . . . finished . . . Get to the ships.'

Erak nodded quickly. 'He's right,' he said, straightening up from beside his friend. 'There's nothing we can do for him.' The others nodded and Erak grabbed first Will and then Evanlyn and shoved them along in front of him.

'Come on, you two,' he said roughly. 'Unless you want to stay here till Morgarath gets back.'

And, moving together in a tight little group, the five of them shoved their way through the milling crowd of Wargals, all trying to move in the opposite direction.

Morgarath was stung by the impact of the heavy leather glove on his face. Furious, he turned to stare at the challenger who had ruined his plan. Then he allowed that thin smile to spread over his face once more.

His challenger was no more than a boy, he realised. Big, certainly, and muscular. But the fresh face under the simple conical helmet couldn't have been more than sixteen years old.

Before the startled members of the King's council could react, he replied swiftly.

'I accept the challenge!'

He was a second ahead of Duncan's furious cry: 'No! I forbid it!' Realising he was too late, he appealed to Morgarath. 'For pity's sake, Morgarath, he's only a boy, as you can see. An apprentice. You can't accept his challenge!'

'On the contrary,' Morgarath replied, 'as I've just pointed out, I have that right. And, as you know, once a challenge is given and accepted, there can be no withdrawal.'

He was right, of course. The strict rules of chivalry and knighthood, by which they had all sworn solemn oaths to be bound, did decree just that. Morgarath smiled now at the boy beside him. He would make short work of him. And the boy's quick death would serve to infuriate Halt even more.

Halt, meanwhile, watched the Lord of Rain and Night through slitted eyes.

'Morgarath, you're already a dead man,' he muttered.

Halt felt a firm hand on his arm and he turned to look into Sir David's grim eyes. The Battlemaster had his sword drawn and resting over his right shoulder.

'The boy will have to take his chances, Halt,' he said.

'His chances? He has no chance!' Halt replied.

Sir David acknowledged the fact sadly. 'Be that as it may. You can't interfere in this combat. I'll stop you if I even think you're going to try. Don't make me do that. We've been friends far too long.'

He held Halt's angry gaze for a few seconds, then the Ranger agreed bitterly. He knew the knight wasn't bluffing. The codes of chivalry meant everything to him.

The byplay hadn't been lost on Morgarath. He was confident that the moment the boy fell, Halt would accept his original challenge, King's orders or no King's orders. And then, at least, Morgarath would know the satisfaction of killing his old, hated enemy before his own world came crashing down around him.

He turned now to Horace.

'What weapons, boy?' he said in an insulting tone. 'How do you choose to fight?'

Horace's face was white and strained with fear. For a moment, his voice was trapped inside his throat. He wasn't sure what had come over him when he'd galloped forward and issued his challenge. It certainly wasn't something he'd planned. A red rage had seemed to overtake him and he had found himself out here in front of the entire army, throwing his gauntlet into Morgarath's startled face. Then he thought of Morgarath's threat to Will, and how he'd been forced to leave his friend at the bridge and he managed, at last, to speak.

'As we are,' he said. Both of them carried swords. In addition, Morgarath's long, kite-shaped shield hung at his saddle and Horace carried his round buckler slung on his back. But Morgarath's sword was a two-handed broad-sword, nearly a foot longer than the standard cavalry sword Horace carried. Morgarath turned now to call once more to Duncan.

'The whelp chooses to fight as we are. You'll stand by the rules of conduct, I assume, Duncan?' he said.

'You'll fight unmolested,' Duncan agreed in a bitter tone. Those were the rules of single combat.

Morgarath nodded and made a mocking bow in the King's direction.

'Just be sure that murderous Ranger Halt understands that,' he said, continuing his plan of driving Halt to a cold fury. 'I know he has little knowledge of the rules of knighthood and chivalry.'

'Morgarath,' said Duncan coldly, 'don't try to pretend that what you're doing has any connection with real chivalry. I ask you one more time, spare the boy's life.'

Morgarath feigned a surprised expression. 'Spare him, your majesty? He's a lump of a boy, big for his age. Who knows, you might be better served asking him to spare me?'

'If you must persist with murder, that's your choice, Morgarath. But save us your sarcasm,' said Duncan. Again Morgarath made that mocking bow. Then he said casually, over his shoulder, to Horace:

'Are you ready, boy?'

Horace swallowed once, then nodded.

'Yes,' he said.

It was Gilan who saw what was coming and managed to shout a warning, just in time. The huge broadsword had snaked out of its scabbard with incredible speed and

Morgarath swung it backhanded at the boy beside him. Warned by the shout, Horace rolled to one side, the blade hissing centimetres above his head.

In the same movement, Morgarath had set spurs to his dead-white horse and was galloping away, reaching for his shield and settling it on his left arm. His mocking laughter carried back to Horace as the boy recovered.

'Then let's get started!' he laughed and Horace felt his throat go dry as he realised he was now fighting for his life.

Thirty-five

Morgarath was wheeling his horse in a wide circle to gain room. Horace knew that he'd swing round soon and charge down on him, using the momentum of his charge as much as the force of his sword to try to strike him from the saddle.

Guiding his horse with his knees, he swung away in the opposite direction, shrugging his buckler round from where it hung on his back and slipping his left arm through the straps. He glanced over his shoulder and saw Morgarath, eighty metres away, spurring his horse forward in a charge. Horace clapped his heels into his own horse's ribs and swung him back to face the black-clad figure.

The two sets of hoofbeats overlapped, merged, then overlapped once more as the riders thundered towards each other. Knowing his opponent had the advantage of reach, Horace determined to let him strike the first blow, then attempt a counterstrike as they passed. They were nearly on each other now and Morgarath suddenly rose in his stirrups and, from his full height, swung an overhand blow at the boy. Horace, expecting the move, threw up his shield.

The power behind Morgarath's blow was devastating. The sword had Morgarath's immense height, the strength of his arm and the momentum of his galloping horse behind it. Timing it to perfection, he had channelled all those separate forces and focused them into his sword as it cleaved down. Horace had never in his life felt such destructive force. Those watching winced at the ringing crash of sword on shield and they saw Horace sway under the mighty stroke, almost knocked clean from his saddle on the first pass.

All thought of a counterstrike was gone now. It was all he could do to regain his saddle as his horse skittered away, dancing sideways as Morgarath's mount, trained for battle, lashed out with its rear hooves.

Horace's left arm, his shield arm, was rendered completely numb by the terrible force of the blow. He shrugged it repeatedly as he rode away, moving the arm in small circles to try to regain some feeling. Finally, he felt a dull ache there that seemed to stretch the entire length of the limb. Now he knew real fear. He knew no way to counter the crushing force of Morgarath's sword strokes. He realised that all his training, all his practice, was nothing compared to Morgarath's years and years of experience.

He wheeled to face Morgarath and rode in again. On the first pass, they had met shield to shield. This time, he saw his opponent was angling to pass on his right side — his sword arm side — and he realised that the next shattering blow would not land on his shield. He would have to parry with his own sword. His mouth was dry as he galloped forward, trying desperately to remember what Gilan had taught him.

But Gilan had never prepared him to face such over-powering strength. He knew he couldn't take the risk of gripping his sword lightly and tightening at the moment of impact. His knuckles whitened on the hilt of his sword and, suddenly, Morgarath was upon him and the massive broadsword swung in a glittering arc at his head. Horace threw up his own sword to parry, just in time.

The mighty crash and slithering scream of steel on steel set the watchers' nerves jangling. Again, Horace reeled in the saddle from the force of the blow. His right arm was numb from fingertip to elbow. He knew that he would have to break out of this cycle of battering blows. But he couldn't think how.

He heard hoofbeats close behind and, turning, realised that this time, Morgarath hadn't gone on to gain ground for another charge. Instead, he had wheeled his horse almost immediately, sacrificing the extra force gained in the charge for the sake of a fast follow-up attack. The broadsword swung back again.

Horace reared his horse onto its hind legs, spinning it in place, and taking Morgarath's sword on his shield once more. This time, the force behind it was a little less devastating, but not by much. Horace cut twice at the black lord, forehand and backhand. His smaller, lighter sword was faster to wield than the mighty broadsword, but his right arm was still numb from the parry and his strokes had little power behind them. Morgarath deflected them easily, almost contemptuously, with his shield then cut again at Horace, overhand this time, standing in his stirrups for extra purchase.

Once again, Horace's shield took the force of the sword stroke. The circular piece of steel was bent almost double by the two massive strokes it had taken. Much more of this and it would be virtually useless to him, he realised. He spurred his horse away from Morgarath, scrambling to remain mounted.

His breath was coming in rapid gasps and sweat covered his face. It was as much the sweat of fear as of exertion, he knew. He shook his head desperately to clear his vision. Morgarath was riding in again. Horace changed his direction at the last moment, dragging his horse's head to the left, taking him across the path of Morgarath's charging horse as he tried to evade that huge sword. Morgarath saw it coming and changed to a backhand stroke, crashing it onto the rim of Horace's shield.

The broadsword bit deep into the steel of the shield, then caught there. Seizing the moment, Horace stood in his stirrups and cut overhand at Morgarath. The black shield came up just a fraction too late and Horace's blow glanced off the black, beaked helmet. He felt the shock of it up his arm but this time, the jarring felt good. He cut again as Morgarath wrenched and heaved to remove his sword.

This time, Morgarath caught the blow on his shield. But for the first time, Horace managed to put some authority behind the stroke and the Lord of Rain and Night grunted as he was rocked in his saddle. His shield dropped fractionally.

Now Horace used the shorter blade of his sword to lunge at the gap that had opened between shield and body and drove the point at Morgarath's ribs. For a moment, those watching felt a brief flare of hope. But the black armour held against the thrust, which was delivered from a cramped position and had little force behind it. Nonetheless, it hurt Morgarath, cracking a rib behind the mail armour, and he cursed in pain and jerked at his caught sword once more.

And then, disaster!

Weakened by the crushing blows Morgarath had struck at it earlier, Horace's shield simply gave way. The huge sword tore free at last, and as it went, it ripped loose the leather straps that held the shield on Horace's arm. The battered, misshapen shield came free and spun away into the air. Horace reeled in the saddle again, desperately trying to retain his balance. Too close to use the full length of his blade, Morgarath slammed the double-handed hilt of the sword into the side of the boy's helmet and the onlookers groaned in dismay as Horace fell from his saddle.

His foot caught in the stirrup and he was dragged for twenty metres or so behind his terrified, galloping horse. Oddly enough, that fact probably saved his life, as he was carried clear of the murderous reach of the broadsword. Finally managing to kick himself free, he rolled in the dust, his sword still grasped in his right hand.

Staggering, he regained his feet, his eyes full of sweat and dust. Dimly, he saw Morgarath bearing down on him again. Gripping his sword with both hands, he blocked the downward cut of the huge sword, but was beaten to his knees by the force of it. A flailing rear hoof took him in the ribs and he went down in the dust again as Morgarath galloped clear.

A hush had fallen over the watchers. The Wargals were unmoved by the spectacle, but the Kingdom's army watched the one-sided contest in silent horror. The end was inevitable, they all knew.

Slowly, painfully, Horace climbed to his feet once more. Morgarath wheeled his horse and set himself for another charge. Horace watched him coming, knowing that this contest could have only one possible result. A desperate idea was forming in his mind as the dead-white battlehorse thundered towards him, heading to his right, leaving Morgarath room to strike down with his sword. Horace had no idea whether or not his armour would protect him from what he had in mind. He could be killed. Then, dully, he laughed at himself. He was going to be killed anyway.

He tensed himself, ready. The horse was almost upon him now, swerving away to his right to leave Morgarath striking room. In the last few metres, Horace hurled himself to the right after it, deliberately throwing himself under the horse's front hooves.

A great, wordless cry went up from the onlookers as, for a moment, the scene was obscured by a cloud of roiling dust. Horace felt a hoof strike him in the back, between the shoulder blades, then saw a brief red flash as another slammed into his helmet, breaking the strap and knocking it from his head. Then he was hit more times than he could count and the world was a blur of pain and dust and, most of all, noise.

Unprepared for his suicidal action, the horse tried desperately to avoid him. Its forelegs crossed and it stumbled, then somersaulted in a tangle of legs and body into the dust. Morgarath, managing to kick clear of the stirrups just in time, was hurled over the horse's neck and crashed to the ground. The broadsword fell from his grasp.

Screaming in rage and fear, the white horse struggled to its feet again. It kicked one more time at the prone figure that had brought it down, then trotted away. Horace grunted with pain and tried to stand. He came to his knees and, vaguely, he heard the swelling cheers of the watching army.

Then the cheers gradually died away as the still, black-clad figure a few metres away also began to move.

Morgarath was winded, nothing more. He dragged in a vast lungful of air and stood. He looked around, saw the broadsword lying half buried in the dust and moved to retrieve it. Horace's heart sank as the tall figure, outlined now against the low afternoon sun, began to advance on him, one long stride at a time. Desperately, Horace retrieved his own sword and scrambled to his feet. Morgarath had discarded his triangular black shield. Holding the sword in a two-handed grip, he advanced. Horace, pain racking every inch of his body, stood firm to meet him.

Again came that nerve-jangling, screeching clash of steel. Morgarath rained blow after blow down on Horace's sword. Desperately, the apprentice warrior parried and blocked. But with each massive blow, his arms were losing their strength. He began to back away but still Morgarath came on, beating down Horace's defence with blow after shattering blow.

And then, as Horace allowed the point of his sword to drop, unable to find the strength to keep it up anymore, Morgarath's huge broadsword whistled down one more time, smashing onto the smaller sword and snapping the blade into two pieces.

He stepped back, a cruel smile on his face, as Horace stared dumbly at the shorn-off blade in his right hand.

'I think we're nearly finished now,' Morgarath said in that soft, toneless voice. Horace still looked at the useless sword. Almost unconsciously, his left hand reached for his dagger and slid it from its sheath. Morgarath saw the movement and laughed.

'I don't think that will do you much good,' he sneered. Then, deliberately, he took the great broadsword up and back for a final, mighty overhand blow that would cleave Horace to the waist.

It was Gilan who realised what was going to happen, a second before it did.

'Oh my God, he's going to . . .' he said slowly and felt a ridiculous surge of hope.

The broadsword began its downward arc, splitting the air. And now Horace, throwing everything into one final effort, stepped forward, crossing the two blades he held, the dagger supporting the shortened sword.

The locked blades took the impact of Morgarath's mighty stroke. But Horace had stepped close to the taller man, and so reduced the leverage of the long blade and the force of the blow. Morgarath's sword clanged into the X formed by the two blades.

Horace's knees buckled then held and, for a moment, Morgarath and he stood locked, chest to chest. Horace could see the puzzled fury on the madman's face as he wondered how this situation had come about. Then the fury turned to surprise and Morgarath felt a deep, burning agony pour through his body as Horace slipped the dagger free and, with every ounce of his strength behind it, drove it through Morgarath's chain mail and up into his heart.

Slowly, the Lord of Rain and Night sagged and crumpled to the ground.

Stunned silence gripped the onlookers for a good ten seconds. Then the cheering started.

Thirty-six

What had, a few minutes before, been a battlefield now became a confusion. The Wargal army, released in an instant from Morgarath's mind control, now milled mindlessly about, waiting for some force to tell them what to do next. All sense of aggression had left them and most of them simply dropped their weapons and wandered off. Others sat down and sang quietly to themselves. Without Morgarath's direction they were like little children.

The group struggling to escape up Three Step Pass now stood mute and unmoving, waiting patiently for those at the front to clear the way.

Duncan surveyed the scene in bewilderment.

'We'll need an army of sheepdogs to round up this lot,' he said to Baron Arald, and his councillor smiled in reply.

'Better that than what we faced, my lord,' he said and Duncan had to agree.

The small inner circle of Morgarath's lieutenants were a different matter. Some had been captured, but others had fled into the wastelands of the fens. Crowley, the Ranger Corps Commandant, shook his head, as he realised that he and his men faced many long hard days in the saddle after this. He would have to assign a Ranger task force to hunt down Morgarath's lieutenants and bring them back to face the King's justice. It was always this way, he thought wryly. While everyone else could sit back and relax, the Rangers' work continued, nonstop.

Horace, bruised, battered and bleeding, had been taken to the King's own tent for treatment. He was badly injured after his insane leap under the Battlehorse's hooves. There were several broken bones and he was bleeding from one ear. But amazingly, none of the injuries were critical and the King's own healer, who had examined him immediately, was confident that he would make a full recovery.

Sir Rodney had hurried up to the litter as the bearers were preparing to carry the boy off the field. His moustache bristled with fury as he stood over his apprentice.

'What the hell did you think you were doing?' he roared, and Horace winced. 'Who told you to challenge Morgarath? You're nothing but an apprentice, boy, and a damned disobedient one at that!'

Horace wondered if the shouting was going to continue for much longer. If it were, he could almost wish to be back facing Morgarath. He was dazed and sick and dizzy and Sir Rodney's angry, red face swam in and out of focus in front of him. The Battlemaster's words seemed to bounce from one side of his skull to the other and back again and he wasn't sure why he was yelling so much. Maybe

Morgarath was still alive, he thought groggily and, as the thought struck him, he tried to get up.

Instantly, Rodney's glare faded and his expression changed to one of concern. He gently stopped the wounded apprentice from rising. Then he reached down and gripped the boy's hand in a firm grasp.

'Rest, boy,' he said. 'You've done enough today. You've done well.'

Meanwhile, Halt shoved his way through the harmless Wargals. They gave way without any resistance or resentment as he searched desperately for Will.

But there was no sign of the boy, nor of the King's daughter. Once they had heard Morgarath's taunt, they had realised that if Will were still alive, there was a chance that Cassandra, as Evanlyn was really called, might have survived as well. The fact that Morgarath hadn't mentioned her indicated that her identity had remained a secret. This, of course, Halt realised, was why she had assumed her maid's name. By doing so, she prevented Morgarath's knowing what a potential lever he had in his hands.

He pushed impatiently through another group of silent Wargals, then stopped as he heard a weak cry from one side.

A Skandian, barely alive, was sitting leaning against the bole of a tree. He had slumped down, his legs stretched straight in front of him in the dust, his head lolling weakly to one side. A huge stain of blood marked the side of his sheepskin vest. A heavy sword lay beside him, his hand too weak to hold it any longer.

He made a feeble scrabbling gesture towards it and his eyes beseeched Halt to help him. Nordel, growing weaker by the moment, had allowed his grasp on the sword to release. Now, weak and almost blinded, he couldn't find it and he knew he was close to death. Halt knelt beside him. He could see there was no potential danger in the man; he was too far gone for any treachery. He took the sword and placed it in the man's lap, putting his hands on the leather-bound hilt.

'Thanks . . . friend . . .' Nordel gasped weakly.

Halt nodded sadly. He admired the Skandians as warriors and it bothered him to see one laid as low as this — so weak that he couldn't maintain his grip on his sword. The Ranger knew what that meant to the sea raiders. He rose slowly and began to turn away, then stopped.

Horace had said that Will and Evanlyn had been taken by a small party of Skandians. Maybe this man knew something. He dropped to one knee again and put a hand on the man's face, turning it towards his own.

'The boy,' he said urgently, knowing he had only a few minutes. 'Where is he?'

Nordel frowned. The words struck a chord in his memory, but everything that had ever happened to him seemed such a long time ago and somehow unimportant.

'Boy,' he repeated thickly and Halt couldn't help himself. He shook the dying man.

'Will!' he said, his face only a few centimetres from the other's. 'A Ranger. A boy. Where is he?'

A small light of understanding and memory burned in Nordel's eyes now as he recalled the boy. He'd admired his courage, he remembered. Admired the way the boy had stood them off at the bridge. Without realising it, he actually said the last three words.

'At the bridge . . .' he whispered and Halt shook him again.

'Yes! The boy at the bridge! Where is he?'

Nordel looked up at him. There was something he had to remember. He knew it was important to this grim-faced stranger and he wanted to help. After all, the stranger had helped him find his sword again. He remembered what it was.

'. . . gone,' he managed finally. He wished the stranger wouldn't shake him. It caused him no pain at all, because he couldn't feel anything. But it kept waking him from the warm, soft sleep he was drifting into. The bearded face was a long way from him now, at the end of a tunnel. The voice echoed down the tunnel to him.

'Gone where?' He listened to the echo. He liked the echo. It reminded him of . . . something from his childhood.

'Where-where-where?' the echo came again and now he remembered.

'The fens,' he said. 'Through the fens to the ships.'

He smiled when he said it. He'd wanted to help the stranger and he had. And this time, when the warm softness crept over him, the stranger didn't shake him. He was glad about that.

Halt stood up from the body of Nordel.

'Thank you, friend,' he said simply. Then he ran to where he'd left Abelard grazing quietly and vaulted into the saddle.

The fens were a tangle of head-high grasses, swamps and winding passages of clear water. To most people, they were impassable. An incautious step could lead to a person sinking quickly into the oozing mire of quicksand that lurked on every side. Once in the featureless marshes, it was easy to become hopelessly lost and to wander until exhaustion overcame you, or the venomous water snakes that thrived here found you unawares.

Wise people avoided the fens. Only two groups knew the secret paths through them: the Rangers and the Skandians, who had been raiding along this coastline for as long as Halt could remember.

Sure-footed as Ranger horses were, once Halt was truly into the tangle of tall grass and swampland, he dismounted and led Abelard. The signs of the safe path were minute and easy to miss and he needed to be close to the ground to follow them. He hadn't been travelling long when he began to see signs that a party had come before him and his spirits lifted. It had to be the rest of the Skandians, with Will and Evanlyn.

He quickened his pace and promptly paid the consequences for doing so, missing a path marker and ending chest deep in a thick mass of bottomless mud. Fortunately, he still had a firm grip on Abelard's reins and, at a word of command, the stocky horse dragged him clear of the danger.

It was another good reason to continue leading the horse behind him, he realised.

He backtracked to the path, found his bearings and set out again. In spite of his seething impatience, he forced himself to go carefully. The marks left by the party in front of him were becoming more and more recent. He knew he was catching them. The question was whether he would catch them in time.

Mosquitoes and marsh flies hummed and whined around him. Without a breath of breeze, it was stiflingly hot in the marshes and he was sweating freely. His clothes were soaked and sodden with stinking mud and he'd lost one boot as Abelard had hauled him out of the quicksand. Nevertheless, he limped on, coming closer and closer to his quarry with every sodden step.

At the same time, he knew, he was coming closer and closer to the end of the fenlands. And that meant the beach where the Skandian ships lay at anchor. He had to find Will before the Skandians reached the beach. Once Will was on one of their wolfships, he would be gone forever, taken back across the Stormwhite Sea to the cold, snow-bound land of the Skandians, where he would be sold as a slave, to lead a life of drudgery and unending labour.

Now, above the rotting smell of the marshes, he caught the fresh scent of salt air. He was close to the sea! He redoubled his efforts, throwing caution to the wind as he chanced everything to catch up with the Skandians before they reached the water.

The grass was thinning in front of him now and the ground beneath his feet became firmer with every step. He was running, the horse trotting behind him, and he burst clear onto the windswept length of the beach.

A small ridge in the dunes in front of him blocked the sea from his sight and he swung up into Abelard's saddle on the run and set the horse to a gallop. They swept over the ridge, the Ranger leaning forward, low on his horse's neck, urging him to greater speed.

There was a wolfship anchored off shore. At the water's edge, a group of people were boarding a small boat and, even at this distance, Halt recognised the small figure in the middle as his apprentice.

'Will!' he shouted but the sea wind snatched the words away. With hands and knees, he urged Abelard onwards.

It was the drumming of hooves that alerted them. Erak, waist deep in water as he and Horak shoved the boat into deeper water, looked over his shoulder and saw the green and grey clad figure on the shaggy horse.

'Hergel's beard!' he shouted. 'Get moving!'

Will, seated beside Evanlyn in the centre of the boat, turned as he spoke and saw Halt, barely two hundred metres away. He stood, precariously trying to keep his balance in the heaving boat.

'Halt!' he yelled, and instantly Svengal's backhanded blow sent him sprawling into the bottom of the little craft.

'Stay down!' he ordered, as Erak and Horak vaulted into the boat and the rowers sent it surging into the first line of waves.

The wind, which had stopped them hearing Halt's cry, carried the boy's thin shout to Halt's ears. Abelard heard it too and found a few more yards of pace, his muscles gathering underneath him and sending him along in huge bounds. Halt was riding without reins now as he unslung the longbow and laid an arrow on the string.

At a full gallop, he sighted and released.

The bow oarsman gave a grunt of surprise and lurched sideways over the gunwale of the boat, as Halt's heavy arrow slammed into him, transfixing his upper arm. The boat began to crab sideways and Erak dashed forward, shoved the man aside and took over the oar.

'Pull like hell!' he ordered them. 'If he gets to close range, we're all dead men.'

Now Halt guided Abelard with his knees, swinging the horse into the sea itself and thrusting forward to try to catch the boat. He fired again but the range was extreme and the target was heaving and tossing on the waves. Added to that was the fact that Halt couldn't shoot near the centre of the boat, for fear of hitting Will or Evanlyn. His best chance was to get close enough for easy shooting and pick off the oarsmen one at a time.

He fired again. The arrow bit deep into the timbers of the boat, barely an inch from Horak's hand, in the stern. He jerked his hand away as if he'd been burnt and yelped in surprise, then flinched as another arrow hissed into the water behind the boat, not a foot away.

But now the boat was gaining, as Abelard, breast deep in the waves, could no longer maintain his speed. The little horse thrust valiantly against the water, but the boat was drawing alongside the wolfship and was still over a hundred metres away. Halt urged the horse a few metres closer, then stopped, defeated, as he saw the figures being hauled up from the boat.

The two smallest passengers were led to the stern steering position. The Skandian crew lined the sides of the ship, standing on the rail to shout their defiance at the small figure who was almost obscured by the rolling grey waves.

On the wolfship, Erak yelled at them, diving for cover behind the solid bulwark.

'Get down, you fools! That's a Ranger!'

He'd seen Halt's bow coming up, then saw his hands

move at incredible speed. His remaining nine arrows were arcing high in the air before the first one struck.

Within the space of two seconds, three of the Skandians lining the rail went down under the arrow storm. Two of them lay groaning in pain. The other was ominously still. The rest of the crew flung themselves flat on the deck as arrows hissed and thudded around them.

Cautiously, Erak raised his head above the bulwark, making sure that Halt was out of arrows.

'Get under way,' he ordered, and took the steering oar. Will, temporarily forgotten, moved to the rail. It was only a few hundred metres and nobody was watching him. He could swim that far, he knew, and he began to reach for the railing. Then he hesitated, thinking of Evanlyn. He knew he couldn't abandon her. Even as he had the thought, Horak's big hand closed over the collar of his jacket and the chance was gone.

As the ship began to gather way, Will stared at the mounted figure in the surf, buffeted by the waves. Halt was so near and yet now so impossibly out of reach. His eyes stung with tears and, faintly, he heard Halt's voice.

'Will! Stay alive! Don't give up! I'll find you wherever they take you!'

Choking on tears, the boy raised his arm in farewell to his friend and mentor.

'Halt!' he croaked but he knew the Ranger would never hear him. He heard the voice again, carrying over the sounds of wind and sea.

'I'll find you, Will!'

Then the wind filled the big, square sail of the wolfship

and she heeled away from the shore, moving faster and faster towards the north-east.

For a long time after she'd dropped below the horizon, the sodden figure sat there, his horse chest deep in the rolling waves, staring after the ship.

And his lips still moved, in a silent promise only he could hear.

About the author

John Flanagan's bestselling *Ranger's Apprentice* adventure series originally comprised twenty short stories, which John wrote to encourage his twelve-year-old son, Michael, to enjoy reading. Now sold to more than twenty countries, the series has sold over one million copies worldwide, has appeared on the *New York Times* Bestseller List and is regularly shortlisted for children's book awards in Australia and overseas.

John, a former television and advertising writer, lives with his wife, Leonie, in the Sydney beachside suburb of Manly. He is currently writing further titles in the *Ranger's Apprentice* series. Visit John Flanagan's website, **www.rangersapprentice.com**, to find out more about John.

The adventures of Will and his friends aren't over yet! Visit the official Australian *Ranger's Apprentice* website for news about upcoming books, plus competitions, quizzes, games and more.

www.rangersapprentice.com.au

THE ICEBOUND LAND
BOOK THREE

Help can arrive from the most unexpected places . . .

Will and Evanlyn are bound for Skandia as the captives of
the fearsome Skandian wolfship captain, Erak. Halt has
sworn to rescue Will, and he will do anything to keep his
promise — even defy his King. Expelled from the Rangers,
Halt is joined by Horace as he travels through Gallica
towards Skandia. On their way, they are constantly
challenged by freelance knights — otherwise known as
thieving thugs. But Horace knows a thing or two about
combat, and he soon begins to atract the attention of
knights and warlords for miles around with his uncanny
skill. But will they be in time to rescue Will from a life
of slavery?

Out now!